I LOVED YOU FIRST

SUZANNE ENOCH   MOLLY HARPER
KAREN HAWKINS

I LOVED YOU FIRST

Take Two by Suzanne Enoch

Pasties and Poor Decisions by Molly Harper

The Last Chance Motel by Karen Hawkins

Copyright © 2020 Suzanne Enoch, Molly Harper, Karen Hawkins

Ebook ISBN: 9781641971478

KDP POD ISBN: 9798678760784

IS POD ISBN: 9781641972024

NYLA Publishing

121 W 27th St., Suite 1201, New York, NY 10001

http://www.nyliterary.com

TAKE TWO

SUZANNE ENOCH

"Cafferty, when's the Charlotte Maybury interview?" Eleanor Ross yelled, tapping her finger on the edge of her phone. *Please let it be Thursday,* she repeated to herself, eyeing her calendar's open skies at the beginning of the week. Three days without a make-up appointment, without a fitting or a reading or a camera test or a schmooze dinner with a producer.

"Tuesday," Cafferty returned, his voice echoing up from the office.

Shit. "Can we—"

"I think we can shift it to Thursday," he interrupted. "That would give you a three-day break before you dive in again."

"Yes, please." Brian Cafferty, the magnificent beast, always anticipated her every need, even if it was only for a bit of breathing room. No wonder she'd nearly married him. And no wonder she'd changed her mind about that; what woman wanted to be married to a man who could read her like an open book?

Instead, they'd found the perfect niche for Cafferty. He could keep her schedule, book her appearances, and give her pep talks, and she could tell him to back the fuck up when she needed some space and a moment or two when her life wasn't scheduled to the millisecond. Hell, she'd fired him six times over the past four years since they'd become un-engaged, which she couldn't have done if they'd been married. And she'd hired him seven times, so he liked something about the arrangement too.

Eleanor tapped in next Thursday's date for the e-news interview, leaving the time blank for the moment. That left her with a FaceTime chat in an hour with Enrique Vance so he could tell her—how had he phrased it—"the window he wanted to open into Teresa Woodward's soul." All directors were like that, with their own favorite method of communicating their vision to the pesky actors who had to pantomime it, but for crying out loud, some of them were pretentious little shits. She liked what she'd seen of Enrique and the fact that he wanted to make a superhero movie with soul, but that didn't stop her from sending up a quick prayer every morning since she'd signed onto the project that she'd made the right choice.

"El," came from the open doorway of her upstairs sitting room, and she jumped.

Cafferty leaned there, a sculptor's wet dream of manliness hidden beneath a Star Wars T-shirt and faded jeans. Yeah, it hadn't been just his gift for anticipation that she'd fallen for. That was past tense now—though she did still like to look. She wasn't dead, for crying out loud. Eleanor shook herself. "Did the new pages show up?"

He straightened, bringing an envelope around from behind his back. "Yep. Figured you'd want to take a look before Vance's call."

"Thanks." She pulled out the two dozen pages, flipping through them. "Huh. Teresa Woodward's drinking problem is now a shopping addiction. Dolce and Gabbana. Can you say product tie-in?"

"You're so cynical." Brian leaned over her shoulder. "It's difficult being a high-powered lawyer with a mutation that lets her detect lies. A new purse helps dull the pain." He reached down to flip over a page of the script. "She is still a lawyer, right?"

Eleanor snorted. "Yes. And I've always wanted to play a superhero. Don't make fun."

"Uh-huh. Speaking of fun, Rod the Bod called twice while you were on the phone with the summer camp people. Something about dinner."

"You shouldn't call him that."

"Sorry. Mr. Bannon, then."

Since Roderick Bannon's last movie had very nearly gone straight to the Walmart five-dollar DVD bin, Rod had been spending extra time at the gym, with Chris Hemsworth's ex-trainer. Personally, she thought the movie had floundered because Rod, with his sun-bleached blond hair, eight-pack abdomen, and trademark piercing blue eyes, hadn't made for a very convincing blind, reclusive professor of literature. Then again, she happened to have inside information that Rod detested reading, so that might have prejudiced her a little on the believability scale.

She liked Rod. He told a good joke, they shared friends, and he happened to be very pleasant to gaze upon—though in her line of work, she knew a lot of guys who fell into that very same category. Still,

they'd been dating for three months, and she hadn't fallen out of the starry-eyed, mushy stage yet. Maybe this time she wouldn't. It could happen; it nearly had four years ago when she'd met Brian Cafferty. The three other men in between those two kept trying to prove her wrong, but hell, if an actress couldn't imagine a different life, she was in the wrong business.

"Am I giving him an excuse, then?" Cafferty prompted. "An early wake-up call? A production meeting first thing in the morning?"

She shook herself out of her whimsy. *That* was something

that didn't belong in her line of work. Whimsy led to heavy-assed costume dramas just so you could play a princess, even if the script was a bloody train wreck. Or a carriage wreck, rather. "Anticipating my every need again?" she quipped, a little too sharply.

"Not your *every* need."

Now she wanted to dive into that damned whimsy again. "Boundaries," she muttered, stacking the script pages in her lap again. Too many people clawed at her, wanted bits of her. It felt…safe, being able to tell one of them off.

"Sorry. What do you want me to do with Bannon?"

"Ask him when he wants to come by or if we're meeting somewhere." She stretched. "A night out will be nice."

"And then three days of catching up on *Secrets of the Zoo* and finally seeing the third season of *Stranger Things?*"

"God, yes. I need to know what happens to Hopper and Joyce before I fly off to Brussels for four months. Why can't Chicago be in Chicago anymore?"

"Because it's cheaper to make Brussels look like Chicago than it is to film in actual Chicago," he pointed out.

"Yes, I know. Just let me complain a little. I can't do it in front of anybody else; they think spending four months away from my house while wearing spandex and hanging by my waist from a piano wire is glamorous."

"So Teresa Woodward can fly, now?" he asked, lifting both eyebrows this time.

"Not yet. By the time I get the next rewrites, who knows?"

He grinned. "I'll let Rod the…Mr. Bannon know you're available tonight."

"Thanks, Cafferty. Tell him he can call me after five, or text me before that."

With a mock salute, he strolled out of the room. Eleanor sank back in her comfy chair and read through the script changes in more detail. It wasn't exactly what she would call edgy, but it did look fun. Clever. And after her last gig playing a no-nonsense factory worker uncovering a flaw in car seats in *Carrier*, fun had a great deal of appeal. And Enrique Vance had directed the very well-regarded *Last Bus to Providence* last year, so she tended to think he could help her pull off being a superhero.

Before he called, she sent off a quick email to Cafferty, instructing him to double her endowment to the Wild Wind Summer Camp so they could send an additional fifty kids camping this year now that they had the permits to expand the campground facilities. City kids visiting lakes and mountains, fishing and experiencing nature for the first time—in the four years since she'd started the foundation, she'd never had a second of regret for either the time or the money spent.

Her phone vibrated and abruptly erupted with Arnold Schwarzenegger's voice yelling "Get to the choppa!" She jumped, looking down at the number. "Dammit, Cafferty," she yelled, "quit changing my text tones!"

Okay, it was a little funny, given Rod's current obsession with being physically fit, but he was also sensitive about it. She read through the text. Rod wanted to pick her up at six sharp, and she was to dress for a fancy dinner so they could celebrate her getting the lead in *Prosecutor*. That was nice, since he'd just lost out to Zac Efron on his own superhero bid. As soon as she texted back her agreement, she went into the phone's contacts and edited his text tone back to the old-fashioned car horn it had been previously.

Brian didn't generally mess with her phone, or her private life, but he'd made it fairly clear that he wasn't a fan of Rod Bannon. She wasn't quite sure why; she'd gone out with a handful of guys in the four years since she'd ended their engagement, and Brian had never so much as batted an eye. Then again, Rod was the first one who'd made it past the four-date mark.

Before she could decide whether that was progress on her part or just a really sad commentary on her high-profile life, her phone rang, and she spent the next forty minutes discussing the psyche of a superhero who'd been happy with her pre super-powered life. God, she'd been after this part for so long, and even with the script changes, or perhaps because of them, the role seemed just…perfect. Or perfectly imperfect, rather. Fun, sarcastic, a bit unsure of herself—a female Tony Stark but with confidence issues and no flying. And then Enrique texted her the photo for the costume prototype, and she began to believe this might actually be her Tony Stark moment.

Yeah, she'd had some hits—some big ones—and a couple of rough patches, but this could be it. *The* it. The part that meshed hard work and skill and craft with fun and pure joy. As she tapped off the call, she felt nearly read to burst out singing. Her gaze on the full-length photo of her costume prototype, she uncurled from her chair and practically bounced to the top of the stairs. "Cafferty! Come look at this!"

"On my way." Brian's voice came from downstairs, the last syllable drowned out by her phone ringing with the theme from *The Terminator*. Damn it, she hadn't checked to see if Cafferty had changed Rod's ringtone too.

"Hey," she said into the phone, jabbing a finger in the direction of her grinning assistant—or handler, as she generally referred to him—as he topped the stairs. "Thanks for waiting to call until after five."

"Your voice is happy," Rod's melodic voice came back to her. "Good news?"

"Yep. I'll tell you what I can at dinner."

"I get it. Confidentiality and all."

That was the nice thing about dating somebody in the business. She didn't have to explain why blabbing about as silly a thing as the color of her superhero uniform could cost her the entire job and her future as an actor. "Thanks. See you in fifteen?"

"I'm on my way now. Just tell me you at least got a peek at the costume. You don't want to get Green Lanterned."

Eleanor snorted. "It's an actual costume, not CGI. And it's gorgeous." She took a breath. "Rod, this could be it."

"Damn. I wanna be your date to the Golden Globes, then."

That made her laugh, the excitement in the sound audible even to her. God, she was giddy. "You're on. I'm hanging up now. I need to get dressed."

"'K."

She ended the call. "Have you messed with any of my other contacts on my cell?" she asked, waggling her iPhone at Cafferty.

"Nope."

"Good. And don't do it again. What are you, twelve?" Turning left, she headed along the upstairs balcony to her bedroom.

"He gives me the willies," Brian countered, following behind her.

"You're my assistant. You help me schedule things, keep my calendar straight, and make sure I don't miss appointments. You field phone calls for me. You *assist* me. You do not get to pass judgment on my boyfriends."

His footsteps slowed. Good. She was serious, dammit. The last thing she needed was to be in a meeting and have somebody forward her something only to hear the *Three Stooges* theme in response. Eleanor turned to face him.

"You're my employee, Cafferty. Stop being so...familiar."

"So you're being independent again?" he asked, an eyebrow lifting.

"I *like* being independent. Remember?"

"Yeah. Not likely to forget that. Do I get to see the costume?"

"Nope. Maybe tomorrow, when I'm not pissed at you."

Narrowing her eyes, she backed into her bedroom and shut the door.

She hoped they were going to Dillard's for dinner. God, she loved the steak there. Together with some wine and a very handsome man saying adoring, supportive things to her, that steak would be just the thing to celebrate her becoming the anchor of her very own movie franchise, if she permitted herself a bit of whimsy for just a minute. Or an entire evening.

BRIAN CAFFERTY LEFT ELEANOR'S HOUSE WHEN SHE DID, MAKING sure Rod the Bod saw him lurking beside his Jeep. At twenty-eight, a year younger than he was, El could stand on her own two feet, but it seemed to him that every single young lady should have someone standing at her side to give the evil eye to every potential boyfriend who looked her way. Eleanor had lost her dad when she was twelve, and she didn't have any brothers. So that left him to deliver nonverbal threats as necessary.

The Bod had driven his Maserati, bright yellow and practically screaming "look at me!" Maybe that was what had attracted Eleanor to Rod Bannon—she liked the shade, and he could blind the sun with his giant personality.

It wouldn't last. At least he hoped not. To his fans, Rod was open and charming and friendly and never too busy for a photo or two, so they all adored him. But Brian had seen him up close and for more than the space of a handshake. Rod fed off the adoration. It literally sustained him, and he had nothing else going on but being famous. Ever.

Or maybe that was just his own ego talking. Scowling, Brian climbed behind the wheel of his four-year-old blue Jeep and headed the five miles southwest to his own condo. Yeah, El paid him a good salary, and he could have afforded one of the nice houses between her mansion and his condo, but he spent so little time at home that the additional expense seemed stupid.

Five years ago, he'd been just shy of becoming a junior partner in a big-name law firm, but his life had made a serious left turn on a warm, windy day in February. That was when a truck towing a giant marquee sign advertising the new romantic comedy movie *Mating Dance* had overturned a hundred feet in front of him. In a weird, Hollywood-style coincidence, the star of the movie, Eleanor Ross, had been driving one of the cars right behind the sign and had subsequently found herself trapped between a forty-foot image of herself in a duck costume and a hundred surprised commuters and shoppers along Artesia Boulevard.

She'd been totally gracious and good-humored about it, too, taking pics with fans in front of the toppled-over truck, until some of them had gotten too zealous and started grabbing at her. He'd moved in between her and them before he'd even realized he'd decided to get out of his car. For a bare second he'd thought she'd believed his line that he was the driver the studio had sent over, until she sat down in the passenger seat of his BMW next to him and commented that until that moment, she'd never believed in the Blanche DuBois line about relying on the kindness of strangers—and her hands had been shaking.

It had never occurred to him that anyone in the acting profession would be personally shy or introverted, but Eleanor Ross was a classic crowd-a-phobe. He'd choked back the abrupt, idiotic desire to ask her to dinner or to drive her to some quaint ice cream parlor out of a '50's romantic comedy, and instead had simply asked where she wanted to go. He'd then embarked on some inane chitchat he couldn't even recall, just something to give her time to pull herself back together. And when they'd arrived at Paramount Studios, she'd asked for his name and phone number, offered to pay him for his trouble like he'd been an Uber driver, and then with a quick smile and thanks, hurried off into the executive building.

Nobody at the firm had believed his story, though they gave him points for the creativity of his excuse at being late coming back from lunch. That night he'd pulled one of her DVDs out of his TV cabinet. As he watched her trying to avoid running out of air while staying ahead of alien-infested Chris Evans in *The Fourth Day*, he wondered if he hadn't imagined the whole thing, after all.

But then the next day she'd called him. Two months later, he'd popped the question, and she'd said yes. Four weeks after that, she'd broken it off—because he'd been too "in tune" with her or some other such crap. A month after that, she'd offered him the job, and because he was an idiot, and because she'd seemed so very alone for someone so popular, he'd quit his job at the firm and gone to work for her.

And now she was on her fifth date with Rod the Bod Bannon, and *he* was sitting on his couch eating takeout and watching a game show. Yeah, whoever thought Hollywood was glamorous saw the tuxedos and gowns on Oscar night and didn't consider the other three hundred sixty-four days in the year.

"You're an idiot, Brian Cafferty," he muttered around his burger.

A game show and a half later, *TMZ* came on, and he shifted to change the channel. Now that he knew a fair share of celebrities, the news rags didn't seem so much like a peek behind the scenes as they did vultures waiting to find the damaged and then feed off them.

"—Breaking news tonight. We have some pics just coming in of the superhero costume Eleanor Ross will be wearing in her first superhero flick. I haven't seen them yet, but apparently, they're really something. The—"

"Shit. Shit, shit, shit." Brian grabbed for his cell phone just as it started ringing to the tune of *Raindrops Keep Falling on My Head*. El's ringtone. "El, what the hell happ—"

"I'm at Almuerzo," Eleanor's voice came, hushed and tight. "He left me here. I'm in the kitchen. Brian, press is everywhere, and I don't know what happened. The—"

"Sit tight," he cut in. "I'll text you when I get there."

2

*H*e was already halfway out the door as he hung up. Almuerzo was on Sunset, a swanky Mexican food place with a Michelin-star chef and a reputation for being a celebrity hangout. Not somewhere she would have chosen to eat, much less to be stranded. Wherever the hell Rod Bannon was, he needed a swift kick in his grade-A ass.

His phone rang again as he backed out of his garage. Paramount Studios this time. Fuck. If they were calling him, they were also calling Eleanor. By the time he got to Almuerzo, she would know why the press was there. For the moment, he ignored the call. Before he and her agent, John Radley, started a war with the studio, he wanted to know the whole story. John would need to know it too.

Thankfully the nine-to-five work traffic had mostly cleared out, but Sunset Boulevard teemed with cars and pedestrians twenty-four hours a day. Rod had left her there. Every molecule he possessed knew this had something to do with the costume photos getting out to TMZ, but for now that was only a suspicion. First things first. One of the most famous faces in the world had been dumped into the middle of tourist central.

Flooring it between lights like a maniac, he managed to get to Almuerzo in fifteen minutes. As he pulled within a block of the restaurant, he started counting. TV vans from three networks were already there, and the damned street was practically closed down with onlookers and jackasses with expensive-looking cameras. Parking, a joke under the most ideal of circumstances, was now impossible.

Swearing again, he swung up the closest side street then pulled halfway onto the sidewalk and stopped in front of a dress boutique. He yanked open the shop's door, flinching at the volume of the Taylor Swift music reverberating through the small, cluttered space. "You have a back door?" he asked the stick-thin girl behind the counter.

"Not for customers," she retorted. "And get your Jeep off the damned sidewalk before I call—"

He pulled a hundred-dollar bill from his pocket and plunked it down in front of her. "I'm performing a rescue. Nothing illegal. I need your back door propped open for a couple of minutes. When I get back, I'll give you another four of those." He gestured at the bill.

"Damn," she breathed and scooped up the money to tuck it into a bra strap.

"Cameras in here?"

"Yeah."

"Turn them off."

"Not until I get another one of these." She patted her chest.

Brian handed one over. "Off. Now. They don't go on again until I say so."

"Okay. Jeez, dude. Chill out."

"I am chill. Go prop open the door. Just enough for me to be able to get it open."

Turning around, he left the boutique and trotted back up the side street and onto Sunset. Then he took a deep breath, squared his shoulders, and charged.

"Hey, you're with Eleanor Ross, aren't you?" came at him from several directions at once, but he ignored it and the jostling and the flashing phones and cameras. His phone began vibrating again, and this time it didn't stop.

Brian pushed to the front door and then inside, only to be met by a hostess shaking hard enough that she was either about to have a heart attack or an orgasm. "Excuse me, sir," she said, wrinkling her cheeks rather than bothering with an actual smile, "we are presently not seating any guests for the dinn—"

"I'm Cafferty," he interrupted in a low voice. "The person in your kitchen called me to come get her. I work for her." At the same time, he lifted his phone and texted "I'm here" to her number.

"Can you prove that?"

He shifted from one foot to the other, reminding himself to be grateful that they were keeping people out, even if that included him. "Send someone to ask her. Cafferty."

One of the waiters nodded and vanished. Just beyond the foyer, the low volume of the voices and clink of utensils on china made it clear that something unusual was up. Half the diners were probably thankful somebody else's scandal was taking up air-time, and the other half were probably jealous of El getting headlines.

The waiter returned. "She says he's okay," he informed the hostess.

"Maybe *he* is," the hostess responded, still keeping her voice low, "but what are we supposed to do about that?" She gestured past his shoulder. "Some of my guests are very private. They can't leave with this going on."

"I'm taking Ms. Ross out the back door," he said, already moving past her. "Give it ten minutes or so, and then tell the mob she's gone, if they haven't figured it out by then."

"You think they don't know we have a back door?"

"Unless you also have a helicopter pad, I'm doing the best I can," he retorted.

She lifted her chin. "What about the bill? They had lobster tacos. And a bottle of chardonnay. Expensive chardonnay."

So Rod had stiffed El on the bill too? Whatever the dickweed was up to, he and Eleanor needed to have a strategy meeting about standards. He pulled out his company credit card. "Put it on here, with a good tip."

Without waiting for her to complain about something else, he moved past her into the dining room. Tuxedos were out except for major award ceremonies, but this was a well-dressed crowd. And he was wearing a BB-8 Star Wars T-shirt and jeans. Ah, well. If they didn't already know something was up, they were probably zombies.

He locked eyes with Julia Prentiss, the current scream queen, and she gave him the up-and-down assessment, bit her lip, and returned to her conversation. Yeah, she was pretty and all, but he'd listened to her try to have a conversation, and he wasn't impressed.

The kitchen consisted of a lot of people in white chef's jackets standing around. With no new customers coming in, Almuerzo was swiftly grinding to a halt. That wouldn't earn El any sympathy, but they still parted reluctantly to allow him into the back corner where she sat on a stool and sipped at a glass of water.

"Hey," he said, squatting in front of her.

Hazel eyes met his, and a tear rolled down one cheek. "He took my phone," she whispered. "I showed him the costume pics, and I think he sent himself the photos. Why would he do that, Brian?"

"Because he's a prick who hasn't had a hit in three movies," he returned. Straightening, he held out one hand. "Let's get out of here."

"I can't. You saw what it looks like out there."

"I've got it covered." He reached out and took her hand, felt her shaking as she set aside her glass and stood. Damn Rod Bannon. Whatever the jackass thought he was getting out of this, it couldn't possibly be worth it.

Keeping her close beside him, he pushed open the back door. Phones and cameras began flashing, and he put an arm around her shoulder, trying to protect her from the crowd and the noise. The boutique's back door was cracked open an inch or so, and he yanked it wide to half shove El inside before he shut and locked it behind them.

The girl behind the counter gaped like a dying fish as he ushered Eleanor past her into the front of the tiny shop. "Three hundred, right?" he said, pulling more bills from his pocket and setting them in front of her.

"Um, yeah. You're—"

"Thanks," he cut her off. "You can turn the cameras back on as soon as we leave."

"O...Okay. I loved you in *Obsidian Nights*," she called after them.

"Thank you," Eleanor managed, sending her a quick smile as they ran for the door.

The paparazzi would be charging out of the alley and around to the front of the shop, so he practically flung her into the passenger side of the Jeep before he continued around to hop behind the wheel. "Stay low," he said, turning the key and jamming it into drive.

For three blocks she sat doubled over beside him, her pretty honey-colored hair curtaining her face. "I am so stupid," her muffled voice came.

"You trusted him to be human," Brian countered. "Which in your line of work is an iffy proposition. But it's admirable that you do still trust people."

"Not anymore." Straightening, she took a breath. "I don't

want to go home. The wolves will be waiting. Paramount's entire team of lawyers is probably on my driveway too."

"They've been calling. I haven't been answering."

"I turned off my phone after I called you. How did everybody find out so fast, though?"

"He sent the photos to *TMZ*, is my guess," Brian answered. "They started the episode with breaking news."

What he didn't say was that for *TMZ* to go live on the West Coast, they had to have known ahead of time that something big was coming. Rod hadn't just given them the photos. He'd told them he would be getting them. What Brian couldn't figure out was what was in it for Bannon. Why ruining Eleanor Ross equaled a payoff for Rod the Bod. Because Rod didn't do anything that didn't serve himself.

"I'm going to lose the part," she said into the silence, sitting up again. "They'll either replace me or shut down the movie altogether."

"Maybe. We need to make some phone calls, but not while we're fleeing the horde." Checking his mirrors, he shifted right and then turned them up the ramp onto the northbound 110 freeway.

"Where are we going? The border and Mexico are south."

He snorted. "It's not fleeing-to-Mexico bad yet."

"Says you."

"Yes, I do say. You don't want to go home. I know a place we can hole up and regroup."

Eleanor closed her eyes for a moment. *Regroup.* This wasn't a football game they were losing. A pep talk wouldn't put those photos back into her phone. And all those people suddenly surrounding her, yammering and pointing and camera lights flashing—the only thing she could think of was to call Cafferty and run.

"You rescued me again," she said aloud.

"It's my job, this time."

Whether he meant that to hurt or not, it did. The implication that he'd shown up because she paid him to do so... After she'd pretty much told him to stay in his lane and leave her to choose her own friends and romantic partners, she probably deserved it, but his timing sucked. "Sorry."

She heard his intake of breath. "No, *I'm* sorry. You've got enough on your shoulders right now. I'm not going to dump on you."

Yes, everything sucked right now and would only get worse, but in the grand scheme of things she supposed she was a great deal more fortunate than most people. "You might as well. There'll be a line later."

"But there isn't one now. Keep your phone off, unroll the window, and breathe. We've got two or so hours before we stop."

Wherever they were headed, it was out of Hollywood, and for the moment that was enough. God, she'd picked the wrong career. Standing in front of a couple of bored guys with cameras and lights was one thing. That was her pretending to be someone else, and she enjoyed that. She was good at it. The other part, the publicity tours and interviews and all the people picking at her like crows on a corncob, that part sucked. Literally. Just like a vampire.

Cafferty fiddled with the radio then shut it off again. He was probably worried that she would be featured on the next news break. "Did he say anything?"

"Who? Rod?"

"Yeah. Before he took off on you. Did he say anything?"

"No. He handed me back my phone, chatted for a minute or two about being up for the next James Bond villain, which I didn't believe, then said, 'I have to go, babe,' and walked away. At first I thought he meant he had to go to the restroom, but then he didn't come back. And then my phone started ringing, and the shit hit the fan." She pounded her fist against the armrest. "Who does that? I mean, I...I liked him."

She knew exactly why Cafferty didn't answer that; she surrounded herself with professional liars. *She* was a professional liar. Evidently that didn't mean her bullshit detector worked better than anyone else's. But did that mean that Rod had only been looking for a way to use her all along? Or to sabotage her career? She'd slept with the guy, for God's sake. He was exciting, bold, and everything she thought a shy, introverted woman like herself should be allying with.

Rod was the opposite of Brian Cafferty, in fact, who at the moment seemed content to let her stew in her own thoughts without a word of encouragement that her career wasn't circling the drain even as they drove away from Hollywood. Cafferty, who'd asked her to marry him, then had stuck around to work for her even after she'd changed her mind about him.

"Why do you work for me?" she asked abruptly, the second she spoke wishing she'd kept her mouth shut.

"Nope. I'm not having that conversation right now. The only mistake you made tonight was trusting somebody you thought was trustworthy. No wallowing in self-pity. Not in my car. I don't have waterproof cushions."

"Oh, ha ha. Fine. I'll be wallowing silently while you drive us God knows where."

"I'm following orders. If you want to go home after all, just say the word."

She thought about it. Her stuff was there. Her toothbrush, her overnight bag, her pajamas. And her house phone, laptop, the TV—three of them, actually—her doorbell, and all the other ways people would know to get to her. "Keep driving."

"I thought so."

Of course he knew she wouldn't change her mind. Brian Cafferty knew everything about her, made every effort to keep her safe and cocooned and protected and unchallenged. As her handler, that was a good thing. As a lover, as a husband, it would stifle her. She knew it.

Eleanor shook herself. She was only hurt and scared right now. That was why the H-word had suddenly shown up in her brain again, when it hadn't for four years. Oh, she needed to get ahead of all this, or at least get back on the game board. "We need to call John."

"I texted him on my way to Almuerzo, to let him know this wasn't your doing and that you'd be in touch as soon as you could."

Yep, as an employee, that anticipating-her-needs-and-requests thing was pretty much priceless. "Thanks again, then, even though I'm not sure at least part of it *wasn't* my doing. Or my fault, anyway."

"Well, I think you need to get over that before we jump into the fight."

He was right about that. If she claimed anything other than complete innocence, her next acting job would be a shoe commercial—if she was lucky. And dammit, she *had* trusted Rod. She would still be trusting him, if he hadn't turned tail and run just in time for the news to break. Her first impression on meeting him, that he wasn't the sharpest knife in the block, made her scowl now. His lack of keen insight had been part of his appeal; her work was challenging enough. She didn't need to be challenged in a relationship. But if she'd settled, what did that really say about her? Firstly, he'd outsmarted her, and secondly, why had she told herself that a long-term relationship with someone whose intellect she didn't respect was okay?

Oh, shut up, El. Brian was right about one thing. She needed to focus, decide on her plan of attack. No fumbling when she got on the phone with Paramount or the two executive producers. Bernie Machinak and Fiona Valenti had been big admirers of hers, but that was before she'd leaked—allowed Rod Bannon to leak—the biggest secret of the movie. Merchandisers wouldn't like that, and merchandise was where a superhero movie made its money.

She sank down in her seat and turned to face the side window. Light and dark streaked by, broken by the side panels of trucks and the longer-lasting light of neighborhoods and storefronts. Those dropped away as they left the freeway for a succession of side roads, and then the street-lights drifted farther apart until they stopped too. "Where are you taking me, the Grand Canyon?"

"Nope. We're almost there. If they don't have rooms, though, it'll be back to that Motel 6 we passed on the Interstate."

"As long as they have a toothbrush, I don't care."

She felt his glance at her. "I can do better than that, I think."

Five minutes later, he turned up a still narrower road that curved through dark trees and up a hill before the way ahead of them opened to reveal a Victorian-style house with a wrap-around porch decorated with string lights, a porch swing on either side of the wide front, and a six-car parking lot to one side. If not for the parking lot, she would have thought they'd arrived at somebody's pretty impressive private residence.

"We're here," he said unnecessarily, sliding into the nearest parking spot and shifting into park. "Do you want to wait here while I check to see if we can get in?"

She looked toward the front the porch, finally spying the shadowed sign that read "Starlight Bed and Breakfast Inn" in neat blue lettering. Eleanor wanted to go with him, both because she felt safer with Brian Cafferty and his lean six-foot-two well-muscled body around, and because everything so far tonight had been out of her control. But people tended to take to Twitter and Instagram when they spied her, and going anywhere private had become virtually impossible about seven years ago. "Yes, I'll wait here."

"I'll be right back. Keep your phone off, and don't turn on the radio."

If she'd felt up to arguing that she was an adult and could make her own decisions, she would have done so. After this catastrophe, though, maybe she should be listening to somebody else's advice. To Brian's advice. He'd disliked Rod Bannon from the beginning, anyway.

When Brian opened his door and stepped out, the sound of crickets and frogs poured into the car, only to be silenced again when he shut her in. God, how long had it been since she'd heard frogs? Not since the Hawaii shoot for *Primitive*, probably. That was when she'd had the idea for the Wild Wind Summer Camp, in fact. And Brian hadn't laughed when she'd told him about it, even though they'd just broken up. Instead he'd used his real estate attorney contacts to help her get the deal put together.

The driver's door opened, and she jumped as Brian sat again. "Well?"

"They only have one room available," he said, closing them in and starting the Jeep. "I'll find us somewhere else."

That would mean more driving, more moping, and longer without taking care of this mess. Eleanor reached over and covered his hand before he could shift into reverse. "Take it," she said.

He cocked his head at her. "You heard me, right? One room. If anybody recognizes you, the—"

"What, I'll be ruined? We've spent time together before, Cafferty, and I'm still here. I want to start pushing back against this before it's all completely out of my hands. I'll take the couch or rollaway or whatever they have."

Cafferty narrowed his eyes a little then shut off the car again. "What they have, El," he said, exiting the car and coming around to pull open her door for her, "is a king-size bed."

3

"That's fine," she said, not even hesitating as she walked around the Jeep to join him. For dinner at Almuerzo she'd worn a pretty pink V-neck T-shirt with streaks of silver beading running down it like rain, black capris, and black sandals that sparkled with silver beading that matched her top.

Eleanor Ross always looked good, but even tonight with her career ready to fall down around her ears, she still made the Kardashians look gaudy. It was all about class, about being a woman who was comfortable with herself even if she didn't trust the rest of the world. The woman to whom he'd tried to give the moon, until she'd decided she would rather fetch it for herself. Or that was the impression she'd given him, anyway. He'd spent several sleepless weeks trying to figure it—and her—out, and still wasn't satisfied with the answers.

"Cafferty?"

Brian shook himself, realizing he'd been staring at her as she stood on the porch waiting for him to get his ass back into gear. "Right. We'll go with the usual."

He passed her to hold open the screened-in front door, then followed her inside. The man standing at the short counter set

into the house's foyer blinked twice, his expression going from
mildly annoyed at people arriving so late in the evening and
without reservations to less annoyed and intrigued.

Celebrities had stayed here before, Brian knew, because he'd
heard about the Starlight Bed and Breakfast Inn from Rita
Wilson's assistant when El had played Tom Hanks's grand-
daughter in *Grampa Henry Likes to Bake*. Under normal circumstances, he would have done more vetting, made some phone
calls to make certain their reputation for discretion was legiti-
mate. Tonight, though, wasn't normal.

"We'll take that room after all," he said, pulling his personal
credit card from his back pocket. "Brian and Rose Cafferty."

"Phillip Eaton, owner and proprietor of the Starlight Bed
and Breakfast Inn," the guy behind the counter replied, nodding.
"My wife Joan is cleaning up the kitchen. We have eight rooms
here, walking trails, a pond for fishing, and a staff of four. We
serve breakfast from seven to nine, and you can arrange for
other meals if you let us know ahead of time. The fee, as I
mentioned to you earlier, is four hundred per night per room,
with a minimum two-night stay."

"Sounds good," Brian returned, handing over his Visa. He'd
repay himself from her business account later, but keeping this
in his name would make her harder to trace. "You wouldn't
happen to have any toothbrushes or anything, would you? Or is
there somewhere close by I could get some stuff?"

Eaton's jaw twitched, and Brian clenched his own in return.
He knew what the guy was thinking—that one of those flighty
actresses had run off for a one-night stand with some dude and
they were in such a hurry to get naked that they hadn't even
remembered to bring luggage. Defending El's honor against
some random man's imagination wouldn't do any good, but he
still wanted to say something. He still wanted to protect her,
even after her troubles were already out in the world.

"We have spare toothbrushes in the rooms, along with soap

and hand lotion, but I'm afraid we don't stock miscellaneous clothes or deodorant or hairbrushes. There's a CVS Pharmacy three miles down the road."

"That'll work," Eleanor said, flashing her famous disarming smile. "Thank you, Phillip. I just really need some peace and quiet."

The proprietor returned her smile; not doing so, Brian had discovered, was a physical impossibility. "You'll find that here in spades, Mrs...." He glanced down at his computer screen. "Mrs. Cafferty. We value our guests' privacy. We wouldn't continue to be in business if we didn't."

Well, that at least sounded reassuring. "Where's our room?" Brian asked.

Eaton picked up two key cards, inserted them into a scanner slot, then handed them over. "All our guest rooms are named after painters, so you'll be in Renoir, up the stairs here and all the way to the back on your left. The other rooms are all occupied tonight, but we do have a parlor on the main level here just through those doors if you have need of some work space, an ethernet computer connection, a fax machine, or phone chargers."

"Perfect. W—"

"The Wi-Fi password is on the back of your door," the proprietor continued, clearly not about to prematurely end his recitation, "along with this week's breakfast menu. If you have any special requests, please fill out the form hanging on the inside of the doorknob and put it outside your door before six a.m. Anything else I can do for you this evening? Your key card will also work on the front door, so you can come and go as you please. There won't be anyone manning the desk here between eleven at night and seven in the morning."

"I think that covers it." Brian started to reach for Eleanor's hand then stopped himself and clenched his fingers. They weren't dating, they weren't a couple, and just this afternoon she'd reminded him about boundaries and basically told him to mind his own business. Of course these days his business was her, but he wasn't going to forget that she'd basically called him a glorified secretary. He just didn't think it was necessary to remind her about that tonight.

"Shall we?" he said instead, gesturing her to precede him up the polished black oak stairs.

The Victorian feel of the house continued on the inside, with busy blue-and-gold floral wallpaper and oil-style table lamps, ornately carved dark furniture, and lacy window curtains. It was a little froufrou for his taste, but they weren't there to visit the décor.

"How did you find this place?" El whispered as they topped the stairs and continued up the narrow hallway. "I've never heard of it."

"I keep a file of getaway places people recommend," he answered in the same tone, leaning around her to slip the key card into its slot and then pushing down the door handle at the corresponding click. "I figured it would be out of the way but close enough to get back into town on fairly short notice."

"It's perfect," she said, stepping past him and flipping on the light. "There you go anticipating my every need again, even when crazy shit happens."

"It's my job," he reminded her again, noting the burgundy couch with a thousand mismatched pillows piled on top of it, the small writing table and pair of chairs, the door to the small bathroom with its clawfoot tub and small shower, and the giant king-sized brass-framed bed with its burgundy-and-silver duvet and another million complementary pillows. "You don't need to flatter me for doing what you pay me for."

"I wasn't... Oh, never mind. I'll call John if you'll start with Fiona. She thinks you're gorgeous."

"You're okay calling?"

Eleanor shrugged, sitting on the sofa and curling one foot

beneath her. "I have to be." She held down the power button on the side of her phone and watched the screen light up again. "Wow. Thirty-one missed calls and...seventy-two messages. In what, two hours?"

"Something like that." Brian powered up his own phone. His numbers were pretty close to hers.

"There's no television in here."

At El's abrupt comment, he looked up. Paintings all over the walls, along with bookshelves and knickknacks and silk flowers everywhere, but she was right. No television. No place for it even to drop down from the ceiling or up from the floor, and no remote anywhere. "Maybe that's good."

"It's not going to stop me from obsessing." Hunching her shoulders, she tapped the photo of John Radley and lifted the phone. "Hi. Yeah, it's me. This is a nightmare, John. I don't know if I should name names, or if that'll make me look like I'm trying to worm out from under something." She paused. "Yes. I'll tell you the whole story, and then please, advise me. Cafferty's calling Fiona." Eleanor scowled, gesturing at him to pick up his phone and get to work.

Right. Work. Save Eleanor Ross's career while she still had one. Save his own employment by rescuing hers. Rod Bannon deserved a punch in his fucking mouth. As for Brian, well, he seemed to be performing this rescue regardless of whether he wanted to bellow "I told you this would happen" at her or not. Because he was an employee. Not a fiancé. Not a lover. Maybe a friend, unless she decided tomorrow that he wasn't that, either.

After this damned thing was over, they needed to have a chat. If he could wait that long.

THE NEXT THREE HOURS, WITH THE EXCEPTION OF THE interruption for delivery of a pair of toothbrushes and a half-dozen freshly baked chocolate chip cookies, were quite possibly the worst in Eleanor's life. Well, in the top three, anyway.

After her first phone call put John Radley on her side and on the attack, she apologized to five execs at Paramount for "the mistake of trusting a new assistant," which was the tack John had suggested they take with this. Getting into a shouting match with the currently less popular but ultimately more bankable Rod Bannon wouldn't help anybody. That line of thinking was probably what Rod had figured on all along. Yeah, his last movie had tanked, but he was gorgeous *and a man*, so his next movie could be gold.

The rest of his line of thinking, as she and Cafferty and John considered it, was more than likely that getting *Prosecutor* derailed or delayed would give another superhero movie room to exist—and that superhero movie could well be his. She knew he'd been chasing a role in *Crimewave* since he'd lost out on *Fallen Angels* to Zac Efron. That would fit the bill.

It was all petty and stupid and ego-driven, but the fallout, for her and her career, at least, was deadly serious. The worst phone call was the one to Enrique Vance, whom they'd had to awaken in Brussels where he was doing pre-production scouting. He'd sent her the pictures, and she'd allowed them to be stolen less than an hour later. She'd fired the mythical Judy Howard, her nonexistent new assistant, immediately, and the young lady would never find another job in the industry. The fact that somebody, real or not, had been punished seemed the most mollifying to everybody else.

"What's her name again?" Cafferty whispered, lowering his phone to press it against his thigh.

"Judy Howard," Eleanor whispered back, sinking onto the couch and throwing her feet up over the back of the overstuffed monstrosity as she finished apologizing to Enrique for the ten-thousandth time.

"Judy Howard," he said aloud, lifting his phone again. "No.

She's gone. Miss Ross knew immediately where the leak had to have come from, and Judy admitted to it. Apparently, she was dating somebody on the *TMZ* staff."

"Nice touch," Eleanor mouthed.

He shrugged at her, rolling his eyes as he continued elaborating on the life of the nonexistent traitor. "Yes, she's still in shock. I mean, this is her dream role, Mr. Machinak. She's in hiding right now, yes. She wanted you and Mrs. Valenti to settle on a course of action before she says anything publicly. Of course. No, *she's* the grateful one. And she told me to assure you that she will remain one hundred percent behind whatever you decide."

After a chorus of more "of courses" and "thank yous," he hung up the phone and dropped onto the couch beside her. "I hope there isn't a real Judy Howard working anywhere even entertainment-adjacent," Eleanor commented, sipping at her complimentary bottle of water and wishing it was something stronger.

"I checked all the lists I could and didn't find anybody with that exact name." Leaning forward, he set his phone face down on the table and sat back again. "At least you're banned from any interviews now until you hear from Machinak or Valenti. Nothing to do but wait."

"That suits me just fine. You're sure no one followed us here?"

"For the last five miles I didn't even see another pair of headlights."

"It's so stupid when you look at it from outside," she commented, curling her legs beneath her. "Millions of dollars in flux, careers threatened, because people saw a photo of a blue-and-purple spandex bodysuit."

Cafferty glanced at her. "I haven't even seen it, so I can't comment on whether the uproar is warranted or not."

"I thought you saw it on *TMZ*."

"Nope. They teased it, then you called."

Eleanor opened her phone, pulled up the pics Enrique had sent her, and handed it over. "There you go. You should at least have an idea why you're spending the night in the boonies without a TV or clean pants."

A fleeting smile touched his mouth. For a lawyer—ex-lawyer —he had a keen sense of humor, and a wicked awesome kiss. And a couple of other very nice qualities that had nearly lured her into a marriage. He was perfect. And that had been the problem. She wasn't anything close to perfect. Sooner rather than later he would have realized that, would have gotten tired of cleaning up her messes and anticipating her every need and whim. She would have relied on him for everything, and when he left, as he inevitably would, everyone including her would know that she was a big, helpless fraud. This way she could at least pay him for his trouble—and keep him from blabbing about her and her disaster of a life.

He'd switched gears pretty easily, too, going from fiancé to employee/handler with only a four-week break in between the two, or so she'd told herself anyway. And she only occasionally needed to remind him about boundaries. She took a breath. "What do you think?"

"I think if they don't find some way to keep you in this suit or something really close to it, they're all idiots. This thing is *you*, El. Wow. I can see why you were so excited about it. And I'm sorry it might not happen." He gave the phone back to her.

"Thanks. Me too." She checked the time. Nearly eleven. "We'll need some stuff for tomorrow. Stuff other than free toothbrushes."

"Right." Cafferty pushed to his feet. "I'll go see what CVS has to offer." His phone buzzed, and he checked the screen. "*TMZ*. Sorry, kids, not happening. Not tonight."

"Not ever."

"I'll be back as soon as I can. Should we coordinate a secret knock?"

That made her grin. "You have a key card. Nobody else is getting in here."

"Okay. No phone calls. Unless they're from me or John."

"I know. I do try to learn from my mistakes."

With another glance at her, he left the room, closing the door softly behind him. Without his solid, safe presence the room immediately felt too quiet. The whole building was silent, in fact. Jeez, had the other guests heard all the phone calls? She hoped not. Some of them were bound to see her tomorrow, and she didn't need anybody ratting out her location to the press.

Perhaps she could comp their stay here at the Starlight Bed and Breakfast Inn. That might buy her some privacy. She'd leave that to Cafferty, though; he would have a better sense of whether they needed to take any extra steps for security. He could still go out and not have people pointing phones at him or demanding photos or refunds for past movies they hadn't liked.

It was definitely a weird life, and however much she enjoyed the acting, the slipping into other people's heads and other people's lives, she wasn't entirely convinced she was cut out for all of it. Actors were supposed to be extroverts, feeding on the energy of their audience. Public appearances, though, made *her* nervous as hell. Who were these strangers expecting to meet? Tori from *Primitive*, capable of escaping jungle plane crashes with Daniel Craig? Jen from *Mating Dance*, who went to Hallmark stores to cry over the sympathy cards? She certainly had next to nothing in common with either of them, except for Jen's dislike of tuna.

Well, this was getting her nowhere. Cafferty—Brian—would be back soon, and she would ask him for some small talk like he'd excelled at the first time they'd met. Then she would feel safe again, and calm, and tomorrow would make much more sense than today had. And she would stop remembering what a good kisser he was, because that didn't help anything.

4

The pickings at CVS as far as deodorants and toothpastes were concerned was exceptional. Their selection of clothing, though, had Brian wondering if he could purchase a dozen emergency sewing kits and throw something together using all those frilly pillows and curtains back at the B and B.

El had thanked him for performing another rescue. She was always polite and genuinely grateful, which definitely set her apart from some of her fellow A-list coworkers. He hadn't fallen for her five years ago because she was polite, though. Eleanor Ross, unlike some of the characters she played, was kind, generous, whip-crack smart, and funny to boot. She knew exactly what kind of odd, wildly unpredictable career she'd chosen and delighted in both its flaws and its surprises.

At the same time, she frustrated the hell out of him. When had learning someone's likes and dislikes and attempting to see that person happy come to mean that he was—how had she put it—too intuitive? "Intuitive" hadn't been what she meant. No, she'd meant that he was some sort of weird spy going through her underwear drawer to discover all her secrets and then using them to woo her. As if understanding her automatically made him wrong for her.

Had he gone overboard with making sure she was happy? Maybe. But then when they'd first met she'd been fleeing fans who'd been so rabid at seeing her trapped on the street they'd scared *him* a little. It had been like a horde of zombies yelling "Eleanor" instead of "brains." She'd been shaken, and he didn't want to see her that way again, especially after they'd begun dating.

But after she'd called off their engagement, she'd unfailingly gone for pretty, confident asshats who only noticed that other people existed because those people went to the movies and made them money. Rod the Bod was only the latest of them, and yeah, probably the worst. Nice guys seemed to be stuck in last place in Eleanor's world.

Brian parked the Jeep outside the Starlight and grabbed the pair of bags he'd filled with the best of the crap available after midnight. As an employee, he was *supposed* to keep her happy. And she felt comfortable with that arrangement because she was paying him to be nice. And he stuck around because… Because he still loved her. Yep, he was an idiot. A hopeless one.

What was the saying about insanity? Repeating the same action over and over and expecting a different outcome? He tried not to be an idiot, but taking action meant taking a chance. She'd fired him before when he'd tried pushing her a little toward things that made her uncomfortable. Until now, she'd hired him back, and he'd been grateful to have more time in her company.

Was that enough, though? Holding her car door and buying deodorant, keeping her calendar and watching her go out with losers who wouldn't try getting inside her head because they were too concerned with their own egos?

Brian blew out his breath, locked the Jeep, and climbed the trio of steps to the front door. In a way he was fortunate—he had three choices, after all. Status quo, which was silent torture but meant he could still see her daily; quitting before she fired him this time and going back to the firm and finding someone else; or being who he truly was, not putting up with her shit, and risking her turning him away for good this time.

Yeah, it was probably really bad timing, but sitting back and watching her find someone else, someone who wouldn't challenge her or expect anything more from her than a pretty picture for the cover of *The Inquirer* was worse.

"Okay," he muttered, using his key card on the front door of the Starlight, "no more Mr. Nice Guy."

He climbed the stairs as quietly as he could, because even if he was finished with being nice, he'd still been raised to be polite. Without the noise of televisions, the place felt practically Amish. That could be really fortunate, though, as long as none of the guests used Twitter or Instagram or Facebook. They might not know what had happened. Hell, they might not know who El was, though the proprietor Phillip had seemed to recognize her.

The room he shared with Eleanor was dark when he slipped inside. Halfway across the floor, he bumped his shin on the edge of the coffee table. "Fuck."

"Cafferty?" Her voice came from the direction of the giant bed. A moment later the nightstand light went on, the brightness searing into his brain.

"I have supplies," he said unnecessarily, hefting the bags. "Not much in the way of fashion, but they're clean."

She'd shed her slacks and T-shirt and lay beneath the covers presumably in just her bra and underwear. "Thank you for doing that. I put one of the bed pillows on the couch for you."

Brian cocked his head. *Do it*, he ordered himself. "What happened to *you* taking the couch or the rollaway bed or whatever they have?" he asked aloud.

"I was stressed out," she returned, propping her head up on

one arm and looking very comfortable. "I didn't want to keep driving around looking for someplace safe."

"Well, you're not stressed out now, but I'm still six-two. I'm not sleeping on the couch."

At that, she sat up. "My business is paying for this room."

"I'm paying for the room, as per our usual secrecy procedures. And I'm not sleeping on the couch."

Whether this was the ideal approach or not, it helped that he was tired, worried, and still kind of pissed off that she'd ignored his advice about Rod Bannon. Anyway, he'd drawn his line in the sand, and he was okay with that. Sleeping on that unicorn-barf couch would give him nightmares.

"I don't like this," El stated. "I'm the boss. I get the bed."

"I'm not the one whose phone had the photos on it. I *am* the one who was off work for the night and then had to drive downtown, bribe a boutique lady and a hostess, and then flee with nothing but the clothes on my back. And I'm still too tall for the couch."

For a long moment she glared at him. "Fine," she finally snapped, flinging off the covers and standing. "You take the bed."

"Thank you." He tossed her a bag, partly so he wouldn't stand there staring at her in her cute pink bra and matching panties. "There's toothpaste, deodorant, a pair of sweatpants, and a Hello Kitty T-shirt that might fit you. I'm going to take a shower."

"I—Fine. I'm going to sleep. Don't wake me up."

She hauled a blanket off the bed and dragged it over to the couch, then punched the pillow there a couple of times so he'd know she wasn't happy with the arrangement. But she hadn't threatened to fire him, and she'd given ground. It might mean something, but then again, she'd had a really bad evening and might be averse to losing an ally. And maybe he wasn't above using that against her tonight.

Or maybe they were both just tired and cranky, and tomorrow they'd both fall back into their old, comfortable roles. Brian regarded himself in the bathroom mirror as he shed his T-shirt. No, he didn't think that would be happening. Things had shifted tonight, and he wasn't going to let them shift back, whatever the consequences.

El in ordered isolation didn't happen very often. And nobody but him with her? Even more rare. Which made it literally now or never. And never was too damned far away.

Eleanor awoke from a dream that she was taking orders at McDonald's for some customers who wanted everything custom, and that she was doing it while wearing her awesome superhero outfit—except that everybody behind the counter was wearing an identical uniform.

For a moment she blinked at the unfamiliar ceiling, trying to remember where she was. Not Brussels yet. Maybe not Brussels at all. No, she was a couple hours north of L.A., sleeping on a psychedelic Victorian couch while Cafferty snored six feet away on the giant, comfy bed.

She sat up. Yep, there he was, black hair tousled and handsome face relaxed as he snored away. God, he was gorgeous. She wasn't the only one to tell him that he could find himself starring in Syfy Channel crocodile-versus-anaconda movies without ever taking an acting lesson just because of his looks.

It hadn't been his appearance that had appealed to her, though. It had been his kindness and the way he'd known she wasn't up for talking or being clever the day he rescued her from some really aggressive fans. He'd just…chatted until she'd found her footing again. And he hadn't hit on her but had just treated her like a normal person. No one had done that for a while.

He'd done the normal-person thing again last night, though, and she hadn't appreciated that at all. But fine, if he wanted to be cranky and take the bed out from under her, she could live with that. Whether it had been his job or not, he *had* rescued her. Really efficiently too.

The room had blackout curtains behind the frilly burgundy bordering the windows, but she could still see a crack of light along one edge. Sunrise, or close to it on one side or the other. Glancing at Cafferty again and refusing to imagine what it would be like to be there again, lying beside him, she picked up her phone.

It remained on mute, but she still had nine phone calls and thirty-one messages. Scowling, she hesitated with her finger over the icon before she opened up Twitter. Immediately she wished she hadn't.

She was trending. Four times over. #EleanorRoss, #Super-heroine, #CostumeMalfunction, and #RossMalfunction. And photos of the costume were just...everywhere. That cat was so far out of the bag it couldn't even see the bag anymore.

Okay, she needed to work with what she had, not what she wanted. Clenching her jaw, she started reading through the hashtags. Paramount would be, and so would Machinak and Valenti. According to various musings such as @snowleopard37 and *Variety*'s @JoeNesco, *Prosecutor* looked to be approaching its superhero in the right way. *Variety* even speculated that Teresa Woodward might be a realistic heroine to whom today's women could relate.

At least there was some good news, then. Of course the other half of Twitter was full of speculation about whether the notoriously cagey Enrique Vance would leave the project now that the costume had leaked, or if Paramount would pull the plug on its first big-budget superhero film if it was plagued with leaks before cameras had even begun rolling. And of course the Basement Boys were out in force, angry that a stupid girl would be attempting to move focus away from the next Batman and Superman movies, and arguing about how a female's tensile muscle strength was simply less than that of a man's, so any male superhero could easily overpower a female one. Jerks who lived in their parents' basements or not, the Basement Boys were loud and demanded to be listened to.

"You dove into Twitter, didn't you?" Brian's voice came from the bed.

She looked up. "Four hashtags. Including hashtag Ross Malfunction. I'm a girl and so shouldn't be attempting to play with the big boys."

He put both hands over his face then ran them through his tousled hair. "Oh, God, not the Basement Boys."

"Yep."

"Well, you're braver than I am, because I'm not even looking at my phone until I've had some coffee. What time is it?"

She closed Twitter to check. "Seven eighteen."

"Breakfast is ready, then."

Shoving aside the covers, he rolled to his feet. *Damn.* Wearing nothing but a pair of plaid boxers, Brian Cafferty didn't exactly scream "lawyer." Beach bum, maybe, one of those guys who surfed from dawn to dusk. Or soccer player, because he just looked...fit. Not with the bulgy pecs actors went for—something to give them the appearance of fitness rather than actually being fit—but just active. Well-toned.

"What?" he asked, lowering his hands to look at her.

"Nothing."

"Okay."

"You look good."

His lips curved just a little. "Thanks. So do you. You want the bathroom first?"

Eleanor shook herself. "Yes. Thanks. I won't be long. I have no make-up."

"I put some lipstick in your bag. It looked close to your color, I think. There's some eyeliner in there too."

And there he went, anticipating her needs again. She picked up the plastic CVS bag and headed into the bathroom. A quick shower, a good toothbrushing, and a pink Hello Kitty T-shirt and blue sweatpants later, she felt a little absurd—and a little more ready to face the day. The lipstick and eyeliner served adequately as warpaint, and if she didn't feel terribly composed on the inside, at least she looked it on the outside. Kind of.

"Anybody who takes my photo today is going to make some money," she commented as she emerged into the bedroom again.

"I wouldn't worry about it," Brian returned, hefting his own bag and moving around her into the bathroom. "You would make these curtains look good."

That was probably an exaggeration, because they were hideous in daylight, but she appreciated the compliment. Especially this morning. But a picture of her this morning wouldn't hurt because of the silly clothes. It would hurt because once a photo of her got out, the press would figure out where she was, and the wagons weren't circled yet.

When Brian emerged fifteen minutes later, he wore matching sweatpants and a black T-shirt featuring a unicorn farting a rainbow. She laughed. "Wow."

"Just be glad they didn't have one of these in your size," he commented, tugging down the front of the shirt and rubbing his palm over the unicorn. "Ready for breakfast?"

She heaved a deep breath. "Yeah. Let's get this over with."

He trotted down the stairs in front of her so that she had to hurry or be left behind. Whatever the hell had started with him demanding the bed last night seemed to be over with, or so she'd thought, but as he pulled opened the doors to the big dining room, she abruptly wasn't so certain.

"Good morning," Cafferty said to the room. "I'm Brian, and this is El. We're in hiding."

"Good morning," a chorus answered, followed by a good dozen pairs of eyes doing double takes as they spied her in the doorway. Great. Anybody who might not know who she was at least knew something weird was going on. *In hiding.* If he kept this up, she was going to have to…do something.

"Coffee, El?" a smiling older woman with her purple-streaked gray hair in a ponytail asked.

"Please. Lots of creamer."

"Of course. I'm Joan, Phillip's wife. You met him last night, yes?"

"Yes. This is your place?"

When Brian gestured at her, she frowned. She knew how to make polite chitchat. She just didn't like it very much. But she fell in behind Joan Eaton, who led her over to a large Keurig setup. *Hmm.* She'd half expected the coffee pot would be hanging in the large fireplace, rustic fashion.

"Just pick your brew of choice," Joan said, pointing at the rack of coffee pods, "pop it in here, and press the middle button since you want to add creamer. And you'll find that over there." Turning, she indicated the closest end of the long sideboard, where the coffee accessories led a trail of stacks of pancakes, trays of bacon and sausage, toast, jams, honey, bowls of fresh fruit, and some cannisters of what looked like cereal and granola.

"Thanks. Everything smells delicious."

Joan smiled. "It had better, or we wouldn't be in business." The proprietor handed Eleanor a pretty mug decorated with hummingbirds and fuchsias. "You can eat in here, or we have some tables out on the patio overlooking the pond. It's very pretty this morning. Phillip says he spotted our herd of deer an hour or so ago back in the pine trees."

Wow. Here there were pancakes and deer and hummingbird

coffee cups, while two hours south there would be board meetings and crazy, yelling phone conferences, and probably some serious groveling going on. Groveling she would no doubt have to participate in later. "Thanks," she said again. "Outside sounds wonderful."

Brian was busy gathering food, so she poured herself a cup of coffee, added the creamer and sugar, then headed out through the patio doors to go sit at one of the tables outside.

The air was crisp, cold by Southern California standards, but for the moment, at least, she liked it. Hollywood felt very insular and bottled-up, especially at times like this, and the Starlight Bed and Breakfast Inn was its exact opposite. Eleanor sipped at her coffee and watched a pair of birds playing tag over the small, reed-rimmed pond.

Brian set down a coffee cup, a heaping plate of food, and then himself opposite her. "It's pretty here," he commented and took a tentative drink of coffee.

She looked from his plate to the empty spot in front of her. "Did you forget something?"

Setting down the cup, he picked up his fork. "Don't think so. Aren't you going to eat?"

"But—"

He took a big bite of pancake. "I'm not your butler, El," he said around it. "I do the calendar, remember?"

"You're not still mad about that, are you? I just didn't like you sharing your opinion of who I should or shouldn't be dating. Don't be a baby."

Swallowing, he pinned another bite with his fork. "Fine. No opinions, no fetching. I'm either your secretary, or we're going to have to make other arrangements. You don't get it both ways."

Her throat tightened. "You're not leaving me here alone, are you?" she asked, leaning forward and lowering her voice to a whisper as another couple sat at the table across from them.

"No. I wouldn't do that, for Christ's sake."

"Then why are you stomping on me?"

"I'm not. I decided this current arrangement isn't satisfactory to me, so I'm opening negotiations."

She looked at him. As good as he was at figuring out what she needed before she asked, he'd have to be blind and deaf not to realize that she needed support right now. Not a rebellion. "Your timing sucks, then." Pushing away from the table, she stood and went to get her own breakfast.

Brian watched her go and let out his breath as she stopped at the sideboard. She'd heard all the rumors about her profession over the past few years, that actresses were empty-headed, flighty, and ditzy. She was none of those things, except maybe for being a little flighty. When something bugged her, she avoided it. That was better than making a scene, and for her, "scenes" extended to her own personal life.

So there he was, pushing for something he couldn't even define, muddling through with trying to be supportive and pushing her into looking at him differently all at the same time. Yeah, it was bad timing, but watching her go out with the next Rod the Bod while he made sure her dress would be ready for the Golden Globes—that wasn't happening again.

His phone vibrated for the zillionth time, and he checked his texts. This one was from John Radley, updating them that the studio was less pissed off this morning—probably because the unplanned uniform reveal had gone over much better with the public than they'd anticipated—and reminding him that El needed to keep a low profile and not say a word publicly until all this was settled.

Good. Low profiles and staying away from cameras fit in pretty well with his own half-baked plans. When Eleanor sat down opposite him again, he nodded, pocketing his phone. "John says so far so good, and keep up what you're doing."

"That being hiding?"

"Yep."

"Okay, I can do that. What the hell are *you* doing, though? Do you want a raise? Help? I told you that I don't want a mob or posse or whatever it's called around me. All those people hovering just makes me nervous."

"I know that, and no, I don't want help. I like my job."

She bit off a piece of bacon. "Really? Then what's with the stomping and scowling? I don't need more damn drama, Cafferty."

This would be the tricky part; all of this, such as it was, was based on the idea that she A, still liked him in more than a professional way, and B, hadn't sworn off men yesterday after Rod the Bod's fucking nonsense. "Why did you hire me?"

Cocking her head in the way that had made a million teenage boys fall in love with her in *Obsidian Nights*, she stirred her strawberry yogurt. "I told you, the qualities that made you wrong for a husband make you perfect for a handler."

"Right. And which qualities were those, exactly?"

Beyond her, the middle-aged woman plowing her way through a stack of pancakes lifted her cell phone like she was answering a text, except that she pointed the phone at El while pretending not to and hit a button a couple of times.

"Hold that thought," he murmured, standing and strolling over to where the woman sat with two female companions. "Hi," Brian said, putting a hand on the back of her chair and flashing a bright smile.

"Hi," she and one of her friends said in near unison, and she abruptly dropped her phone into her lap.

"That's Eleanor Ross over there sitting with me. She's an actress, if you didn't know that, and she's been in a couple of pretty popular movies. Anyway, last night some stuff kind of went crazy, and she's pretty upset about it. Actresses, you know, they hide things pretty well, but today is not going to be easy on her."

"So you're going to warn us not to take photos of her and offer us tickets to her next premiere or something?" the third lady suggested, sending El's profile a cool glance.

God, lady, I deal with you guys seven days a week, and twice on Sundays, was right on the tip of Brian's tongue, but he kept his mouth shut. Eleanor's mantra had always been that she'd found herself living a privileged life, which made her fortunate, and part of a teeny-tiny minority of people on the planet. She had no intention of forgetting that, and none of her employees were allowed to do so, either. He tilted his head. Maybe he could get a little help out of this. "I was going to do that, yeah, but... Can I sit down for a sec?"

"Sure," camera lady returned. "Are you her manager?"

"No. I'm her secretary, I guess you'd say. She calls me her handler." Brian pulled out the fourth iron patio chair and sat down, leaning in on the table so he felt more conspiratorial. "Brian Cafferty."

"You were engaged to her," friend number two whispered.

Ah, a big fan, then. That was good. "I was, for about five seconds. We just get along really well."

"So do we get tickets to *Prosecutor* or not? Or the next one she has coming out. What is it? *Carrier*, right?"

"Right. At this point, we're not even sure *Prosecutor* is going to get made. I'll make you a deal. If you keep her visit here to yourselves for another twenty-four hours, I'll share some gossip that'll make *you* go viral."

"What? I thought you worked for her."

"I do. It's not about her."

Camera lady picked up her cup of tea and then set it down again. "OMG, I'm so nervous I'm shaking. What gossip?"

"Twenty-four hours. Deal?" He folded his hands on the tabletop. "I have to watch out for her, first. That's my job."

Number three frowned, probably at the eager expression on number two's face. "You better not be yanking our chain."

"I'm not. But we need to be away from here before you start sending photos and the press vultures fly in."

She blew out her breath. "Fine. Deal."

He nodded, turning his attention to the other two. "Ladies?"

"Deal."

Once they'd all agreed, he leaned in a bit more. "Okay. You know her costume for *Prosecutor* got leaked yesterday, right?"

"I saw it. It's gorgeous. Better than Wonder Woman's."

"Well, we're publicly saying that a new assistant she hired is the one who took her phone and stole the photos. But…it wasn't an assistant. It's not public knowledge, but they're finally making a movie based on *The Fallen Angels* comic series. Rod Bannon and Zac Efron were up against each other to play Omega, the leader of the Fallen. Bannon lost out."

"No way. He's so…pretty!"

"He's dating Miss Ross," camera woman put in.

"Exactly," Brian agreed. "They went out to dinner last night, and suddenly *TMZ* has Eleanor's top-secret photos. So probably no *Prosecutor* for her, which leaves Paramount with a big, fat empty superhero space to fill for next summer. And Rod Bannon totally available."

Number two gasped. "*He* did it? To sabotage her! While they're dating? That's horrible! She's always so nice and funny in interviews!"

"I always thought he was too arrogant for his own good."

"All we have is your word, though," the cynical third friend countered.

"That is true. You could wait and see if Paramount drops *Prosecutor* and green-lights a movie going by the working title of *Crimewave* and featuring a beach-bum superhero, though. It's kind of Rod Bannon's dream job. Of course by then it'll be too late for Eleanor Ross and her female-led superhero movie."

Number three narrowed her eyes. "You sure you're not just

jealous that Rod Bannon is dating Miss Ross? Like Tiffany said, you were engaged to her."

"I might be a little jealous," he admitted, noting that El had shifted her seat and was within earshot now. "But I'm not making this up. And honestly, as long as you wait twenty-four hours, you can say whatever you want. My story has the benefit of being verifiable by both *TMZ* and Paramount, though."

"Okay," camera lady said, holding out her right hand. "If I get a selfie with her."

"If all of us do," Tiffany put in.

Abruptly a pair of hands gripped his shoulders from behind, and not very gently. "Hi, there," Eleanor said smoothly. "I'd be happy to take some photos with you ladies. I don't know what else Mr. Cafferty has been saying, but you have no idea how much I appreciate your giving me twenty-four hours to regroup. I'm just—Ugh, and I'm wearing a Hello Kitty shirt."

"It looks good on you," Tiffany said firmly. "I'm Tiffany Diaz. This is Hillary Mason," she went on, pointing at the camera woman, "and Poppy Heinz."

"Thanks for saying so," El returned, tugging at the front of the shirt and favoring them with a ruthful grin. "It was this one or the unicorn farts one Brian's wearing."

"Hello Kitty wouldn't fit me," he said dryly. "Photos first, then breakfast?"

"That would be perfect, if you don't mind. We're going to tour Hearst Castle in an hour."

"Sure."

For the next few minutes, Brian juggled a trio of phones and took pictures of El with each of her new friends, together and separately. If it gave her some peace of mind for the next day or so, the use of her image as currency was worth it.

As he handed back the last phone, El wrapped her hand around his arm. "How about a walk so I can regroup before the next round of phone calls?" she suggested.

Eleanor had an Oscar nomination in showing emotions and concealing them, but he didn't need a doctorate in acting to know she was pissed at him. Well, he had a slightly larger goal in mind than keeping her safe from prying eyes until the studio figured out the backstory for the photos leaking. "Sure. Want to bring your coffee?"

"That sounds like a good idea."

He picked his up from the table and stepped back. "I thought so."

Tightening her lips, she retrieved her own cup and led the way between the other two tables and out to the gravel path that disappeared where the pond widened out behind a low hill. The two of them worked out together these days, now that the studio had engaged a personal trainer to get her into superhero shape. Even taking that and his longer stride into account, she was setting a pretty impressive pace.

"Correct me if I'm wrong," she said, striding away from the Starlight, "but didn't we spend several hours last night making sure that an imaginary woman was the one who leaked the uniform photos?"

"You're not wrong."

"Then why the hell were you gossiping about Rod to those women? Are you trying to make me lose this role?" She glared at him over her shoulder and continued stomping up the hill.

"Because the Bod doesn't deserve to earn a role in *Crimewave* for what he did to you."

El stopped, the defiant hands-on-her-hips pose diminished because she still held a coffee cup in one hand. "No one will incriminate him, including me."

"Doesn't matter. The people in the industry know he's a prick, and they'll figure out he actually did try to sabotage you to make a space for his own movie. Especially when you stop seeing him after a public date at Almuerzo the night the photos leaked."

"You're sabotaging him, then."

"I'm getting even."

"He didn't do anything to you."

Brian cocked his head. "He put your dream part in jeopardy, he abandoned you in a public place, and he stiffed you with the dinner bill. Even if he hadn't done the other shit, I'd be out to kick his ass."

"Cafferty, you are m—"

"I know," he cut in. "I'm the guy who keeps your calendar. I'm your secretary. You don't need a knight in shining armor. You don't want a knight in shining armor, because you can defend yourself. Sorry. I guess I'm more vindictive than you are."

"You're not just a secretary, Brian," she said, using his first name for the first time in months. "You're my friend, and I do appreciate your...righteous anger at that jerk. And I appreciate you. But you can't go behind my back like that."

Brian took a deep breath. "The better interpretation would be that I've got your back, El."

"Fine. Call it what you want. But I need your assistance right now, not this...whatever it is you're doing." She gestured at the air around them.

"So no independent thoughts, no advice-giving, and no brain-usage on my part?" Yeah he was being an ass, but dammit, if she didn't start thinking differently about how she approached men and relationships, even if she decided that she truly didn't want anything more with him, her next romance would be even worse than Rod Bannon.

"That's not what I said." She turned her back and resumed striding along the trail. "God, you are so—Argh!"

"I'm a pirate?"

She snorted. "Shut up."

"El, when you called off our engagement, you said I was too

intuitive. That I smothered you by doing everything you needed before you asked me for it."

"Before I even knew I needed it." She slowed down but kept moving away from him. "Is that what the crap about Rod was for? You're jealous? You said you could deal with me going out. I asked you that before I offered you the job."

"I can deal with you going out." Brian scowled. "I *could*," he amended. "But when you keep choosing jerks like Bannon, it makes me wonder what the hell must be wrong with me that I came in second. Or third. Or fifth."

"That's not—" Eleanor stopped. Her shoulders rose and fell with the breath she took before she faced him again. "You really want to do this now?"

"Yep."

"Okay. You're fired."

Brian blinked. He'd expected pushback, and he had a ton of opposing arguments, well-thought-through arguments, waiting to counter whatever she said. But he *had* expected a fight. Not her just shutting him down. He probably shouldn't have been so surprised. This made the seventh time she'd fired him in the four years since she'd hired him to be her handler. "For how long this time?" he retorted. "Twelve hours? A week?"

"Permanently. It occurred to me just now that if you weren't...you, I might have listened to your warning about Rod Bannon. But I didn't listen to you, because always in the back of my mind I figured you were a little harder on my boyfriends because you used to be one."

"So this is *my* fault? Wow. You should go on Broadway, because that was some first-class gaslighting, El."

"I'll give you a nice parting bonus so you can take a vacation before you go back to the law firm or whatever you decide to do next. So excuse me, but I'm going to finish my walk."

"You do that."

He stood there, half-empty cup of coffee in one hand, and

watched her take the curve behind the low hill and vanish from sight. When she decided to go for something, Eleanor Ross jumped in with both feet, sometimes without considering all the angles. That was generally where he came in, to figure out the logistics and make sure it happened the way she wanted.

This time, though, she'd forgotten a couple of major details. And he wasn't above using them to his own advantage. Because he knew why she'd fired him. He'd pushed her to make a statement about his place in her life, one that couldn't just be answered by saying he was an awesome employee, and rather than answer truthfully, she'd shoved him away. Again.

Well, this time he wasn't ready to go. Not when he still had questions about how he fit into all this, and whether it could be not just for her, but with her.

5

*S*tupid Cafferty. How typical. Just like every other man in her life, Eleanor reflected, he waited until he figured she really needed him and then decided it was time to move the goalposts. Jerk.

His timing could have been worse, she supposed, taking a second lap around the pretty pond amid the pretty trees and pretty meadows. He could have done this last night at the restaurant and left her to find her own way to a safe place and to make all the preliminary phone calls that had at least made today bearable—so far.

That business of telling people that Rod had done all this— yeah, the first second she'd heard it, she'd kind of been…thrilled that somebody was making sure Rod the Bod would pay for his selfish jerkiness. But that wasn't how this needed to work. According to her agent, it would be better if nobody got the blame. Nobody real, anyway. No blame, no retributions, no burned fingers down the line. Smooth. Or as smooth as it could be, considering.

What the hell was Brian thinking, anyway, doing that to her

now? She had enough crap on her plate right now, for crying out loud. Jerk. "Jerk," she said aloud, while a hummingbird in front of her continued doing whatever it was that humming-birds did to suck nectar out of flowers.

She stayed away from the Starlight until she figured Brian had had enough time to pack his non-bags and leave. She'd have to put in a call to John to come pick her up and find her another place to stay, but they had the room here for two days. She wasn't in any hurry to return home to find someone who could replace Brian—Cafferty, she meant.

Damn it, things had been fine as they were. Why had he decided they needed to change? And asking about where he fell in her ranking of boyfriends had just been mean. She didn't rank her boyfriends, anyway. And she wasn't going to think about it now. She wasn't going to think about how she'd only been engaged one time, and it had been to Brian Cafferty. That should say plenty about where he stood in the rankings.

Or where he had stood until that last conversation. Now he would *have* to move on, since apparently he hadn't done so previously. And she would have to move on, because now that he was gone, she could admit that she enjoyed having him around. That maybe from time to time she imagined what it would have been like if he hadn't been so...perfect.

The big old house came into view again, and this time she took the path leading back to the back patio. Nobody sat there; hopefully all the other guests had left to go tour Hearst Castle or see the sea lions on the coast or whatever it was they'd come to central California for.

Phillip Eaton walked through the breakfast room, an armful of dishes in hand, as she stepped inside. "Your friend said you would be in all day, and he arranged for your lunch and dinner," the owner said with a nod. "I hope salad and baked chicken is acceptable."

"More than acceptable," she returned with a smile. Even when he was fired, Brian still managed to be perfect.

"Lunch at one o'clock, then. And dinner at six."

"Thank you, Phillip."

"You're welcome. I put fresh towels in the bathroom, and there's coffee available in here all day."

"Thanks," she said again.

"And Miss Ross? I heard what happened. Some people are just mean."

"Yes, they are. Thank you for not being one of those people, though."

At that, his smile broadened. "I try."

Handing over her empty coffee cup, she walked to the front of the house and up the stairs. It had been quiet last night, but today it felt more peaceful, probably because nobody else was here. If she'd known ahead of time that a disaster was imminent, she might have bought out the entire B and B and not have had to worry about photos and gossip getting out.

Her door opened with the key card, and she slipped inside. Somebody had made the bed, folded the blanket she'd left on the couch, and opened the two windows overlooking the pond. The warmish breeze felt good and had the benefit of lessening the potpourri scent that lingered in every room she'd so far explored.

She sat on the couch. Brian was gone. She'd see him again, because some of his things remained at her house, but she couldn't hire him again. Not if he was thinking in terms of—of what, winning her back again? Of dating her again? Of sex and engagements and a wedding after all?

A clean break was much better. She should have realized that four years ago instead of hiring him so...so she could still keep him around, like a photo of her favorite vacation or something. Of course he'd also been the best assistant she'd ever had, and losing him would hurt for that reason.

"Fuck," she muttered, pounding her fist into the garish couch.

The bathroom door opened, and she nearly jumped through the ceiling. "You probably shouldn't go in there for a few minutes," Brian said, waving his hand. "I opened the window."

She lowered her hands from where she'd instinctively grabbed her chest. "What the hell are you still doing here?"

"I paid for the room for two nights," he returned, sitting at the far end of her couch.

"For me."

"For us."

"I'll pay you back. Go away."

"I like it here. You go away."

They both knew perfectly well that she needed to be here and he didn't, but evidently he didn't care about that any longer. "Fine," she snapped, lifting one haunch to pull her phone out of her pocket. "I'll call John to come get me."

"You should call for an Uber. John's trying to save your movie right now."

"I know what John is doing for me, jerk. That's why you should leave, and I should stay. And I'm not calling an Uber. You know that."

"Then stay here for another night. You can still use my couch."

"Oh, thanks. So how are you going to keep yourself occupied for the rest of the day with nothing to put on a calendar and no phone calls to movie studios for you to make?"

He picked up a book from the end table. "I thought I'd read. They have a nice little library downstairs."

"Your first day of unemployment and you're going to read…" She bent over to see the title. "*Moby Dick?*"

"Call me Ishmael." Sinking down farther into the deep cushions of the couch, he flipped to the first page.

"You can't be serious."

"Why can't I be?"

"You're going to sit here and read." Eleanor stood up, planting both hands on her hips. "Just to spite me."

"I'm sitting here and reading because I like to read and because I don't have a job. I'm politely allowing you to remain in the room I paid for." He crossed one ankle over the other. "Though I've been thinking about doing some fishing. Phillip says the pond is stocked, and he has poles for his guests to use. It's catch and release, but who wants to clean the fish after you catch them, anyway?"

"This is ridiculous. You're ridiculous. I'm calling John."

Before he could say anything else, she hit quick dial, found John Radley's number second under Brian's, and punched it. Her agent picked up after the first ring. "El? How are you holding up?"

"Not great. I had to—"

"Listen, I've got a call in to Paramount, but so far they've come down on your side in all this. We're calling it an unforeseen complication. They do want to redesign the costume, though, since its reveal was supposed to be such a big deal in the film."

Shit. She'd loved that costume. "I get it," she said aloud. "The reason I—"

"I'm trying to arrange for you to have dinner with Enrique Vance to make sure things are smoothed over. As far as everybody knows, you are so upset that you've gone into hiding, and you're willing to leave the film if that saves the project, even though none of this is your doing. So stay where you are. Let Cafferty field your phone calls, but take any from the studio or Machinak and Valenti. I've been giving everybody his number."

Dammit. "John, I—"

"Hey, Molly just walked in. Paramount's on the other line. I'll update you as soon as I know anything. Hang in there, El."

The phone clicked dead before she could respond. "Well,

that's just it," she went on into dead air, "I had to fire Cafferty. Yes. No, he was just getting too wrapped up in my personal life." She paused as if waiting for a response. "Sure. Send her on up. Cafferty told you where I'm staying, yes? No, tomorrow's fine. I'll see her then. Thanks for finding me somebody before I even knew I needed them. Bye."

When she lowered the phone, Brian was eyeing her. "So I'm replaced already?"

"If I like her. Denise Mayo," she made up. "Heard of her?"

"No. Did she go to school with Judy Howard, by chance?"

Judy Howard, her made-up assistant's assistant. "Are you accusing me of lying?"

"Girl, you lie for a living," he responded easily. "You've said so yourself. And whatever. I don't care if Denise Mayo is made up or not, or if she's best friends with Tina Mustard. I'm not working for you anymore. From now on, we're equals."

She hesitated, his choice of words making her skin heat. "We've always been equals." She'd never talked down to him or asked him to do anything stupid or crazy. Really crazy, anyway.

"Except now you can't fire me. I don't have to leave because you don't like where our conversation is going, because I reserved this room with my credit card."

"Just because I don't like you comparing yourself to my other boyfriends doesn't make me unreasonable, you know." She folded her arms across her chest.

"You fired me because you can't make yourself say out loud that you still have feelings for me, just like I do for you."

Oh, this was not fair. "I'm going fishing," she stated and turned for the door.

"Coward."

"Oh, so now we're in a Western, and I'm supposed to turn and fight you because you called me out? Don't be an idiot." Usually Brian kept his car keys right inside the front door. She glanced toward the exit. Yep, there they were. She could grab them and go before he realized she'd taken off. Of course then he'd probably call the cops on her for grand theft auto, but at least she wouldn't have to have this conversation.

Eleanor took a breath. God, she *was* a coward, ready to break the law to avoid saying or thinking anything uncomfortable. She clenched her jaw and faced him again. "I don't have feelings for you."

"Liar."

"Stop insulting me!"

"Stop lying, then."

"Okay, I do have feelings for you. Friend feelings. You've been a good friend. I know I'm high-maintenance, and that didn't scare you away. I appreciate that." She kept her back pressed against the door; knowing she could escape if she needed to made her feel a little steadier. And he stayed on the couch, because he probably knew the same thing about her.

"Of course you didn't scare me away. You just wanted me on your payroll so you could push me away whenever you felt like you were starting to rely on me too much."

"Yes, I relied on you. I don't hire people I don't need. Your problem is you keep forgetting it's a job—a *job*—and you start putting personal feelings into everything."

Brian opened his mouth then shut it again. *Ha.* At least he was self-aware enough to realize she wasn't just spouting nonsense. She had a point. A good point, damn it all.

"Okay," he said after a moment. "Maybe it is all me, then. We had a fling, took it too seriously, and you just saw the light before I did."

Eleanor nodded. "Yes. Exactly that."

"So there really is nothing left between us. No carnal, sexual pull, and no chance of a happily ever after. And you aren't pushing me away because your dad died when you were a kid and you have a thing about any man getting too tangled up in your life."

THAT WAS A CHEAP SHOT. "THAT WAS A CHEAP SHOT," SHE SAID aloud. "Don't use your attorney training on me. I'm not some felon you're trying to get to confess."

"I'm not that kind of attorney, anyway. You just…" He slapped the book closed and dropped it at his feet. "You don't like to yell, so instead you run. If you would just stop once in a while and tell me what the hell is bothering you, maybe I could stop doing it, or it could turn out that my reasons for doing it aren't the ones you think they are."

"All of your arguments seem to hinge on your being right and my being wrong. I'm the first one to admit that I'm not perfect, but jeez, Brian. Look in the mirror for once."

Slowly he climbed to his feet, all six-foot-two of well-toned, capable man, and walked up to her. Even in sweats and a rainbow-farting unicorn shirt, he was nothing to sneeze at, and yeah, she did enjoy looking at him. Maybe it was just physical, then. That argument might make more sense to him. And to her.

When he stopped, she could have reached out and poked him, he was so close. It could have been intimidating, but she'd never felt anything like a physical threat from him. Intellect-wise, yeah, he could probably run circles around her, but he'd never done that, either. She lifted her chin to look him in the eye.

"What? Am I supposed to melt into your arms now or something?"

Blue eyes held her gaze. "Just tell me, straight up, one thing. Am I wrong? Is there nothing here?" He gestured between the two of them. "Because I feel it, every day. Every time I set eyes on you or turn around to see you looking at me. I feel it, and *that* is why I've stuck around for four years. That is why I hate that every man you've gone out with since has been some high-testosterone jackass who's never had a thought beyond how many hours he needs to spend at the gym."

Oh, boy. Brian Cafferty was a smart guy. And at least to herself she could admit that some of what he said made sense. She did have a track record for dating jerks. Rod had only been the latest, and yes, by now she should have known better. Still, Rod was the first one to have actively tried to sink her career to further his own. According to Brian, her next boyfriend would be the actual King Kong. "Being self-centered is a hazard of and a necessity to this profession. I just need to be more aware of that."

"Yeah, you do. But you didn't answer my question, El."

Now would be an awesome time for Enrique or John or Taylor at Paramount to give her a call. A couple of minutes to think, to figure out what she'd kind of been avoiding for a couple of years. "What's wrong with the way we've been doing things for the past four years? We're good together. The kids' camp was your idea."

"It was your idea. I just helped figure out the logistics. And the—"

Somebody rapped at the door. Jumping, Eleanor spun around and yanked it open. *Thank God.* A distraction.

Phillip Eaton stood there, his hand still raised in a fist to knock. "Oh. I—your salads are ready. Do you want them up here or out on the porch? We have a nice breeze going today."

"The porch, please." Eleanor slipped past him before he could step back. A few minutes. Just a few minutes to think. Because Brian had called her out on the running-away thing, and he was right. She did run, avoid sticky situations rather than confront them. But apparently this time he meant to chase her until he had some answers. And honestly, if the past day had proven anything, it was that she needed to figure some things out for herself too.

"Shitty timing, Phil," Brian commented as El darted out the door in the direction of the stairs.

"I—sorry."

"Don't worry about it. I needed a couple of minutes to regroup too."

The proprietor cocked his head. "Are you two a...a thing, then? I thought she was dating Roderick Bannon. And my wife said somebody in here slept on the couch last night."

"We were a thing," Brian said, stuffing his phone into his sweatpants pocket. "What we are now is kind of up for debate."

"They said this morning that her new movie is on hold because of all the costume stuff. That's why she's hiding out here, I presume?"

"Who said?"

"On the TV. *Good Morning America.*"

"You have a television?"

Phillip's face flushed. "Well, a small one, in our bedroom. We like to keep up with the news and everything. Don't let that get around to the other guests. No televisions is kind of our thing here."

"Hey, you keep our secret safe, we'll keep yours." With a quick grin, Brian motioned the older man to precede him down the hallway. With the swiftness that things churned in a twenty-four-hour news cycle, it was helpful to know that El's costume was still national entertainment news even if he wished that wasn't the case. Of course the popularity of Eleanor herself contributed to that, a kind of weird catch-22.

But however much the costume and this part meant to her, for him, all that came in a distant second today. As uncomfortable as the conversation made her—and him, now that he'd realized he had been pushing his own agenda on her this whole time—it needed to happen. They needed to get this mess straightened out. However much it would hurt for him to leave her employment, he'd learned from experience that watching her be happy with somebody else would be worse.

Phillip's wife Joan stood talking with Eleanor on the patio, two very large salads and the one set table next to them. "We're all booked again tonight, but no one new is coming in until tomorrow."

"I was just wondering," Eleanor returned with one of her gracious smiles. "I know I can be a disruptive presence."

"Oh, nonsense. You aren't our first celebrity, Miss Ross. In fact, the lack of televisions here is one of the accommodations we've made for that very reason."

Except for the one they kept in their room. They would need to know who their guests were, though—some celebrities might like a degree of anonymity but hated to be completely unrecognized. Brian took the seat opposite where El was standing. "Thanks for that," he said aloud. "If you could arrange selective internet, that would be even better."

"We've tried, believe me. People and their phones. It's worse than an addiction, I swear." Joan shook herself. "Don't get me started. Anyway, let me know if you need anything else. I'm baking chicken for dinner tonight, if that's acceptable."

"That sounds perfect," Eleanor put in. "Thanks, Joan."

"You are very welcome, my dear."

Once the proprietors had retreated into the house, Eleanor pulled her salad closer and picked up her fork. "They're nice. How much extra are you paying for the lunch and dinner service?"

Shrugging, Brian dug into his own lunch. "I don't know yet. But it's worth it, since our only alternative is a couple of frozen burritos stuck to the ice cream at CVS. And yes, I checked."

"See? This is nice. What's wrong with going on like this?" She gestured between the two of them.

"Because it doesn't go anywhere. Do you just want us to hang out together forever while you date jerks and I... Well, I'm not dating anybody else. Not while I'm around you."

Her mouth tightened. "Brian, I like you. I do. But this right now is—"

"It's safer. Like I said, you can fire me if you start to get too dependent on having me around. But it's not enough for me. So I'm either in all the way or out all the way."

She jabbed at her lettuce and bacon bits. "If it was just you deciding all this, where would we be?"

"You wouldn't be sleeping on the couch, for one thing. And I wouldn't be living in a condo in Brentwood."

"We'd be living together, you mean. And sleeping together." She sipped at her lemonade, which also looked homemade. "And not going anywhere from there would be okay with you? Your requirement is sex and exclusivity?"

If he said yes to that, would she agree to it? For him, it would mean that she would be safe and protected and someone would always be looking out for her best interests. That he could be with her and inside her and that she couldn't fire him. For her, it would mean she could still escape if she needed to, because they wouldn't be bound together by rings or any of that pesky marriage and till-death-us-do-part stuff.

"It's a start," he said slowly. "But it's not enough."

"We went through this before, and we weren't right for each other. What makes you think that we are now?"

"Dammit, Eleanor, *I* didn't think we were wrong for each other. I don't even know why it was you decided that we wouldn't work. It would help if you told me."

That made her grimace, but she didn't stand up or pretend her phone was ringing or something. That in itself had his heart beating a little faster. This might not go the way he wanted, but one way or the other, he would know.

"It was when you flew to New York for your friend Mark's bachelor party," she said, her gaze still on her salad.

"I was only gone for three days. What the hell happened?"

"That first morning I got the call from John saying that Abrams wanted me for the female lead in *Primitive*. That it would mean spending three months on Maui filming, and I would have to drop out of the running for the part in *Midsummer Days*. The first thing I wanted to do after I hung up with John was call you. Not to tell you the news, but to ask if you were okay with me being gone for three months and if you thought *Primitive* would be a better move for me than *Midsummer Days*. I didn't know what to say on my own."

"El, y—"

"It was *my* decision, *my* career. You were still a lawyer and really knew shit about Hollywood back then. But it was like I came second in my own life. In my own head."

Brian looked at her. When she'd called him that day, she'd sounded a little nervous, but then she'd told him about getting *Primitive* and working with Daniel Craig, and he'd figured that had been the reason for any anxiety. And she'd later used the beginning of that three-month absence to call off the engagement, even though she'd hired him as her handler four weeks later.

"You made the decision, though. Without my input."

"Yeah, after I first decided that I couldn't marry you. That I could use *Primitive* to escape the relationship." She shrugged, a tear running down her face. "I guess you were right. I am a coward. But then I've always been a coward, haven't I?"

Things had definitely felt different when he'd returned from New York, but he hadn't been able to put his finger on why, at least not until she'd basically said she couldn't marry him then boarded a plane for Hawaii. Agreeing to work for her had both changed what had become a set path for his life and had given him what he hoped was the opportunity to figure out what the hell had happened.

"Don't punch me," he said slowly, "but I think you weren't used to having a man in your life, and the idea that you could be adding one back in there *for* life did scare you. I mean, I'm not a psychologist or anything, but I know you adored your dad. Most of us as we get older go through the 'my dad doesn't know anything' stage before we realize he's actually kind of midway between superhero and stifled jerk."

"I think it's more that you're too perfect," she countered, her face completely serious, as far as he could tell.

That stopped him for a second. "Dude, you're kidding, right?"

El shook her head. "You always know what to say, and you always know what I need before I even know, and you're funny and smart and kind and gorgeous. I'm a mess. I totally know that."

"Eleanor Grace, I've been in love with you for a little over four years. That's a lot of time to figure out what you like, what you want, and what bothers you. I don't want you to be sad or scared, and so I do what I can to keep those things away from you. That's what love is, you know. Doing your best to protect your partner and help them be happy and successful."

"But then what does that make me? You were an up-and-coming law superstar, just about to become a junior partner, and I hired you to be my handler. Like a dog handler only with a phone."

Brian snorted. "My dad's a lawyer, and my granddad's a lawyer. Yeah, I figured that's what I would do, and I was pretty good at it. Then you dumped me. When you called me again it only took me about ten minutes to decide to quit and go work for you. I haven't missed it for a day, and it's been handy here, knowing lawyer stuff."

"So you don't regret anything since you met me?"

"The luckiest day of my life was when that sign fell off that truck and nearly totaled your Tesla." He stabbed at his lettuce, already halfway to hating himself but knowing it would be worse if he stopped there. "But if you're just grateful or you just see me as a bodyguard or your shopping buddy or something, you need to tell me, El. The truth. Not what you think I want to hear or what makes things easiest on you."

Their eyes met for a moment, and he wanted to swat everything off the table and reach over to kiss her. At the same time, he felt like he had that first day they'd met, that he was the high school math nerd and she was the most popular girl in school and he had no business even talking to her, much less asking her to prom.

"I need to go take another walk," she announced. Eleanor pushed away from the table, took another swallow of her lemonade, and headed off the porch.

Brian sat back. *Dammit.* They still had that connection. He could feel it. But if she wasn't willing to risk herself that far, what lay between them wouldn't matter. It would just wither and die.

"Coming?" she asked from the foot of the steps, stopping to face him.

He shot to his feet. "Yes, ma'am."

"You ticked me off, making me get my own breakfast and stuff," she said, starting off along the pond.

Their last walk hadn't ended well. He hoped this one went a little better. "I was feeling abused."

"I decided I liked it, though. I didn't hire you to be my step-and-fetch guy, anyway. I just always knew you would do whatever I asked, and I started to abuse it. I needed a shake-up."

"This isn't just a shake-up or a ploy for a raise, you know. I totally wouldn't go to this much trouble for a raise." Brian kept up with her, resisting the urge to reach for her hand. He could still get punched—figuratively at the least.

"I know." She sighed. "I was trying to make you into an employee, I think. So I could respect you a little less. Like you a little less. Fire you, eventually, and not hire you back again."

"You fired me this morning, as I recall."

"And I meant it. But I didn't fire you because I stopped respecting you. I fired you because you were right, and I wanted to run."

He stopped in the shade of an old, bent oak tree. "I was right about what, exactly?" he asked.

She continued on for another few feet, slowed, and turned around to slow walk back to him. "I didn't think about it that way until today, but I think I did keep you around as my backup plan. So I could see you and have you in my life without doing anything brave about it." Eleanor scowled, the expression still attractive on her face. "I play all these brave women who fling their hearts into the fire without a second thought, and I can't do it in real life."

"It matters in real life. In a movie, somebody else writes the story, and you take off your costume and go home at the end of the day."

Outdoors like this, her hazel eyes looked more green than brown in the shade as she gazed at him. "Am I really worth all this nonsense to you?"

"Yes," he responded without hesitation. "Look at it this way —I will never compete with you over a part. I will always tell you the truth, and I will never fool around on you. Hell, you know I haven't been on a date in four years."

"Yeah, I know. I was watching."

"Then what happens now?" he asked, because that had to come from her. He was liking this new El, the one who smacked him back in the face with straight answers, even more than the other, more elusive one. But this one might actually walk away from him and mean it.

"The f—"

Her phone rang, and with a quick frown, she pulled it from her pocket. "John," she muttered and lifted it. "Hey." She listened for a few seconds then held up her hand. "John, John, wait a sec. I'm right in the middle of something. I'll call you back in ten minutes, okay?" Another pause. "No. I mean, yes, I get it. I'll call you back. Okay? Bye. Bye." She tapped her phone and pocketed it again.

"Good news or bad news?" Brian asked.

"We're still doing the movie," she said, taking a step closer to him.

Thank God. "That is very good news. This is your *Iron Man*, you know. I think you're right about that. What is th—"

"Shut up."

Brian snapped his jaw closed. "Okay."

"I'm trying to find a clever way to say all this stuff in my head and not sound like I'm quoting from *Romancing the Stone* or something."

The dark and worried lump in his chest melted away, just like that. Just a few hopeful words from her, and he was sane and whole and happy. "El, I'm a sure bet. Just tell me."

At that, she smiled. The rare smile, the one that touched her eyes and shivered warm all the way down his spine. "I love you, Brian Cafferty," she murmured, sliding her arms up around his shoulders and lifting up on her toes. "You are the most patient man in the world. Will you be engaged with me again, with the intention of that leading to a long marriage, a dog, and maybe a couple of babies?"

He looked her in the eyes, wondering if she could feel his hands shaking as he gripped her waist. "You're sure."

"Yes."

"Then I'm all in. For good, El." Brian lowered his head and

caught her upturned mouth with his, kissing her in the way he'd missed doing for four long, long damned years. It was worth the wait. She was worth the wait.

"For good," she murmured against his mouth and kissed him again. "And I even know where we can get married."

Yep, they were going to become regulars at the Starlight Bed and Breakfast Inn. Hell, they might never leave.

THE END

PASTIES AND POOR DECISIONS

MOLLY HARPER

1

*A*nastasia Villiers, socialite and minor reality television star, had hit rock bottom. And that rock was named Espoir Island.

Anastasia pressed her forehead against the cold window glass of the *Woeful Lady*, Espoir's principal ferry to the mainland.

It would be at least another hour of rough, choppy water before Espoir came into view. More than twenty years before, back when she was still Ana Gustavsson, she'd ridden away from that sight on this same rusted, battered passenger boat, promising herself that she'd never see either again. And here she was, right back where she started, with almost nothing.

Her home was a tiny spit of rocks in Lake Superior and technically part of Michigan, though Canada and the States had a brief skirmish over the right *not* to claim it during the 1880s. Originally called *Sans Espoir*, meaning "without hope" by the French settlers, they declared it "unlivable" after a few decades, and it was established as a "treatment colony" for leprosy patients. Blessed with little more than rocky shores, thick forests and isolation, modern tourists who summered on Espoir couldn't rent houses on the more glamorous Mackinac Island or even Sault Ste. Marie. And after one summer, they rarely came back. Anastasia certainly hadn't planned on coming back.

Ana Gustavsson had been an unremarkable student with little discernible talent and few ambitions beyond moving to a big city for some other kind of life. She supposed that she'd done just that. She just hadn't planned for what would come after, which had been a near-fatal error on her part.

She should have seen it coming. After all, she'd seen this sort of thing play out multiple times amongst her social circle. Her husband, Sebastian Villiers, was a self-styled "titan of industry." And titans played fast and loose with trivial things like taxes and trade regulations. Amongst her friends (or, at least the people who had called themselves her friends up until three days ago), raids from federal authorities were just an inconvenience that came up every once in a while—like your facialist getting the flu. And sure, occasionally, that meant fleeing the country for a spur of the moment "vacation" to Switzerland or one of the islands where extradition didn't exist, until the matter could be cleared up. (It didn't count as being a fugitive if you flew a private jet.) Then again, her friends' husbands were usually loyal enough to take their wives *with them* when they made their escape to consequence-free paradise.

But Bash hadn't done that.

Bash had always assured her that he had contingency plans in place, that there were routes planned and resources stashed away for an emergency like say, federal authorities attempting to arrest him for an impressive array of white-collar crimes. Anastasia just always assumed that she was included in those plans. She'd come home from an impromptu Tuesday brunch to find federal agents raiding her Broome Street penthouse, a penthouse she'd been given fifteen minutes to pack what personal items they didn't consider evidence and vacate. Their homes in Miami, the Hamptons, Napa, the apartment on the

Upper West Side Bash thought she didn't know about, they were all being similarly seized and searched. Frantic phone calls to an embarrassing number of the contacts in her phone left her feeling even more alone and adrift. Bash's number was "out of service." His trusted legal team only responded to tell her that while her husband was their client, she was not and should not expect any help from them. Her personal banker pretended not to know who she was.

For the rest of her life, she would remember that moment when she was on her knees in her custom walk-in closet, cell phone pressed to her ear. She was shoving random clothes into a Louis Vuitton duffel bag, while a sympathetic secretary informed Anastasia that Mr. Villiers very recently sold his partnership in the investment firm his family founded. "Recently," as in that very morning.

It was their driver, poor Mark Bingley, who met her outside their building to tell her that he'd dropped Bash and a Pilates instructor named Wren at a private airfield, bound for the Caymans that morning. And there had been a lot of luggage involved.

That was when the weasel-faced process server approached Ana on the sidewalk and handed her divorce papers. All of this had been recorded by ever-helpful paparazzi, and Anastasia could only hope that Bash hadn't been the ones to tip them off, just to give him more time to get away.

For two days, she'd survived on caffeine, panic, and the cash she just happened to have in the handbag she chose that fateful morning. All of her credit cards were cancelled. She only managed to get her plane ticket because Bash hadn't thought to change the login for their American Airlines account. While the credit cards were defunct, they had built up just enough reward points to cover a *coach* seat to the Upper Peninsula. She'd crashed on her hair colorist's couch, for God's sake, contemplating what life choices led to a person's list of acquaintances who would help her out in a crisis being limited to the person who put in her fucking highlights.

Anastasia hadn't even had time to process the emotions involved in her marriage and world falling apart. She couldn't even think about how she felt about her husband's betrayal or how stupidly naive she'd been. The only thing she'd been able to feel through the shock was the overwhelming humiliation. Wren—just Wren, no last name, though she was too damn young to make or understand the Cher comparison—had been *her* Pilates instructor first. Anastasia had been the one to talk Bash into taking sessions because he was always complaining about his weight, but he didn't like lifting or running. She'd been so stupidly pleased when he'd taken to the sessions, even scheduled extra solo lessons with Wren during the week.

Honestly. She should have known something was up.

Anastasia felt the windowpane warm beneath her forehead and leaned away, sliding a navy U M baseball cap over her long blond hair. She angled it over a delicate oval face, as if it could shield her. The last thing she wanted was to be recognized by the dozen or so Espoir Island commuters sitting inside the ferry to avoid the frigid winds. She was still Gustavsson enough to try to find the bright side in all this. In the words of her mother, if your roof leaked, it meant you had a roof. At least she wasn't going to jail like those poor actresses who had paid their children's way into college. She had watched the media coverage for weeks, perplexed as to why so many people had seemed so surprised by those stories, the collective moral outrage.

The elite had access to special privileges *because* they were the elite. They had the money and the connections to make things happen. It was the way things worked. It was the way things had *always* worked. It was why she had worked so damn hard to become a member of the elite in the first place, clawing her way up from discount shoe store clerk to personal shopper to Mrs. Sebastian Villiers.

Ana's mother had also spouted wisdom about heights and pride and busting her proverbial ass combining the two.

In the distance, Espoir Island splayed up from the gray froth like an old woman on her back, trapped forever in the "I've fallen and I can't get up!" position. The waterfront businesses sagged along the shoreline, comfortable as a faded housecoat is welcoming. Graying clapboard houses sprouted from the rocky cliffs like chin hairs. The island's primary tourist "attraction," an enormous old hotel called the Seacliff Inn, known for its authentic Senate bean soup, stood molting on the northmost hill.

On the east side of the island, far out of sight, Ana's late parents had lived in an old fisherman's cottage, which had belonged to her father's family for generations. When her parents passed, her cousin Fred inherited it, as the oldest male in the Gustavsson line, such as it was. Fred had been kind enough to pack her parents' things away in a storage unit near Brimley, because there wasn't any room on the island for something as frivolous as storing things you didn't use every day.

Fred and his wife lived in the cottage now, and with four huge teenage sons, there certainly wasn't enough room for Ana to bunk there. So even if she was coming home, she technically wasn't going "home."

She dialed the security code into her phone, grateful that she'd kept the same number since her single days, and therefore her own phone plan, all because she was unwilling to give up her early-adopted 212 area code. She dialed her daughters; first her oldest, Chloe, then Arden, her chest tightening painfully when both calls when to voicemail. Chloe hadn't answered since Tuesday, insisting that she had no idea where her father had gone to, and she didn't really have time to deal with "all the drama" when she was in the middle of an important internship with a London-based fashion label. Arden had never answered, but her roommate at Brown informed Anastasia that Arden was

"super busy" with midterms and just didn't have time to talk...
or text...or email. If their posts on their social media—involving
new cars and some very expensive jewelry—were any indication, the girls had chosen who "got them" in the divorce. And it
wasn't Anastasia.

It hurt, but in a strange way, she thought maybe she should
be grateful that Bash was making an effort to secure the girls'
loyalty. Ana had watched her friends fight tooth and nail for
child support, to try to prove to their exes that they couldn't just
walk away from their children.

Even if Bash didn't live up to the promises he was making
the girls, they had trust funds provided by their grandfather.
The elder Mr. Villiers had been surprisingly accepting of his son
marrying "so far beneath him" as Ana's mother-in-law put it.
Her father-in-law had been glad of the "good old Midwestern
salt of the Earth stock" mixing with his gene pool, even if Ana
had found the condescension mildly insulting. He'd given both
girls education funds, plus trust funds large enough to support
them comfortably for several lifetimes.

The girls' defection hurt. Ana couldn't deny that. She'd
thought she had a close relationship with her kids. She certainly
devoted more time to them than her peers had to their children.
She thought that meant something. She thought her daughters
were strong enough, smart enough, that they couldn't be
bought. Yes, they'd had a cook and housekeeper, nannies and
special tutors, dance instructors, *dressage* instructors, fencing
instructors—but *she'd* been the one shuttling them back and
forth to those lessons, attending the plays, the doctors' appointments, the parent-teacher conferences. She was the one who
put them to bed every night.

When her schedule allowed.

But that hadn't meant much to the girls, apparently. Like so
many, they followed the money. She supposed she couldn't
blame them. She was terrified of being penniless, but for her, it

was simply a return to the state she'd known as a girl. Her daughters had only known privilege and protection. How could she expect them to give up all that they'd known, out of loyalty to her?

Anastasia would be the first to admit that she'd lost a bit of her identity once the girls started high school. In her twenties, she'd devoted herself to becoming Mrs. Sebastian Villiers, socialite and philanthropist. In her thirties, she was mother to two future debutantes, molding and preparing them for the most cutthroat educational and social circles in the world. But then they'd made it more than clear that they were ready for those circles on their own...she didn't know what to do with herself. Now in her...late thirties, her brief stint as a fringe "friend" on the *True Housewives of Manhattan* lead to some name recognition and D-list celebrity, which she'd been trying to translate into her own haircare line, her own line of household furniture, and a discount fashion label when the bottom dropped out of her world.

She supposed that was all over now. No one wanted to have hair like an acknowledged train wreck, no matter how shiny and bouncy it may be. The same went for clothes and cheap, easy-to-assemble furnishings. Of all the things that were no longer hers, that bothered her the least. She'd never really been passionate about those projects. It just seemed like that's what you *did* when people recognized your name: you turned it into a brand. It was one of the few things about her that Bash had seemed interested in, in the last couple of years, capitalizing on her notoriety, building "their empire," as if decades of indecent success under his father's leadership wasn't enough.

The boat bucked violently as it swerved broadside towards the dock. Ana's stomach roiled and she gripped the seat in front of her to steady herself. It had been far too long since she'd been on a proper boat, without white-uniformed waitstaff and cocktails on hand. She tried not to think of how her father would react to a Gustavsson having seasickness on the fucking *ferry*.

Outside, she could hear the clang of iron and men's gruff voices as the dockhands tied off the ropes. Ana stood on wobbly legs, slinging her duffle over her shoulder. She almost buckled under its weight, smacking her hip against the hard plastic bench. It had been a *long* time since she'd carried anything so heavy for herself. Adjusting the cap low over her wide blue eyes, she followed the commuters shuffling out of the main cabin and into the howling wind.

"It's fucking *March*," she grumbled, pulling the collar of her jacket around her chin. She'd grabbed the Prada trench as an after-thought, just as the jack-booted federal thugs forced her out of her home of fifteen years. The lightweight wool was designed for casually strolling down an urban sidewalk while window-shopping for pretties, *not* braving the breath of an icy northern god who was none too happy to see her return.

Her last-season booties were super cute, but they were not made to navigate the slick patches of ice on the concrete dock. In the distance, through the fading twilight, she could see a semi-sort-of familiar face in Dougie Jergenson under a red plaid Stormy Kromer cap. That face was a little doughier than the last time she'd seen him, but he'd used the same goofy "howdy neighbor" wave since high school. There was a strange sort of assurance in that. He'd been her class president and a Future Business Leader of America, determined *not* to leave the island, to "make his home a better place." Ana had scoffed at the time, but now she couldn't help but envy him. If he failed on Espoir Island, he wouldn't fall that far.

Short, with his mother's stocky build and warm brown eyes, Dougie ran a second-rate property management company on the island. Not second-rate because he did a bad job, but because he literally managed second-rate properties. There weren't that many first-rate homes on Espoir.

"Well, Ana Gustavsson, look at ya! Haven't changed a bit!" he crowed over the wind, reaching for her bag.

She smiled, grateful to hand off her burden, even as she glanced around to see if anyone heard him call her name. "I'd like to think that's not true."

He reached out with his free arm as if he was going to hug her, and then reconsidered. He went for a more professional handshake, even while he frowned at her ungloved hands. And she wasn't sure how she felt about it. She'd known (and been quietly annoyed by) Dougie since kindergarten. The fact that he felt the need to distance himself with a handshake didn't speak well of how she might be received on the island. Not that she was looking for a warm homecoming, but clashing with her former neighbors wasn't going to get her off of the island any faster.

Behind him, Anastasia could see an early model Ford SUV parked behind him on Main Street, a battered magnetic sign reading, "Jergenson and Sons Property Management." Inside, in the passenger seat, another familiar face was practically pressed against the window in eager anticipation.

Dougie followed her eyeline to his wife, who was peering through the glass at Anastasia like she was some sort of zoo specimen. He frowned again, at her unabashedly eager expression. "You remember my Bonnie."

Dougie and Bonnie had dated since their freshman year, and he called her "my Bonnie" even then. Dougie was a sucker for a good folk song-based pun. Anastasia chose not to mention "remembering" Bonnie because she'd been an absolute cow for the entirety of their childhood. How Bonnie had ended up with a lovable goof like Dougie was a mystery for the ages, one Anastasia just didn't have the mental energy to contemplate.

"Of course." She offered Bonnie the barest of smiles through the glass.

"When she heard ya were coming back to the island, she just

had to come see ya for herself. She watched all of your episodes on the TV, ya know?" Dougie glanced over his shoulder at Bonnie and cleared his throat, as if he'd suddenly remembered the connection between her "fame" and what had brought her back to Espoir. "Um, how ya holding up there? With your husband and all?"

"I'd really like to just get to the house and settle in, Dougie, if you don't mind."

"Of course, of course!" he boomed, opening the back passenger door and rounding the SUV to put her bag in the back. Bonnie, who wore a thick knit cap over a severe, heavily blonde-streaked bob, didn't turn to look at her. Because that made sense.

"Bonnie."

"Ana, nice to see ya," she said in a tone that was at odds with the fervent expression on her face just a minute ago. Anastasia just shook her head and cupped her hands over the heating vent. Dougie slid into the driver's seat and thoughtfully turned the heater on full blast.

"We figured you wouldn't have time to shop for groceries tonight, so we brought ya some pasties from mom's shop." Dougie jerked a thumb towards the small Coleman cooler in the seat next to her. Anastasia gasped, removing the lid and letting the sausage and onion-scented steam envelope her. She groaned at the sight of the foiled wrapped packets and felt her mouth water as Dougie pulled onto Main Street without even looking for traffic…because there wasn't any. "Ma labeled them, 'breakfast, lunch, dinner, and all.'"

Dougie's mom, Cheryl, owned the Espoir Island Pasty Shop, the oldest (and only) "pasties-serie" on the island. Pasties, a sort of Cornish-slash-Finnish hand pie that sustained miners during their long subterranean workdays, were a staple of her childhood and a cornerstone of the Espoir diet. Cheryl had tweaked the recipes out of the traditional meat-and-rutabaga range over years, creating breakfast egg and sausage pies, portable chicken pot pies, and even chili pies during the college football season. Whenever Anastasia's mother didn't feel up to cooking, her family would pile into the cozy café and enjoy Cheryl's hospitality and "gravy on tap."

She didn't even want to think of what her nutritionist would say about the dense golden pasties, literally made with lard. But then her stomach rumbled and she remembered she hadn't had anything to eat since an obscenely expensive fruit cup she grabbed while running through LaGuardia that morning.

"Thank you, Dougie." She closed the lid and watched as the familiar, weathered buildings of Main Street passed. Everything seemed smaller, and she wasn't sure if that was the classic "you can't go home again" response or because she lived in one of the biggest cities in the world. Everywhere she looked, she saw that the town was trying *so hard* to appeal to visitors, but everything was just...off. Instead of quaint historical light posts, the utility department installed sturdy steel posts that could withstand the lake winds. The freshly painted signs were the same weird combinations of brown and yellow and orange, something that might have been stylish when she was a very young kid, but now, just looked dingy and dated. Posters screaming *"Explore the Espoir Island Museum of Weathervanes!"* and *"Enjoy authentic Senate bean soup at the Seacliff Inn!"* hung from every available surface...but who the hell wanted to travel to the middle of nowhere for obsolete meteorological devices and bland bean soup?

She closed her eyes and leaned her head back on the seat rest. Nope. Espoir was pretty much the same.

While Dougie was sure to point out all of the other things about the island that hadn't changed—the tiny K-12 school, the movie theater that only showed John Wayne movies because that's what the owner liked, the three fudge shops—Bonnie was silent. They passed the museum, housed in the what was essentially a circa 1800 military fortress, where multiple battles were fought (and lost in spectacular fashion.) On Francis Street, their destination came into view, a graying Queen Anne built in 1873 called Fishscale House, named because of the oval patterned wood shingle siding. While the multiple gables in the roof looked brand new, the rest of the house was shabby and faded. The windows, also new, were as clear and blank as doll's eyes, despondently staring down from the hill on Francis Street.

Once upon a time, when Bash had cared a lot more about Anastasia being happy, he'd surprised her by buying this place sight unseen, promising her that they'd make it their special hideaway for holidays and visits to her family. She'd told him about Fishscale House when they were dating, how it was her childhood dream house with its strange onion-shaped tower turret, topped by a bronze trout weather-vane. And while she'd been touched that he'd listened to her, new connections to Espoir was the last thing she'd wanted. She didn't want to lord her new status over her former neighbors. She didn't want Bash to see how she'd grown up when she'd worked so hard to change so much about herself. She just wanted to stay far away. And then her parents had died and she'd managed to convince him that visiting the island was too painful of a reminder.

Stung by her rejection of his grand gesture, Bash lost enthusiasm for the project, which wasn't unusual for him, and the house sat unused for years. As it was one of the only assets Sebastian put in her name, this was the only place she had left to retreat to—the Miss Havisham of houses.

Dougie parked in the circular pea gravel drive while she stared up at the house through the car window. She took a deep breath before reaching for the door handle.

"Bonnie, honey, we'll just be a few minutes," Dougie said, leaving the car running as he stepped out. "I'll leave ya snug as a bug in a rug."

As Ana slid out of the car, Bonnie turned around and blurted out, "What's Chantrelle like in person?"

Ana's chin retreated as she leaned away from the verbal outburst. "Um…just like she appears on TV? High-maintenance? Emotionally volatile? Refuses to go anywhere without an herbalist in tow? Swears by feng shui and organic foods, and then swills vodka like it's water?"

Bonnie's lips quirked up and her dark eyes narrowed. "I knew it. Welcome back, flatlander."

Ana chuckled as she shut the car door. Dougie had a heavily loaded key ring in his hand, searching for the right set. "Are you sure ya don't want to go to the hotel for the night? It's kind of rough conditions in there. Not at all what you're usedta."

"Thanks, but I'm set on staying here," she said, and he reluctantly put the key into the enormous gray door.

"I came in and turned up the thermostat for ya earlier, to warm it up. And the cleaners did the best they could, but it's been more than ten years since the house was occupied. The dust has been pretty stubborn," he said, clicking the light switch closest to the door. A damaged crystal chandelier overhead blinked to life, casting a yellowed glow over grubby plaster walls and a winding oak staircase whose missing spindles gave the impression of a hockey player's teeth. Off to the left, the empty parlor was dominated by a massive brick fireplace. The kitchen, visible through the foyer, housed a multitude of harvest gold appliances. That seemed…wrong.

Dougie pointed out a big Rubbermaid tub in front of the fireplace. "I put some dishes in there, bedding, towels. I nicked it from the freebies our owners leave out for renters. Nobody will miss it, before the season starts up. The master bed is built into the wall, so you've got that going for you, but you're going to want to replace the mattress before too long."

"Oh, Dougie, I couldn't accept all that," she protested, her stomach dropping unpleasantly. She hadn't even thought of basics like towels and dishes. She'd had people to deal with those little details for *years*. How was she going to get through this if she couldn't remember that linens and dishware were things that were necessary to life?

He waved her off. "It's just a few things to keep ya going until ya have a chance to get your parents stuff out of storage, or go to the store. You can drop the tub off by my office as soon as you're done."

She nodded, biting her bottom lip. It pricked at her considerable pride, having to accept charity for basic creature comforts, while Bash and his mistress were probably attended, at this very moment, by a household staff of twenty. That dinged pride warred with her being genuinely touched by the gesture. She said quietly, "This is just more than I could hope for. Thank you, so much."

He laid a gentle hand on her shoulder. "We're happy you're back Ana, even if it's been rough on ya. How long ya planning on staying?"

"Not long," she said. "Honestly, Dougie, I'm not here to settle long term. This house is basically my only asset right now. What do you think I could get if I were to sell this place?"

Dougie, who also happened to be the island's only real estate agent, pursed his lips. "With the right buyer, ya might be able to get a couple hundred thousand dollars. Maybe even four, which would be a minor miracle and you would have to do a lot of work on the house. No promises, mind. Ya should try to get it on the market before the summer, when people are in love with the idea of having a vacation home in the middle of nowhere, particularly a house with a proper name."

She snorted. "How quickly do you think you could sell it?"

"Well, ya have to understand. There are a lot of places on the island that have been on the market for a good while, and they don't have the...optical issues that your house has."

Ana giggled. "That was very diplomatic of you, Dougie."

He jerked his broad shoulders. "Real estate is a personality-based business. I just want ya to know, Ana, I did send your husband's accountants regular recommendations on what needed to be done with the house. He only replaced the roof and shored up the foundation when he first bought it because I convinced him that the place would fall down without it. That, and replacing the furnace, was about all he did."

"I know you tried, Dougie," she assured him.

"Unless ya want to accept a bottom-dollar, fixer upper price, which I don't think ya do, you're looking at a full reno-vation. Floors, windows, replace the bathrooms and the kitchen, some of the drywall. Ya could do it cheap, but not if ya want to sell for the kind of money that I think you're looking for. And if ya want to keep the historical feel of the house, you're going to need someone who knows how to handle restoration work."

"Any idea who around here would be qualified for that kind of work?" she asked. "Who might be willing to exchange services for an insanely low price? Like he might be willing to take any unspoken for and unnecessary organs I have laying around?"

Dougie's mouth quirked up into a smile and then did an immediate arch in the opposite direction, "Oh sure, but...you're not going to like this."

"What?"

"It's Ned." He sighed.

Ned. Ned Fitzroy. The Ned she'd left in her wake without a second look when she ran from this island in the summer of 1995. Of course.

Dougie nodded, his expression sympathetic. "He went to this program for historical restorations over at Eastern Michigan. He got some fancy degree on top of all of his regular licensing for general contracting. He could be making loads of money under the bridge, but he stays here."

She dropped her bag on the floor, rattling the boards and making a considerable cloud of dust curl around her feet.

"The hotel is still an option," Dougie told her, watching the dust settle on her boots.

"No," she told him. "It's not."

2

*T*he next morning, Ana was crouching in front of the massive oak bed in the master suite, sorting through her socks.

It may have seemed like a strangely obsessive task for someone who had much more important things to accomplish —job one, buy a shower curtain. It turned out that bathing without one was ...challenging. So was sleeping in a dusty bedroom that smelled of damp and disuse. She was basically camping, without the fresh air or feeling of being virtuously "outdoorsy." She should feel grateful for the fact that she'd come to the island in spring.

If this was the middle of winter...she shuddered to think of it. She would be long gone before winter came. The one thing she had was a plan. She'd started with nothing and she tried to tell herself that she could build it up all over again, but honestly, the very idea exhausted her. She was not some nubile twenty-something with endless energy powered by ambition and an empty belly. She was nearly middle-aged. She used to pride herself on the fact that she'd never considered having work done. Sure, she had a monthly appointment with her derm and a bathroom solely dedicated to her styling team's machinations. But she'd refused to re-arrange her face to stave off the inevitable.

Now, she sort of wished she'd taken advantage of the plastic surgeons when she could afford their attention. The gray hairs were creeping in like an invasive species. No matter how much fancy French cream she applied under her eyes, the tiny lines kept showing up. And she couldn't even afford the damn creams anymore.

She couldn't go back to working multiple jobs and constantly scanning the horizon for opportunities. She had nothing. For the first time in almost twenty years, she had no safety net. She'd gotten used to it so quickly, having that cushion that protected her from the reality of her old life. She would get her cushion back. And that started with unpacking her socks. She pulled each pair out of her duffle bag and unrolled them.

Inside each pair was a sizeable diamond piece—a ring, a necklace, a pair of earrings, most of them at least five carats. She'd collected them over the years, when she reached the end of the month without spending all of her "allowance," and stashed them away in her sock drawer. There was enough Gustavsson left in her to believe the good times might not last forever. She'd thought if the worst happened, she could present Bash with her secret hoard and he would be so thrilled with the practical, thoughtful woman he'd married. In her panic, she'd almost run out of the apartment without them. Then she remembered to tell the agent who was supervising her packing at the last minute, "I need socks!" and shoved all of them inside her bag while the agent tried to find a reason to argue.

She hadn't had time to sell them before her exodus from the city. There were too many reporters following her and she didn't want to be seen hocking her jewelry. Agents from the IRS or Treasury Department might see it and come after her for the proceeds of the sale. She planned to go below the bridge somewhere, probably Traverse City or even Grand Rapids—somewhere she could find a jewelry store capable of paying what she needed. Most likely, she would need to find several jewelry stores to avoid raising red flags. All she needed was to get reported to police for trying to sell her own "stolen" jewelry.

She knew she wouldn't be able to get retail price for the pieces, but she hoped it would be enough to fix up the house for sale. Selling Fishscale House wouldn't be enough to set her up for life, but maybe it would be enough to prop her up while she found a divorce lawyer willing to take her case, to get her a settlement she could live on. She understood that might mean working, and while she felt intimidated and unsure of what she could possibly be qualified for, she wasn't afraid of earning her keep.

Satisfied that no one had stolen her sock treasures from her carry-on, she stowed the jewelry in her bag and scrubbed her hand over her face. She was going to have to see Ned today. She wanted to put it off, after selling the jewelry and about a million other moving-in tasks she could use to procrastinate. But getting Ned to agree to work on Fishscale House was an important first step, one she desperately wished she could skip.

Seeing Ned and asking for help meant swallowing more than her pride. Once upon a time, Ned was the man she saw living her dream life with in Fishscale House, her happily ever after. Sure, most of the kids on the island just *knew* it was haunted, but Ned and Ana always saw it as a fairy tale castle. They'd imagined what it would be like to find a way to buy the place and turn it into their home, a place they could raise kids and be happy. Because they were about sixteen at the time, staying up as late as they wanted and controlling the TV were also mentioned.

But then her dreams changed. She told him that she would leave one day, and he'd grin at her and say sure she would, and then go right back to talking about all the improvements he would make to Fishscale House. Ned had been a trap, baited with honeyed promises he might deliver, but would never be enough. She hadn't even said goodbye when she left. She'd just taken her savings out of the bank—cash she'd hoarded ruthlessly while working summers at the Dairy Moo —and boarded the ferry. She knew that if she told Ned, he would have talked her out of it. He would have convinced her to stay just for the summer, just until she saved a little more. And then next thing she knew, she'd be pregnant, living with Ned in the apartment over the pub, stuck there in resentful domesticity for the rest of her life.

Ned seemed to be the only person who was honestly surprised that she left—if the emails he'd sent her AOL address had been any indication. Her parents had been...resigned to the fact that she would never make her life on the island. They knew that she planned on leaving, that there was nothing for her on the island. Sometimes, Anastasia thought her mother had wanted to leave, too, when she was younger, before married life and a child pinned her to the island. They'd been so pleased when she'd married Sebastian, though they hadn't come for the wedding. They were embarrassed, said they didn't feel comfortable with "those type of folks," and asked her to send pictures. They just weren't comfortable leaving what they saw as their place.

But Ned had seemed shocked, like he wasn't listening when she told him she couldn't be content living there. She wanted more than living in a clapboard shack where the wind rattled the windows all winter. Not that New York was warm exactly, but it felt like the center of the universe. It had all of the color and movement and life that Espoir never had. When she'd first arrived, she'd gone down to Times Square like a tourist and sat on the outdoor café chairs, nursing the single black coffee she could barely afford and watching all the people go by.

She'd worked two and sometimes, three, jobs, had five roommates in a two bedroom walk-up apartment, eaten Ramen like she was personally endorsing it. Every cent she could spare went to buying designer staples she could wear frequently without anyone's notice; a classic Calvin Klein sheath dress, a pair of Louboutin heels, a black Chanel clutch. She'd never attended college. She'd devoured etiquette books, Tiffany & Co. catalogues, fashion magazines, interior design textbooks, histories on the Kennedys, the Rockefellers, anything that would help her navigate their world. She'd ruthlessly pared the Yooperneese from her vocabulary, using diction tapes to help her take on a more neutral "newscaster" accent. She'd created her own education from nothing. She'd created her life from *nothing*.

By asking Ned for help, on this project of all things, she was swallowing a Great Lake's worth of regrets and apologies. And she didn't even know if it would be worth it. He could slam the door in her face, and she wouldn't blame him in the least.

He'd never said anything about going to school for construction or restoration. He wasn't even interested in carpentry when she knew him. How was she supposed to approach him after all these years and ask for a favor? Would she just brazen her way through, acting as if she hadn't stomped all over his feelings years before? Or would this require more of a hair shirt and groveling tactic?

Argh, if she approached him at the pub, it would be witnessed by half the town, including Ned's sister, who had threatened to burn off Anastasia's eyebrows via that same AOL account.

"Well, if you're going to be knocked down a peg or twenty, you might as well get it over with," she muttered, digging her travel makeup case out of her bag. "What exactly does one wear to a humbling?"

Before she could find a suitable outfit for the occasion, a

loud knock at the door caught her attention. Since all of her financial eggs were in one basket, er, duffle bag, she slid the bag into the wardrobe in the corner and locked it, pocketing the key.

"Coming!" she yelled, treading down stairs she didn't entirely trust, wondering who the hell could be knocking on her door at this hour. Dougie had sworn that he wouldn't tell anybody she was in town. It was part of "client confidentiality" or some code of property management ethics that he had made up on his own, but stuck to religiously. One thing was certain, it wouldn't be Ned. She'd be lucky if her former high school sweetheart didn't leap over the bar and bolt out of the pub when she approached.

It was when she opened the door and saw said sweetheart standing on her front porch that she realized that while Dougie may stick to his strict property management protocols, Bonnie Jergenson did not.

On those long dark nights when Sebastian was traveling on "business," she'd imagined Ned Fitzroy. She'd told herself that he was probably balding, with a dad bod and a frumpy wife who had to clip coupons to feed their brood of loud, sticky children. The phrase "sour grapes" haunted her lonely marriage bed no matter how many luxurious custom bedding sets she bought.

Well, he still had a full head of dark, almost black, though it was shorn into a tousled sort of style instead of the long waves that once curled behind his ears. He had the same long straight nose, thin lips and hard, gray eyes. While he'd smiled so much when she'd known him in school, he had a stern air now, that reminded Ana of his father. Or it may have just been her. Tom Fitzroy, a stubborn Scotsman who'd insisted on making his living here on an island full of even more stubborn Scandinavians, never seemed too thrilled to clap eyes on her...or anyone really. For a man who ran a pub, he didn't seem to have much use for people, in general.

Still tall and rangy, Ned had the sort of body honed by years and years of hard, physical labor, the sort of body that would have made Bash suck in his middle self-consciously. Hell, she sucked her own stomach in, even if a ruthless diet and exercise regimen kept her in the same size she'd worn since before the girls were born.

Somehow, he looked more attractive in an old blue-gray cable-knit fisherman's sweater and battered jeans, than in any of the bespoke designer clothes her soon-to-be-ex's stylist curated for Bash over the years. Tailoring could only do so much.

And she was just standing there, staring at him, without speaking. It was entirely possible her mental state was making the hormones in her brain think whimsically destructive things. Also, she was wearing yoga pants and not a brushstroke of makeup. Not even lip balm. Had she brushed her teeth that morning? She couldn't remember.

She'd had nightmares like this.

"Ana," he rumbled in that low voice of his that used to make her thighs ache.

Maybe "used to" was giving herself a little too much credit. The new gravelly element of that voice certainly wasn't helping her situation.

He was staring at her as if she wasn't real, though she couldn't tell from his expression whether he saw her as a mirage or a specter from a nightmare.

"Ned, hi. What are you doing here?"

And then his eyes narrowed angrily and she decided it was probably the nightmare. "Really? That's all you have to say to me?"

Her mind was completely blank. She knew she was supposed to be asking him something, something important, but right now, all she could think about was her rat's nest hair and the fact that Ned still smelled like cedar and oak moss after all these years. He didn't even wear cologne. How was that even possible?

"How are you?" she guessed.

"There is something very wrong with you," he told her, turning on his heel and walking out the door.

"Ned, wait, I'm sorry. I'm just in shock, seeing you again after all these years," she said, following him onto the porch as he jogged down the stairs. "I don't know what to say."

His mouth bent into an even more unhappy shape. "How about, 'Hi, Ned, how have you been? What have you been up to since I left without a word and didn't talk to you for twenty years?' Or maybe, 'I'm sorry I didn't trust you enough to tell you what I was planning. It's nothing personal, you just weren't that important to me.'"

"I'm sorry, Ned."

He held up two large hands. "No, I was wrong, 'sorry' was for twenty years ago...you know what, I thought this would make me feel better. Closure and all that bullshit, but I just can't even look at you right now. I thought I wasn't mad anymore, but seeing you? I'm not ready to talk to you."

"Ned, wait."

"Is that what you think I've been doing all these years? Waiting? Did you think I was just going to sit around alone, pining for you?"

"I'm not saying I wanted that necessarily, but did picturing it made me feel better? Yes," she said, shrugging. He stared at her. "OK, maybe now is not the time for humor."

"No. It's not. Are you still doing that?"

"Blurting out inappropriate jokes at the wrong time to make myself feel better? No. I'd kicked the habit until just now," she admitted.

Bash had hated it. He'd never found it snicker-worthy like Ned had, or understood it as a release valve for emotional pressure. He said it was embarrassing, a psychological tic for which she should seek therapy.

"I missed it," he admitted, staring down at the peeling porch boards as if they were the most fascinating thing in the world. When he looked up, his expression was softer, the Ned she remembered, the one who had been the first to touch her, the first to make her laugh so hard she cried. "Bonnie said you would probably want to talk to me."

"Of course, she did."

"Are you all right?" he asked. "I know things have been... difficult for you lately.

She nodded. "I did want to talk to you."

His head tilted as he stared at her. "You don't want to talk. You want something."

She blushed. She liked to think she was less transparent than this.

He groaned. "This isn't like one of those true crime shows where you ask me to murder your husband for you, is it? Because I am a lot of things, but "too stupid to function" is not one of them."

"What? No! I was going to ask you to help me renovate Fish-scale House. Why would I ask you to murder my husband?"

"Why would you ask me to renovate your house?" he demanded, throwing his arms up toward the pile of decrepit wood she was trying to saddle him with.

"Because I'm told you're one of the few people around here qualified for the job!" she exclaimed.

"And I'm just supposed to do this out of the kindness of my heart?" He stared at her, his mouth agape. "Can we go back to the murder thing?"

"I would pay you," she protested. "Not for the murder. There's no murder. I meant the renovation. I don't know how much I could pay you exactly, but—"

"You're insane," he told her and stomped down the stairs to an old red truck advertising Fitzroy Construction.

As he sped away, she pinched her nose, sighing deeply. "That went well."

SINCE SHE'D FAILED UTTERLY AT HER MOST IMPORTANT TASK, ANA hoped she was prepared for something a little easier, like buying the damn shower curtain. Because the island was too small to support a proper supermarket, locals shopped at the Laine Mercantile, a sort of general store that carried everything from canned goods to blue jeans, and whatever the Laine family could special order from their mainland contacts. Fortunately, the house was within easy walking distance of Main Street. If she didn't go too crazy on canned goods, she could carry it back easily enough.

Just outside the low-slung cedar shake building she stopped, wondering for the first time in too many years whether she had enough cash on her to cover the things she needed. She didn't have a credit card as a safety net. She wasn't sure what her groceries would cost. She didn't even know what a loaf of bread cost nowadays. For some reason, she found that to be even more humiliating than losing her husband to a girl with one name and no discernible brain cells.

Maybe she should find a quiet place and do a cash count again.

"Ana? Ana Gustavsson?"

She turned to find Bailey Laine, who had been just a year behind her in school, standing in the doorway to the store. Bailey hadn't changed a bit, with her thick sandy hair, just starting to gray around the temples and wide dark green eyes. Bailey had been one of the sweeter girls in school, carefully packing extra sandwiches in her lunch for the students whose families struggled. If more Espoir Islanders had been like Bailey, maybe Ana would have taken more pains to stay in touch.

Probably not, but maybe.

Bailey opened her arms and enfolded Ana in a hug. Ana relaxed into it, burying her face into Bailey's sweet-smelling shoulder. The tenuous hold Ana had on her emotions snapped completely at the first hug she'd received since finding federal agents in her closet.

"Rough time of it, huh?"

Ana nodded as Bailey patted her back. "Why don'tcha come on in and I'll fix ya a cuppa coffee. You can tell me all about it."

Before shepherding Ana through the door, Bailey stopped to take the weathervane museum poster out of the shop window. She shooed Ana to a small dining table in the back, where the Laine family would scarf down dinner between customers on busy nights. She poured coffee into a mug that read, "Michigan —America's Mitten." "It's good to see ya, hon. Folks have been worried about ya, what with everything that's been on the news."

Ana gave her a skeptical look and Bailey added. "OK, the decent folks around here have been worried about you. Some of the more assholish types have been crowin' over it."

"That's what I thought," Ana muttered into her mug, making Bailey laugh. "It's been really awful, Bailey. I can't even express how awful. I don't have the words. I don't think I've even realized how much I've lost, but it's just about everything—and I know that sounds dramatic and my mom would immediately remind me that I still have my health. But I can't help but feel that I'm just surviving moment to moment."

"Well, the good news is that it can't get much worse," Bailey said.

"I saw Ned this morning."

"Wow, I stand corrected," Bailey retorted, pursing her lips.

Ana laughed. "It was just about as bad as you can imagine."

Bailey grimaced. "So, your first day back was kind of bad, but it's gotta get better, right?"

"I'm not willing to speculate," Ana said, shaking her head. "I have a feeling that would bite me on the ass."

Ana nodded to the poster Bailey had retrieved from outside. It was just as badly designed as the other signage in town, in the same outdated sepia tones, emphasizing the many informative weather vane-related exhibits available at the museum. "What's with the poster?"

Bonnie clucked her tongue. "Oh, I'm trying to figure out how to change it. If we don't get more visitors, we're going to have to close it after this summer."

"You can't close the museum!" Ana exclaimed. "That thing's been open since our parents were kids! How else will people learn how Espoir Island contributed to the development of an extremely outdated method of determining which way the wind is blowing?"

Bailey shrugged. "The numbers have been down for years now. All the tourism numbers for the island have dropped over the years. I'm on the historical society board so I've seen them myself. People just aren't buying what we're selling. And with the museum run by public funds, and we just can't justify the expense. Plus, Mrs. Larsson is getting ready to retire soon, so there's no one to run the place anyway."

Ana flopped back in her chair, feeling even more defeated than she had been this morning. How was she was supposed to a sell house on an island, where nobody wanted to visit, much less live?

"Oh, come on, it's not all bad," Bailey said, patting Ana's hand. "Maybe things will pick up this summer. This last winter was pretty bad, so people will be desperate to get out of their houses and into the sun."

Ana nodded, contemplating the graphically confused mess on the table.

"Do you mind if I take this with me?" Ana asked, picking it up. "I think I might have some ideas to make it...less repulsive."

Bailey shrugged. "You can't make it worse."

"You've always been so relentlessly optimistic," Ana noted. "Please stop that."

AFTER FINISHING HER COFFEE, ANA LEFT THE SHOP WITH A promise to meet Bailey for dinner at the pasty shop some time that week. Bailey said she'd send her nephew, Charlie, along to the house with her groceries later, because Ana bought a bit more than she intended. (It turned out that food prices in Michigan were much lower than New York, even with the trouble of importing groceries to the island.) For just a moment, it felt like her day was looking up.

She decided to walk down to the weather vane museum herself. Surely it wouldn't be difficult to lay out a better poster. She ran her own social media and had enough experience with design software suites to make her graphics. She had a knack for it and even designed her own website without it looking like a thirteen-year-old with Wordpress access made it. And if she was able to draw more people to the museum and more people to the island, maybe one of those people would buy her house... if she could manage to get it renovated.

One of these days, she would learn the lesson about lowering her guard.

"GUSTAVSSON!"

Ana turned to see Ned's sister storming down the sidewalk toward her. Nell Fitzroy's walk had always reminded Ana of one of those cartoon bulldogs in the old Warner Brothers shorts, all shoulder and arm motion while she glared at the world in general. She had the Fitzroy strong jaw and clear gray eyes, but with none of Ned's humor to soften either.

Ana's shoulders sagged. She didn't have the patience for some "explaining herself" conversation in which she promised Nell that she wouldn't hurt Ned again.

Fortunately for her, Nell didn't want conversation. She wanted to punch Ana right in the face.

3

*A*s her head snapped back, Ana realized she really should have seen that coming. At age nine, Nell had been kicked out of the island's Brownie troop for breaking Bonnie's front tooth with a right hook. Ana's teeth felt intact, but her right cheekbone felt like it was going to explode.

How in the hell could such a short woman reach that high?

"You should have stayed your ass in the big city," Nell spat. "We don't need you coming around screwing up people's lives."

Before her head could recover its position, Ana brought her own right hand swinging up in an upper cut, catching Nell under her chin.

"Ow! Shit!" Ana howled, shaking her throbbing fingers. Hitting Nell hurt a lot more than smacking a reality housewife.

Nell yelped, cradling her chin with her right hand as she jabbed with her left. It was a wild swing that caught Ana in the chest. She cursed, clutching her throbbing breast. And pretty soon they were just rolling around on the icy sidewalk, taking swipes at each other. A string of increasingly colorful insults streamed out of Nell's mouth like a profane fountain.

Vaguely, Ana heard the bell over the shop's door jangle and Bailey grumble, "Oh, for cripes' sake."

"What in the hell is wrong with you, Nell?" Ana yelled. She'd never taken a punch to the boob. She didn't recommend it.

"Ladies!" Ana heard a male voice shout through Nell's curses. "Cut it out! Don't make me get the pepper spray!"

A strong hand clamped her shoulder as Nell's weight was lifted off of her. Nell was kicking at Ana as John Ferris, the town's only sheriff's deputy, held her in a half-nelson hold and dragged her away to plop her butt on a nearby truck bed.

"Are you *nuts?*" Ana yelled, clutching at her cheek. She pushed to her feet, leaning against the cedar wall. "I haven't talked to you in twenty years and you punch me?"

"Well, maybe you shouldn't make your face so punchable!" Nell shot back, attempting to dart around John and swipe at Ana.

"Cut it out, Nell!" John shouted, forcing her to sit. John hadn't changed much over the years, same athletic build, same rugged features he'd had when they were kids. He did look a bit more tired around the eyes, though, and Ana could only imagine that came from a lifetime spent wrangling drunken assholes when the winters really started getting to people.

"Now, do either one of you need medical attention?"

"No, but I would love to press charges against her, thank you, John," Ana said, smiling sweetly.

"Oh, please!" Nell snorted. "Like he'd take me to jail over this."

John stood between the two of them, his hands raised. "Now, from what I saw, you were throwing punches, too, Ana. If I take one of you in, I'm going to have to take both."

"My punches were in self-defense!" Ana cried.

"Well, I don't know if I can believe that," John said, clearing his throat before adding, "Given your history of violent behavior."

PASTIES AND POOR DECISIONS

Ana gasped. "History of—since when?"

John's high cheeks flushed pink. "Since episode eight, season twelve of *True Housewives of Manhattan.*"

"I don't think you're allowed to use someone's behavior in another state against them, just because it was shown on television," Ana replied.

John jerked his shoulders. "I know what I saw."

"All right, fine. Take us both in, then." Ana crossed her long arms over her chest, which was still throbbing, not that anyone cared.

"Really?" John asked with a frown.

Nell squawked indignantly, hopping off of the truck. "You can't be serious!"

"Really," Ana said, glaring at her.

John sighed, slapping his EISD baseball cap on his head. "Fine, let's go on down to the station. I'm assuming I don't have to cuff you."

"Not me," Ana said. "But you might consider a muzzle for her."

"You might consider a muzzle for her," Nell mimicked her under her breath as they followed John down the street.

"How old are you?" Ana scoffed.

When Nell didn't respond, Ana grumbled, pulling her collar around her neck, "How is it still this cold? The first day of spring is next week!"

"Spoken like a flatlander," Nell snickered.

The Espoir Island police station was a three-cell, one room jail built sometime in the 1930s. The crime rate on the island had always been rather low, beyond drunk and disorderlies, so the town didn't devote much money to it. Each cell had a narrow cot, covered in a rough wool blanket, and not much else.

Poor John had basically inherited the job from his father, who refused to give up the sheriff job, despite being seventy-five years old. Sheriff Jacob Ferris was sleeping at his desk, his boots propped up on a drawer full of files, a basketball game blasting over the radio. John rolled his eyes and sat at a much smaller desk, tapping on a computer keyboard and bringing it to life. "You know the drill, Nell. Cell Number Two."

John opened the door to the third cell, and motioned for Ana to step through the barred gate. She dropped onto the narrow jailhouse cot, the springs screaming in protest. Still, she thought maybe it was more comfortable than her old mattress at home. Now that she was no longer fueled by righteous indignation, she was starting to doubt how smart it was to insist on charging Nell. She didn't have anyone to bail her out. She wasn't sure anyone on the island would be willing to risk bail money on her.

"How often do you get arrested?" Ana asked Nell, leaning against the bars between them.

Nell shrugged as she crossed her ankles on the cot. "Less, since John and I started dating."

Ana's head whipped toward the deputy, who gave a resigned shake of his head, as he pulled some forms out of his desk. "Damn."

Nell shrugged.

"Do you feel better?" Ana asked. "Now, that you've vented your anger all over my face?"

"A little bit," Nell admitted. "I'd say I'm sorry. But I'm not."

"I guess I respect that," Ana muttered. "And really, that was a greeting a bit more in line with what I was expecting here. I'm kind of glad to get it over with, to be honest. So, how have you been? Good to see you. You haven't changed a bit, you lunatic."

Nell threw her head back and laughed, wincing at the pain in her chin. "Good to see you, too. You come back here to screw with my brother's head again?"

"Not specifically."

"Well, that's something, I suppose," Nell admitted, plucking at the gray blanket. "When you left, it wrecked Ned. He likes to pretend that it didn't, but I know him better than anybody. He never took up with anybody after you left, not one single person. It was like he couldn't trust anybody enough to let them close. And it made him a downright grumpy bastard."

"I never meant for that to happen. I thought he would move on, get married. I thought it would be easier for him if I didn't leave any ties."

Nell sniffed. "Well, you were wrong."

"Obviously."

Nell let out a long breath and her shoulders seemed to relax. "So what's it like being on TV?"

Ana laughed. "Not all it's cracked up to be. That fight in the lash bar?"

"Episode eight, season twelve," John called while filling out his paperwork.

Ana rolled her eyes. "I thought Dakota and I were—well, not friends, none of the women on that show even understand the meaning of the word 'friend' but I thought we understood each other. She started that weird, contrived argument with me because a producer told her it would get her more attention and more storylines that season. And they were right, it did. Me punching her in the face got a lot of attention, and the trips to the plastic surgeon, the reconstructive surgery on her nose, the lawsuit, they were all big plot points for her."

"It was a pretty good punch," Nell conceded, rubbing her chin.

"I let my temper get the better of me. She said something about my daughter. I just couldn't let it go. And of course, they edited that part out, no one heard her making that awful comment about my Chloe having a learning disorder, so I looked like an unstable bully."

"Nope, she went after your kids, she had it coming," Nell reached through the bars and patted her shoulder. "That's the line you don't cross."

Ana shook her head. "It was stupid of me. No matter what she said, adults don't solve problems with their fists."

She sent Nell an arch look, making Nell raise her hands. "Point taken."

After a long pause, Nell asked, "What the hell is a lash bar?"

Ana burst out laughing, whacking her head against the bars. "Ow."

That was how Ned found them when he walked through the jail door, two idiots behind bars, laughing on jailhouse cots, covered in scrapes and bruises. Ned stared at them both and shook his head. "What in the hell is wrong with you?"

"Are you asking me or her?" Nell asked.

"I haven't decided yet." He glared at Nell. "Mom and Dad never should have taught you how to talk. Clearly, you're not meant to be around people."

Ana snickered and tried to cover it with a cough. Ned turned and pinned her with a dark look. "And you.

"Easy," Ana warned him.

"How do you keep getting into fights?" he demanded.

"Technically, in this case, I was *punched* first," Ana insisted.

"It's true. I punched her right in the face," Nell said, nodding. "She didn't even try to guard."

Ana threw her arms up. "I didn't see you coming!"

"Well, that's *your* fault," Nell told her.

John sighed from his desk. "You do know you have the right to remain silent, right?"

"Maybe the right, but not the wisdom," Ned replied, turning to them. "You're two grown-ass women. Use your damn words. I have a mind not to bail either one of you out."

"That's fine, John will just take me home with him later," Nell said.

Ana looked to John, who sort of shrugged helplessly.

"Gah!" Ned scrubbed his hand over his face. "I don't want to picture that!"

"I'm flattered bailing *me* out is even an option," Ana said. "I'm sorry, for earlier."

Ned shook his head. "No, I let my temper get the best of me. I said things that were…"

"Not wrong," Ana told him. "I'm sorry I hurt you."

He nodded. "Why don't you show me this house of yours and we'll see what we can do."

"Really?" she gasped. "Does this mean you're willing to work for me?"

Even the phrase put a sour look on his face. "No, it means that I have always wanted to work on Fishscale House, see it restored to its former glory. It's one of the most interesting houses on the island and I have spent years watching it fall apart. It's about the project, not you."

She tried not to let that hurt her feelings, she really did. Then again, he didn't mention that the house was falling apart all of those years while her husband owned it…so she guessed that was a wash.

"You're not just trying to get me in a secluded location with power tools?" she asked, her brow arched.

"I could leave you here," he retorted.

She smiled her best and brightest smile. "Let's go see the house."

NED SAID VERY LITTLE AS THEY WALKED THE FLOORS, SURVEYING the damage that time and neglect had done to Fishscale House. He made notes on a very official looking clipboard and frowned a lot, which made Ana more than a little nervous. Having slept in the house the night before, she knew what to expect—the chipping paint, the water damage, the leaky windows. She wondered what her neighbors thought the house looked like inside now, having been sealed up for so long.

It was so strange to trail behind Ned, seeing him after all these years, to see all the changes and what was still the same, and not *speak*. It was like he had put a wall between them. Ned was scribbling, and frowned some more. The frowning was very disconcerting.

She sighed. She was going to have to get *so* creative with the Zillow photos to sell this place.

"So you're not going to say anything about the fact that you went to school for this?" she said, as he jotted down his notes. "That you actually have a degree in restoring historical homes?"

He glanced up at her, dark brows raised. She added, "Dougie told me. He's very proud of you. You could have said something this morning."

"I have two degrees in 'this,'" Ned told her. "And why would I talk about that? You weren't interested in my plans when you left. I assumed you wouldn't be interested now."

Well, that point was pointed.

"General human interest? The whole 'catching up' conversation," she said, sitting on the bottom step of her staircase. "Filling the awkward silence?"

"I don't know if I'm ready for that yet," he said. "I am sorry for what I said earlier, because I shouldn't have shouted at you like that. I always told myself if I saw you again, I would be an adult about it, show you that you hadn't hurt me, that you'd missed out on a mature, successful adult man. And I failed pretty miserably at that, I guess."

He flopped down on the stairs next to her, a boneless habit that had driven her crazy when they'd dated. He took out his phone and tapped numbers into the calculator app.

Finally, he looked up at her. "It's not going to be easy. And it's not going to be cheap...and I'm not sure how long it's going to take me."

"That's a lot of 'nots,'" she said as he handed her the phone. She grimaced at the sum shown. "And that is a lot of digits."

He grimaced. "Um, that's just a rough guess. There could be other expenses, as I take the house apart. I could find problems we don't know about. I could bring on other restorationists, call in some favors from people who would want to do the work just for the chance to work on a house like this, but that could still increase the cost. Do you have enough to cover that?"

He nodded to the calculator.

"I think so," she said, mentally estimating what she might get for her emergency jewelry stash and wincing. There was so much wincing. "Maybe."

He sighed, pinching the bridge of his long, straight nose. "I will probably regret this."

She wanted to nudge him with her shoulder, like she used to. But she got the distinct impression than they were not at that place yet. "If it makes you feel better, I regret it already."

"That does make me feel a little better," he said, turning and pinning her with his most serious expression. "I will work on this house. But you have to help me. You will pound nails and paint and lift and tote whatever I say."

"This could take months," she told him. "You want to trap yourself in this probably haunted wreck of a house on an isolated island with me for *months*? Have you even seen a horror movie?"

"Well, I get to leave at night," he said. "And you don't, so... yeah, I can live with that."

"That's not nice," she told him.

To her surprise, he leaned against her side, bumping shoulders with her. It was the first time he'd touched her in twenty years and she felt it in every cell in her body. It was as if she had been in a coma and someone plunged a needle full of adrenaline into her heart. She was suddenly awake and aware of every sound and scent. Her eyes went wide and she inhaled sharply, that damn cedar scent flooding her lungs. He leaned closer, his nose bumping hers. It was so familiar and so alien to everything she'd known for decades. She knew those lips, their shape and the way they would slant against hers, and she knew that it would feel more real than every kiss of her marriage—even those heady early years when she loved Bash. She wondered if her husband had ever loved her back.

Why was she thinking of her soon-to-be-ex right now? It was probably a sign she didn't need to be kissing Ned. Before she could say so, he broke away from her. She couldn't help the way her mouth followed his as he moved. Her rational brain could only control so much.

"I'm sorry," she said. "Wait, I'm not sorry. You kissed me… and I shouldn't have kissed back, because we're just drunk on the nostalgia of seeing each other again. This isn't real. It's a stress response. At least, for me."

Ned groaned, tilting his head against the stair rail. "I can't believe I let myself fall for it again. I can't do this with you. Not if you're just going to leave. I can't live through losing you all over again, Ana."

"Well, who says that you would lose me?"

"So you're saying you would want to stay? That this isn't some sort of rebound revenge sex to soothe your ego after what your husband did to you?"

"Trust me, at this point, this is anything but soothing for my self-esteem. That's not what this is!"

"Then what is it?" he demanded.

"I don't know, it's not like there are guidebooks for how to gracefully reconnect with the 'one that got away' while going through extensive personal crises!"

"You don't get to call me that," he told her, standing. "You're the one who left. You left and your damned husband bought *our* house and left it to rot. And now you're asking me to fix it for you? Do you have any idea how fucking awful that is?"

"Yeah, and the next couple of months are going to be really rough if you're going to throw that in my face the whole time," she said. "We can't do this. I can't do this. I don't have the emotional reserves to walk through the minefield of memories and blame and bullshit every day. So if you can't do this, we might as well stop before we start."

"No!" he exclaimed, his expression shifting from angry to anxious in a blink.

Now her brows rose. Ned really wanted to work on her house. She wasn't entirely powerless in this situation.

"OK, so we're agreed that you will do this work on my house. I will keep my face away from your face. And you will stop throwing my heartless and total abandonment of you in that face at every opportunity," she said.

He pursed his lips. "Fine."

"Thank you."

She gestured toward the door as she opened it. He said, "I'll get a contract to you tomorrow," and extended his hand.

She shook her head. "We're not there yet."

He titled his head. "Funny."

He descended the porch steps. She was just grateful that his foot didn't go through the wood. The tension she'd been carrying since she'd basically begged him to work on Fishscale House melted from her middle. While her situation with Ned wasn't exactly comfortable, she wouldn't have to walk on eggshells around him. He seemed to want access to her house far more than he wanted to avoid her. He glanced over his shoulder as he climbed into his old red truck. This was what Bash liked to call "leverage." She waved back and worked to keep her expression neutral.

She really needed to turn that reptilian part of her brain off if she was going to move in polite non-predatory, non-New York society.

4

*N*ow that she was semi-settled on the island, there were things that Ana missed about the city—reliable wifi, her day spa, that vegan Turkish place that delivered to her building even though they weren't technically supposed to, coffee that she didn't have to mix from freeze-dried crystals with an old iron kettle. Her household staff. Good God, did she miss her household staff.

She never realized how much of the tiny, annoying details of her daily life those dear, dear people protected her from—making her own food, doing her own laundry, the thousand thankless tasks that it took to maintain existence as an adult. Hell, it had taken her two hours to get the utilities switched over to her name when Larry Cooper, the local meter reader, informed her that Bash's accountants were closing the house's accounts.

Those hours spent on hold gave her a lot of time to think about her character and just how much of an asshole she'd become. Those people—the ones who'd worked in her home for years, making her life easier, learning all that information about her life and her children—she wasn't even sure she knew some of their last names. No matter how much money she'd had, she didn't think she'd changed on the inside. She thought that she'd held onto the values her parents had instilled in her—working hard, knowing the value of money, being kind to people. She'd tried to share those same values with her children…obviously, that blew up in her face on several levels as those children weren't currently speaking her.

Ana wanted to write apology letters to each and every one of her staff, like some sort of privileged twelve-step program. But she didn't know how to contact any of them, what with the last name issues…also, she suspected that none of them would want to hear from her. And it made her more than a little sad that none of the other things she missed about her old life included people. The friends that she thought might not be calling or contacting her over social media because they were giving her space? Or maybe they thought she was too embarrassed to talk? Well, at this point, she'd figured out that they weren't calling because they weren't really her friends. She knew that she'd developed a tendency to hold people at a distance, after being burned by too many *Housewife* types, but she thought maybe she'd made connections with some of the other moms from the girls' school…whose husbands Bash had put out of business…or maybe some of her neighbors…who Bash had sued over co-op association rules…

Yeah, her life was a strange, toxic stew of not-quite-relationships.

On the subject of non-relationships, Ned started work on the house on the very day she signed the contract, tearing out rotten floorboards and stairs, sanding down plaster and other messy, aggressive work that seemed to involve a lot of dust and noise. He had absolutely held her to the agreement that she would tote all of the debris to the giant garbage bin out front labeled Fitzroy Construction. There were work gloves involved and muscles that were not prepared by extensive hot yoga for this sort of exercise. But there was no talking.

Ned communicated mostly through grunts and pointing— which was way sexier than it should have been, when combined with Ned wearing dirty, tattered jeans and a gray Fitzroy Construction t-shirt that hugged every long line of him. There were moments when she would pause in the doorway to the parlor, watching the muscles of his back work as he pried the baseboards from the walls. But then she would shake herself out of that frame of mind because that way laid madness. And Ned seemed absolutely content having nothing to do with her or her face.

The best part was that she was exhausted and therefore, had never slept better. She couldn't remember working so hard since those early days in New York, when her feet were so tired from waiting tables and running retail that they *burned*. It was good though, to lay her head on a pillow at night, feeling that she'd accomplished something. It was something that she hadn't felt for a long time.

She'd only ventured off the island once, bumming a ride from Nell to Grand Rapids to sell her jewelry. It was a grueling drive and she'd gotten...significantly less than she'd hoped for, but she also knew she was dealing with market forces of the Midwest. And there were drawbacks to wanting a quick sale. She had just enough to cover Ned's estimate and her relatively minor living expenses, plus a tiny margin of error for any "extra problems" he might find.

Going back to a larger city was strange. It had taken her very little time to get used to the quiet of Espoir again. Everything seemed too loud and too crowded. The signs were garish and too bright. She'd tried to soak up as much noise and traffic and people as she could but it felt just as foreign to her now as New York had been in the beginning.

She was standing at her bay window, staring at the full

garbage bin and contemplating the sore muscles in her back, when Ned walked up behind her.

"I'm all done for the day," he said, making her yelp and whack her forehead against the glass.

"Ow!" She'd gotten so used to "silent Ned" that human speech almost sent her tumbling out a picture window.

"Easy," he said. "That glass is pretty old. It can't take much in the way of headbutts."

"And I'm fine, thank you," she said, glaring at him while she rubbed her forehead.

"I figured. You've always been hard-headed."

She reconfigured her hand so just her middle finger rested on her skin.

"Charming," he said dryly. "I'm going to cut out early. Nell needs me to tend to the bar tonight and I need to get there before seven. She's got her meeting over at the library."

"Oh, sure," she said, rolling her neck and wincing at the crackling of her vertebrae. "What kind of meeting?"

"The historical society. Nell's on the board."

"Nell's on the board? Is everybody from our high school class on the board?"

Ned slipped into his jacket. "We own the oldest bar on the island. It's in her best interest."

"So how do you have time to help run the pub and work on houses like this?" she asked,

"Nell's running things more and more these days, giving me more time to do the construction work," he said. "If anything, I'm just part-time. I tend bar when she needs help. She's always been better at the paperwork, the licenses and managing people, believe it or not. Also, I always order the wrong beer kegs. Drives her crazy."

"OK, well, I hope it goes well and you don't...spill anything?" she suggested.

"That works as well as anything else," he said, opening the

door. He paused there and gave her a little half-nod. "You've been working hard, Ana. You're keeping up your end of the deal."

She smirked at the reluctant tone with which he was praising her. "You didn't expect me to, did you?"

He scowled. "I'm not going to hand you an 'Employee of the Month' plaque, woman. I'm just saying, I've noticed and I appreciate it."

"You're welcome. I appreciate you working so hard and making the first floor look less like a Scooby Doo-style nightmare in such a short amount of time." She sighed. "This feels like a very awkward couple's counseling exercise."

"I wouldn't know," he said. "I've never been in couple's counseling."

"Ohhhh, I've been to every marriage therapist on the Upper West Side," she said. "I am a connoisseur of couples counseling styles—the Gottman Method, attachment therapy, narrative therapy, imago therapy. I tried it all."

Ned grimaced, and she got the impression that it was related to not wanting to know anything about her marriage rather than any sympathy for her. "And none of that…worked?"

"Generally speaking, if therapy is going to save a marriage, both people need to show up for the appointments," she said.

"Well, that sucks."

"Really does," she agreed. "So, you're really good at all this," she said, gesturing towards the chaos of construction."Thank you for not sounding surprised," he said, leaning against the door.

"Why didn't you tell me that you'd gone to school? Gotten all of your qualifications?" she asked.

He rolled his eyes. "Why does it matter?"

"It doesn't really, I guess. Other than it's a big part of your life and I'm interested."

"Because there were more options than you thought," he

said, staring through her with those frank gray eyes. "You saw your future two ways—staying on the island and being unhappy or leaving the island and having everything you wanted. We were young and you didn't see all of the different possibilities in between. I found one of those possibilities—I left for school, saw some of the outside world, experienced something different, and realized how much I liked life here. You...you didn't talk to me, Ana."

"It was no secret I was planning to leave," she said.

"Yeah, but you talked about it like it was 'someday.' Everybody we knew talked about it as 'someday.' Except for Dougie, of course. You could have told me it was going to be the day after we graduated high school. I went to your parents' house and they were just sitting at the kitchen table, staring at your note. If you hadn't left it, they might have dragged the lake for your body. You didn't call. You didn't write. You didn't answer when we called or wrote to you. Did you even think about how that would make us feel, to be completely cut off like that? Did you think about me at all over the years? Or was I just some stepping stone on the 'Ana Gustavsson path to better things?'"

"No, and yes. Too many questions at once. No, I didn't tell you when I was leaving because I wouldn't have been able to leave you. You would have convinced me not to go. You were the only one who had the power to do that. So I stayed away. And I didn't come back or call or write, because you were the only one who could talk me into coming back too. It wasn't because I didn't think of you, it was because I thought of you too much."

She'd decided to diplomatically omit the part about imagining him bald and surrounded by sticky children.

Ned pressed his lips into a thin line, nodding. "Goodnight, Ana."

And with that, he closed the door behind him.

"Once again, you are a stunning conversationalist—stunned

him right out of the damned house." She sighed, lightly thumping her sore forehead against the door.

Turning to her disarrayed, achingly quiet house—no staff, no family, not even a TV to make her feel like she had company, she was suddenly desperate to escape all that silence. She walked into the kitchen to make herself some tea and spotted the museum poster. She'd left it splayed across the kitchen table after marking it extensively with one of Ned's red grease pencils.

"No," she told herself, crossing to the stove to heat water in the old iron kettle.

There would be people there, because there was very little else happening on the island that night. And those would be people she'd known since she was a kid, some of whom would be more than happy to laugh at Ana's misfortune. Or some of them might do worse. She'd felt like she'd sort of neutralized Nell, but that didn't mean some other former classmate wouldn't come out swinging.

She would make herself some tea and try to call the girls. It was probably masochistic, considering that they'd yet to answer, but she dialed their numbers every other day, just to make sure their numbers were still in service.

When both calls went unanswered, she opened Chloe's Instagram. Ana was grateful, she supposed, that her oldest hadn't blocked her there, and Ana could still see how she was enjoying London. New posts assured her that both girls were, at least, safe and functioning. She tapped on Chloe's account, opening what appeared to be a classic "beach feet" picture—Chloe's delicately painted coral toes peeking out over a linen beach lounge with turquoise water in the distance.

"What the?"

Chloe was supposed to be in London. She said she was so busy, she couldn't even take her mother's calls. And yet, here she was lounging on a beach in a hashtag-less picture where the location services were clearly turned off...right next to a pair of feet she was almost certain belonged to Arden. She'd recognize the small diamond-shaped birthmark on the instep of her daughter's left foot anywhere.

And in the far corner of the picture, a pair of slim, tanned legs practically posed in the romantic "foot pop" position, toe to toe, with hairier male legs dusted with gray. On the female calf, Ana could make out a tattoo—an infinity symbol with what Wren claimed was the Sanskrit word for "inner peace." Ana had noticed it often enough during her Pilates, wondering if Wren would ever regret such a cliché, probably misspelled tattoo.

Her girls were with Bash, wherever he was hiding. They'd taken a fugitive vacation with their father and his mistress. They'd more than left her on read. They had more than chosen him in the divorce. They'd written their mother off completely.

"Fuuuuuuuuuuuuck," Ana gasped.

———

She wanted to wallow. So badly.

Ana had wanted to crawl under her borrowed covers and cry out her hurt and horror and the bone-deep betrayal into a pillow. She figured she'd earned the right, but amongst Irma Gustavsson's pearls of wisdom were several sayings about feeling sorry for yourself and crying over spilled milk. She wondered what pithy advice her mother would have had about spilled cheater fuck-face husbands who lured one's daughters out of extradition territory with free first- class flights and unlimited room service.

So instead of wallowing, she slipped into the nicest of the cashmere sweaters she'd shoved in her duffle and into the Eddie Bauer down jacket she'd found at a...*internal sigh*...consignment store in Grand Rapids. It was as light as a croissant, but was a definite improvement over her too-thin trench. She let her anger propel her down the sidewalk to Main Street, around slushy islands of ice frozen to the concrete. The forecast might not have called for snow this late in March, but Ana could smell it on the wind—a sort of sixth sense all islanders developed that never left her, even when she lived in New York.

She glanced toward Fitzroy's Pub as she passed, spotting Ned standing behind the bar, pouring pints for the crowd cemented to the barstools. With little else to do in the winter, the pub was one of the main social outlets for locals. Tom Fitzroy had resisted putting in a TV for games up until Ana left the island, but she could see ESPN playing on a wall-mounted big screen through the window. Ned and Nell had to wait until Mr. Fitzroy passed, which was...not at all surprising.

A strange pang of loneliness hit her right in the gut as she walked by, feeling very separate from the warm cheer inside the pub. It made no sense. She'd rarely spent time at Fitzroy's when she lived on the island. She'd been too young and Mr. Fitzroy couldn't stand her, what with her "dangerous ideas" about living off-island. Maybe it was because she passed without Ned so much as looking at her. Which was ridiculous, because they'd spent weeks together in the house without Ned so much as looking at her or speaking beyond the instructive grunts. Ned might be willing to fix her house, but he wanted nothing to do with her beyond barely civil conversation. She needed to stop looking to him for notice or...companionship...or anything beyond carpentry. If she did, it would be twice as hard for her to leave again. It had been hard enough the first time.

Her boots crunched over the snow as she approached the Espoir Island Public Library, a tiny cement block building that shared walls with the county courthouse, for heating purposes. They'd only built it in the 1950s because the old library burned in an incident involving old books being stored near a coal furnace...which should have surprised her more, but it never had.

It was very intimidating, walking into that humble little building. Just as she suspected, it was crowded with her former classmates and neighbors, and it felt like they were all staring at her. And whispering. While Nell gave her a friendly nod and Bailey waved enthusiastically, Ana scanned the chairs arranged in the children's section for other less friendly, familiar faces.

She realized that she'd either done something very right or very wrong by staying in Fishscale House, mostly isolated, since she'd returned. Given their shocked expressions, it was if people didn't really believe she was back on the island until they saw her with their own eyes. She recognized her former history teacher, Mrs. Larsson, who'd once told her she'd be a much more pleasant girl if she wasn't so mouthy. And Terri Boylan, former head cheerleader—the school only had three—who had given an interview to the New York Daily News and E!Online stating that she hadn't been surprised by the lash bar fight, because Ana was a violent, erratic teenager who frequently terrorized her classmates. And Mrs. Eskind, a friend of her mother, who had sent her a condolence card reading "SHAME ON YOU" in bright red ink, when Ana's parents died.

"Well, this was a huge miscalculation on my part," Ana muttered to herself, turning back towards the door. Suddenly, an arm slipped through hers. Ana jumped at the sight of Jackie Sanditon, class president and valedictorian, grinning at her. Jackie was wearing a thick navy wool coat, not by a designer Ana recognized, but exquisitely cut, with a Burberry scarf even New York Ana would have envied.

"So good to see you, Ana!" she said—loudly and with very deliberate cheer as her mother, Bette, passed and sat with Mrs. Hotchner in the back row.

"Come sit next to me!" Jackie shooed a smirking Terri Boylan down the row of folding chairs to make room for her and Ana. The spell of staring and whispering seemed to have broken and the twenty or so people seated were content to review the mimeographed copies of the meeting agenda. Ana didn't even know mimeograph machines still existed.

"Thanks," Ana whispered out of the side of her mouth.

"No problem," Jackie murmured, keeping her eyes trained on the agenda in her hand. "I remember in eighth grade, I had a nosebleed all over my shirt in English class. You were the one who offered me your gym clothes to change into, instead of laughing at me."

Ana's brows rose. "Wow."

"What, you didn't remember that?"

"No, not really," Ana said, tugging her knit cap off of her head and shaking out her hair. "It's just nice to have a good deed thrown back at me instead of fist-fighting and general self-ishness."

Jackie patted her arm. "I'd like to talk to you after the meeting, if you don't mind. How about we go get a beer?"

"That is the best offer I've gotten in weeks," Ana sighed.

"That's really fucking sad, Gustavsson."

"All right, all right, let's get down to it," Nell told the crowd. She stood at the head of the room, her Fitzroy Pub baseball cap firmly in place. "We're here to review the press package and poster designs for the upcoming tourist season. Mrs. Larsson suggested that we reuse last year's posters in order to save some money and devote that to new shelves at the museum. I'm sure that has nothing to do with the fact that Mrs. Larsson's grandson designed the posters."

Light laughter ran through the crowd, and Nell's expression became more serious. "We all know that tourism doesn't bring a *lot* of money onto the island, but it brings in enough to keep us afloat. And if we can't bring in better numbers, it's gonna hurt us all."

Ana watched as fear and dread rippled across every face in the room. With that, Nell launched into an explanation of the historical society's public relations strategy for the next year. It seemed that—in the absence of a real tourist commission on the island—the historical society had became a sort of de facto commission, attempting to draw tourists to town. And now that Ana saw the full package of posters and planned advertisements set up on easels, she could see that the situation was much worse than she thought. It was like they were planning some sort of bizarre Opposite Day campaign where they were trying to talk people *out* of visiting the island.

The message was inconsistent and emphasized the wrong things. For instance, almost every ad mentioned how cheap the island was. Ana knew from experience that people might want low prices, but they didn't like the word "cheap." They wanted to feel they were getting high quality for a low cost, that they were beating the system.

Ana sat squirming as these bad ideas were being bandied about like casually unpinned grenades. But when Nell got to the museum poster, Ana couldn't take it anymore.

"OK, OK, hold on." She stood up. Nell shot her a displeased look. "Nell, I have a little bit more experience with branding than most of the people here. Would you mind if I pointed out some issues with the posters?"

Mrs. Larsson harrumphed. "I don't see why the flatlander gets to speak at the meeting."

"With all due respect, Mrs. Larsson, my family's been here for five generations and you just moved here thirty years ago. If anybody here is the flatlander here, it's you," Ana shot back. "Also, your grandson couldn't design his way out of a maze with no turns."

"Are you going to let her take over this meeting, Nell?" Terri barked.

"Well, I did check her Facebook page a couple weeks back and she does have about fifty times the likes as the Espoir Island page, so yeah, she has a little more expertise than we do," Nell said, gesturing for Ana to join her at the front of the room.

Ana took her copy of the poster and attached it to the easel. "If you want people to come to the island, you need to change your focus. This poster emphasizes nothing...really. I can't see anything that would make me want to visit the island versus literally any other place in the greater Midwest. Also, people can eat bland bean soup, pretty much anywhere, including from a can in their kitchens. Bean soup isn't exactly a treat or a delicacy, and frankly, it kind of reminds me of prisons and suffering. Suffering is always bad and again, not the sort of thing people leave their homes to seek out... unless we had some sort of serial killer that operated on the island and the people who visit those sort of sites..."

When no one responded, Ana shook her head. "Never mind. My point is, what's the one thing this island has?"

"Mold?" Nell suggested.

"Artisan *lutefisk?*" Jackie guessed, her lips twitching.

"A collection of weather vane-specific blacksmithing tools from throughout the years?" Bailey shouted from the back of the room.

Ana laughed. "No. Struggle. Espoir Island has struggle out the ass. Battles, hardships, illness. And people *love* struggle. What do people build museum exhibits around? Struggle. What inspires young people to shit all over their parents and rebel? *Songs* about struggle. What do they give Oscars for? *Movies* about struggle. The people who have lived on the island have struggled from the moment they set foot on the godforsaken rock. And yes, it's more than a little depressing, but it's also inspiring."

"How is 'struggle' different from suffering?" Nell asked. "You said suffering was bad."

"Struggle means you're working to overcome the suffering. There's a happily ever after," she said.

For the briefest moment, she allowed herself to feel the shame of a complete fraud for even muttering the words "happily ever after" in public. Why was she trying so hard? She couldn't say that she felt a great wellspring of pride or loyalty to her hometown. She didn't owe these people anything. Hell, some of them had celebrated when she hit rock bottom. Terri actually mentioned the word "celebrate" in her interviews. She supposed it was because she knew what it was like to be discounted, discarded. And if she could use her limited skills to keep other people from feeling that way, she should.

"So we reframe the history around the theme of 'The Winds of Fate,'" Ana said, and seeing Nell opening her mouth to protest, she raised her hands. "We keep it true, but we put the emphasis on how the people of Espoir Island won in the end, that no matter how the wind blew the weather vane, we found our way. Surely, there are some stories hidden in the archives, some people who succeeded here, when all else failed."

Nell turned to Mrs. Larsson, who was frowning. "I think I could find some stories like that."

"If you give me access to a decent laptop with a basic design software package, I could lay the posters out myself. No charge. Because I'm not a professional and I wouldn't feel right charging you," she said. "Also, I know we don't like to change things around here, but I would seriously consider renaming the weather vane museum. You've still got all the archive stuff there, right? Old family trees, marriage and birth certificates, baptism records moved over from the church?"

"Yeah," Nell said, nodding.

"Well, I would rechristen the museum the Espoir Island Historical and Genealogical Center. People go crazy for all that family tree-tracking stuff. How else do you explain spitting in a tube to find out where they come from?" Ana said. "You can keep all of the weather vane exhibits intact, but emphasize how all of these wonderful families sprang up from the island. They may have been scattered by the winds, but Espoir Island never forgets its own.'"

"Yeah, but what are the odds that people's families came from Espoir?" Bailey asked.

"Are you kidding? More families have moved *off* of Espoir to greener pastures than have ever stayed on it," Ana scoffed. "And even if they don't find connections here, at least we get them on the island long enough to buy stuff. The rebranding would be fairly easy and cheap. All you would have to do is print up some new signage, posters, and maybe register a new domain name. You're going to have to redesign all of the websites on the island. All of them. Oh, and the social media, too. And while you're at it, please consider all of the other tourism type signs in town because...damn."

Everybody was staring at her.

"What?" Ana asked, checking her sweater for offending stains. "Do I have to make a motion or something to make the proposal official?"

"No, I can do that, since you're not officially a member," Nell said. "The motion has been made to redesign the posters and advertising plus rebranding the museum into a genealogical center?"

"That seems like a lot for one motion," Ana said.

"I'm in charge. I do what I want," Nell told her. "Do I have a second?"

"Second!" Bailey called.

"All in favor?" Nell asked.

Most of the room voted "aye" with the notable exceptions of Terri and Mrs. Larsson.

"Motion passes," Nell said, grinning. "All in favor of Ana Gustavsson handling the redesign and rebranding?"

"What, what?" Ana cried.

Again, with the exception of Terri and Mrs. Larsson, the motion carried.

Ana shook her head, her expression horrified. "I think this is a violation of how the 'motion' thing is supposed to work."

*a*na walked out of the meeting responsible for a lot more than she intended, but honestly, a part of her was proud that she'd been asked to handle something so important to the island after all this time. Of course, she was also acutely aware that she'd been asked because no one else wanted the job, but still…

Yeah, she didn't have a follow-up to that.

She tried to see the silver lining. Having a project, other than Fishscale House, would keep her busy. It would keep her from wallowing…and maybe she wouldn't come across as someone who was using and abusing the island for her own gain if she left the island a little better this time around.

Nell patted her on the shoulder. "We're never going to get you to come to another meeting again, huh?"

"Let that be a lesson to me," Ana said, though she was smirking. "Nell, people here still *make* weather-vanes, right?"

"Sure," Nell said. "We have six or seven people who make the vanes for demonstrations, but we hadn't had enough demand for more than one person to work the old forges. And no one was really buying them from the gift shop."

"I need them to make a lot of them. As many as they can—shiny and stately as possible. If they need money for materials... I think I have some in my house budget," she sighed. "I'll have to give up some of the upgrades I was thinking of—granite counter tops and this absolutely divine tiling for the bathroom. But I can't sell a house on an island with no attractions, can I?"

"And why would we make a large stock of weather vanes that no one will buy?" Nell asked.

"I have a plan," Ana said, grinning broadly.

"I am serious when I say this—I have never been so frightened in my entire life," Nell told her. Ana wriggled her eyebrows.

"You still up for that drink?" Jackie asked, slipping her arm through Ana's. "I just need to drop my mom at home."

"Oh, you go have your beer," Bette Sanditon said, waving her arthritic hands towards the door. "I'm gonna go by Inga's for a few hands of euchre. Pick me up when you're done."

"OK. Goodnight, Nell." Jackie kissed her mother's cheek, and a pang of longing struck Ana so hard, she thought she might double over. Her parents worked so hard every day, they never seemed to have time for anything beyond quick, quiet dinners and dozing in front of the TV. Her own relationship with her mother had been cordial, but distant. They'd never had the warmth between them that Jackie and Bette so casually enjoyed.

Jackie wrapped her arm through Ana's again, as if she sensed that Ana might bolt as they walked closer to Ned's family bar. She wasn't too far off, carefully securing Ana to her side as she talked about attending law school at Michigan and living near Whitefish Point. She traveled into town about once a week to check on her mom, who didn't want to admit how bad her driving was getting.

And if Ana thought that her entrance to the library was awkward, walking into the pub was practically accompanied by a social record scratch. People were staring, openly, their faces lit by blue and red neon beer signs. Even Ned looked uncomfortable for her. Ana made a little waving gesture. "Hi, everybody."

"All right, all right. Quit your gawking," Ned yelled. "Or I start calling in tabs."

Heads bent obediently over their beers while Jackie threaded her way through the tables for a booth at the back, the wooden benches nestled carefully against the ancient oak paneling.

"Two Stroh's, Ned!" Jackie called. "And my usual!"

Ned nodded, holding up two clean glasses. Jackie slid into the empty booth with a sigh, shrugging out of her coat. "So, who's handling your divorce?"

"That's…direct," Ana said, drawing off her hat.

"I've practiced family law for the last ten years," she said, shrugging. "And your case is one of the more interesting ones I've seen in a while."

"Oh, sure, if you think 'interesting' is another word for 'grotesque' and 'riddled with asshole-ry,'" Ana said, making Jackie laugh as she took a notebook out of her purse.

"I'm assuming you don't have representation."

"No, because so far I haven't been able to find any divorce lawyers who are willing to take magic beans as payment."

"What about old friends, who happen to be able to practice in New York—plus a good number of states in the northeast just for job flexibility and bragging rights—and feel like they owe you some kindness?" Jackie asked.

Ana sputtered. "You already paid me back earlier, not letting the crowd burn me at the stake in the library. And we're not talking about a couple of hours consulting over a weekend. My case could involve months of work, Jackie."

"So, you pay me a very, *very* small percentage of your settlement when it comes through," Jackie said, shrugging. "And then we go after that bitch Dakota and the producers for damages for that lash bar fight. It was clearly engineered and did demonstrable damage to your reputation."

"You're insane!" Ana laughed. Jackie did not. She looked absolutely serious, prompting Ana to add, "If you're sure about this. Let's just start with my ex."

"I'm sure," Jackie said crisply. "Now, just so I walk into this with eyes open, do we need to be worried about you being drawn in on any of Sebastian's charges?"

"No, once I convinced them that I knew absolutely nothing about Bash's activities or whereabouts, the feds informed me that I'm of no interest to them. I was free to go. They didn't even ask me for a forwarding address. My almost-ex was paranoid about keeping things to himself. Bash had seen too many guys trying to hide assets in their wives' names, only to lose them in a divorce when the wives wised up. And I filed my taxes separately, because I barely earned enough income on my own to pay anything. It was another point of pride for Bash. Sure, I might earn 'fun money' with endorsements or product lines, but nothing that reach the kind of money that would support us. He didn't ever want me to feel like I contributed to his business, or the household income."

"Why would that be a point of pride?"

Ana pressed her lips together, unsure of whether she was prepared to admit something she'd never really spoken aloud. As a venture capitalist, Bash made his money off knowing what investments would pay off and which ones wouldn't. Years of selling to people, listening to conversations in cafes while she waited tables helped Ana hone a sharp sense of what people wanted, what they would convince themselves they had to have. Over the years, he'd asked her what she thought of proposals and took advantage of that sense. She'd kept him from investing in several absolute bombs—Google Glass, Wow! Chips, that weird ketchup that came in purple and green to appeal to kids—

but Ana's interest in social media had prompted him to join on the ground floor of several of the world's most popular apps, not to mention the leading brand of selfie stick and an up-and-coming electric car company.

"Bash made his money predicting trends," Ana said, fiddling with a coaster. "I don't think he wanted to admit to himself how much he relied on my advice. In the last year or so, he started pulling away. He didn't talk to me about potential investments anymore. He started making his own calls, choosing his own proposals. And he picked some real stinkers. I thought maybe that's why he was distant, because he was ashamed and didn't want to come back to me for help. But I guess that's when he started seeing Wren. Boinking your mistress on every available surface requires a certain level of emotional detachment from your marriage."

"Hmmm." Jackie scribbled in her notebook. "And how do you see yourself after this divorce is over? What's your ideal situation?"

"Are you asking how much money I'm hoping to get?" Ana asked. "Because I don't think my chances are very good there. Bash moved most of his assets to secret places we will not be able to track."

Jackie shook her head. "Not necessarily. What are you hoping for in your life?"

Ana sat back in the booth. Honestly, she hadn't thought that far ahead. She'd been in survival mode for so many weeks. She didn't really know what she wanted beyond some security. Jackie seemed to sense her hesitation. "OK, first things first. *Where* do you want to live?"

Her mouth dropped open as she searched for the response that felt right.

"Gustavsson, these are not difficult questions." Jackie laughed.

"I don't think I'll have the means to live in New York, at least not in the way that I was before. I think maybe I could stay on the island, which is more than I could say a few weeks, even a few days, ago. I'm still trying to figure out what I want to do when I grow up."

It surprised her that she meant it. She wasn't as desperate to escape Espoir as she had been only recently. And of course, that was the moment Ned came to the table with two beers and burgers. If he was having any reaction to her desire to possibly stay on the island, he wasn't showing it.

"Ladies, two Stroh's and an olive burger—"

"Yay!" Jackie cheered, making grabby hands at her plate.

"I have never understood the olive burger, in terms of Michigan specialties, that is just gross," Ana said, cringing as Jackie carefully cut through a burger bun slathered with mayo and chopped green olives. "Then again, I couldn't eat olives when they were soaked in booze, so if that's not enough of a reason…"

"I told Smitty not to let an olive within a foot of yours," Ned told her, rolling his eyes. "It's Swiss and bacon, your favorite."

"Thank you," she said, trying to remember the last time she'd eaten a damn burger, much less cheese or bacon. And Fitzroy's were seasoned by virtue of a grill that probably hadn't been cleaned since before Ana was born. But considering how much ramen she'd eaten over the last few weeks, she decided to just shut up and eat the burger.

She would choose to pretend no one heard the indecent noises she made while chewing the first bite.

"Tell Smitty my offer of marriage still stands," Jackie said, waggling her fingers flirtatiously at the grizzled sixty-seven-year-old cook, who waved back with his spatula. "He will be mine. *Oh, yes*, he will be mine."

Ned looked to Ana, who shrugged. "I'll witness the ceremony in exchange for more burgers. Hell, I'll even be flower girl."

"Enjoy your burgers, ya weirdos," Ned said, shaking his head as he walked away.

Jackie took a huge bite of her briny burger, chewing thoughtfully. "So you don't want to live in New York and you don't want to stay here. Somewhere in between, then?"

"Wherever that may be. I don't expect to live at the same level I was, but I just want to be comfortable. I don't want to have to worry about where my next meal will come from or whether I can pay my living expenses. I know that sounds entitled, considering I haven't worked since I was twenty-five—"

"No, no. You were married to the man for twenty years. Food security and being able to pay your utilities seems more than reasonable, especially when you take into account that you were basically an unpaid consultant whose advice resulted in financial gain," Jackie agreed. "What about your daughters?"

"Arden turns eighteen in May, so I don't see the point in asking for child support," Ana said. "She had early admission to Brown. She's brilliant and terrifying, and it turns out, very loyal to her father."

When Jackie frowned in confusion, Ana quickly explained about the Instagram post, which she had almost forgotten in the hubbub of the historical society meeting. Jackie winced, sliding half of her fries to Ana's plate. "Damn. You need these more than I do."

"You're a good woman, Jacqueline Sanditon."

"Not when I'm in the courtroom, I'm not."

"Well, when you're up against Bash's legal team, you'll need it," Ana told her. "They're good. Like 'pre-programmed into OJ's phone' good."

Jackie grinned at her. "You ever been to a divorce court in Detroit?"

"No. No, I have not."

Jackie started snickering, and suddenly, Ana was sort of

afraid for Bash—not bad enough to do anything about it. But still, the feeling was there.

Temporarily.

6

Ana had forgotten how good her neighbors on Espoir could be to each other.

Once word spread that yes, Ana Gustavsson was really back and living in Fishscale House, her doorbell started ringing.

Also, her doorbell desperately needed to be replaced, because it sounded like something out of *The Addams Family*.

John Mohlen had dropped three cords of firewood into the storage box on her porch, waving his Stormy Kromer at her when she called out her thanks. Fileted whitefish and apple bread showed up like clockwork every few days. Eddie Burgess and Art Giddner—a couple of "confirmed bachelors" who owned the hardware store together for the last forty years and probably the most functional couple on the island—showed up one afternoon to help Ned with the wiring. Bette Sanditon came by with some extra pots and pans and kitchen stuff. Nell and Smitty came to help with tearing out the cabinets and fixtures.

Combined with the specialists Ned recruited to replace the scale-shaped siding, and replace the staircase spindles, (not granite) countertops, and cabinets, the house was almost unrecognizable. A crew painted the siding a soft gray while the trim was painted a deeper slate color and then white to emphasize the different dimensions. The awful appliances were replaced with units that were not quite luxurious, but they were energy efficient and *not* harvest gold.

Slowly, day by day, the house became livable, particularly after Ned found a huge soaking tub on claw feet. It was a lot easier to see her herself living on the island permanently— without the usual debilitating despair—while up to her chin in warm, scented water.

And while the cynical part of her thought maybe the sudden outpouring of support had something to do with her taking over the historical society's efforts, she also knew that people on Espoir helped each other not so they had leverage to hold over each other in a never-ending game of social chess. They helped each other because alone, no one survived on Espoir.

Speaking of which, Jackie had already contacted Bash's lawyers and filed several motions in divorce court on Ana's behalf. She seemed to know what she was doing, considering that Bash's chief lawyer, John H. Houston, had called Ana to say that 'surely, rushing a divorce process wasn't what she wanted' and telling her that it might be best just to wait awhile and let Bash's lawyers ease the proceeding through court quietly. Houston promised he would represent her interests fairly. All she had to do was "stop complicating the situation." Ana told Houston to direct all contact to her lawyer before hanging up on him.

She tried to help Ned with the house as much as possible, but eventually he realized that while the spirit was willing, the flesh was an enormous risk to herself and others while handling power tools. There was an incident with the nail gun and poor Smitty's foot. She was sure it was the talk of Fitzroy's for days.

Ana carried things and helped him set up or clean up. But eventually, he pretended not to notice while she wordlessly slipped out of the room and into the library. It was a fancy term for what was basically a large office with a ton of built-in bookshelves, and an enormous oak desk decorated with carved, writhing fish that looked like something off of one of those maps that warned, "Here there be dragons." Ana suspected that the original owners left it behind because they couldn't move the damn thing.

Still, it was a good place to work on the historical society's project, if for no other reason, than it didn't require a lot of work. It was quiet and had been built to let the island's limited light in. Somehow, Nell had wrangled a laptop and a stack of historical records that provided the sort of information she needed to frame her "struggle narrative." They were spread across the desk in a banquet of romance and heartbreak and joy.

She'd found surprises in those pages, which was the most surprising part of all. She thought she knew everything about her island. But she'd never heard of Rosalee Nilsson, a teenage girl who managed to save a ship carrying her betrothed in 1823 by maintaining signal fires on the beach in a storm. Ana knew that beach was called Sweethearts Beach, but she thought that was because kids went there to make out. It was because of Rosalee that the town eventually built a lighthouse to lead ships away from the rockier shores of Espoir. She'd never heard of the Espoir Canning Club, a group of women who had taken to harvesting, canning and selling what fruit that grew on the island to keep their families going during the Great Depression. Their men tried to object, according to a record from the church aid society logs, and in response, a woman named Roberta Laine threatened to "irreparably change" her husband with a pair of jar tongs. Apparently, the menfolk decided to put their pride aside fairly quickly after that. And in the most shocking turn, she'd never been told about the winter in 1963, when a local boy nearly died from pneumonia, forcing the local fire department into a borrowed sleigh to drive across the frozen lake, risking their lives on ice they weren't quite sure would hold them, just to get Petey Gustavsson to the mainland.

How had her father never told her about that? She wasn't sure she could use it, but seeing her dad's name written in the fire chief's duty log was jarring enough to knock open that little door in her heart that she'd tried to close to Espoir. How had these stories been neglected on the school's Historical Days? How had she not heard those stories around a campfire, instead of Dougie's attempt at scaring her with "The Hooked-Handed Man on Pine Street?" How had she closed herself off to something that was such a part of her make-up as a person? And what had it gained her? Damn near nothing.

The "new" material made her job easier. Within three weeks, she had enough stories and historical pictures to revamp the posters, the brochures and set up a few pages of the historical society's new web site. And while she knew that what she'd put together was better than what the society had before, she felt the need to show someone what she was doing, to confirm that it was as good as she thought. And that's how she found herself walking into Fitzroy's on a relatively warm Friday night with a laptop bag over her shoulder.

For the first time since she moved back to the Espoir, she walked into a building without group conversation stopping entirely. A few people waved, including Nell, who was standing behind the bar pouring a pint, but it was the least awkward entrance she'd made in months.

She passed the bar, and postmaster Gill Swann, who had occupied the far corner seats every Friday night as long anyone could remember. "Hey, there, Ana, how are ya, honey?"

"I'm doing all right, Mr. Swann, how are you?"

Gill's prodigious gray brows waggled. "Oh, you know me, Friday night's meat loaf night, so here I am."

Liddie Swann was a lovely woman, but her meat loafs had been known to double as door-stoppers on particularly cold winter nights. Avoiding those meaty bricks had spurred Gill's Friday night patronage for more than forty years.

"Tell Mrs. Swann that I said hello," Ana said, laughing and patting him on the back. Nell pointed to a table near the back. "Will do."

Nell delivered a pitcher to a crowded table of barely-twenty-somethings and brought Ana a Diet Coke. "What brings you out tonight? I thought you were being all hermit-y and contemplating your poor life choices in your lonely haunted house."

"You know, I think I liked it better when you just punched me in the face as a greeting?" Ana said.

"It's still an option," Nell offered as Smitty brought a bacon cheeseburger to the table, kissed Ana on top of her head and walked off without a word. Ana stared after him, her expression fond, as she took her laptop out of her bag.

"I'm good," she said, taking a bite of cheeseburger as she fired up the computer.

"You know, Smitty bumped a *paying* customer's order out of the way to give you your burger first—without you even ordering." Nell nodded to the burger basket.

"I can't help it that I'm adored," Ana said around a mouthful of cheesy goodness.

"Yeah, you're still paying for that burger," Nell muttered.

Ana opened the poster design file to show Nell a colorful view of the cliffs on the south shore, where the striped lighthouse loomed amongst the tallest and thickest trees on the island. She'd used a clean, modern font in a gold metallic to write "Espoir Island." It popped nicely against the blue of the lake. She'd inset several photos of landmarks around town in the less interesting "blank spaces" of the scene—historical houses, blooming fruit trees the courthouse, statues. Under the gold town name, she used a subtle script font to write, "Espoir Island—Let the Winds of Fate Send You Here."

"And I carried the theme through web site and the brochure

—though the brochure talks a lot more about the genealogy center," Ana said, scrolling through the documents.

"I really like the pictures. Pretty without being too pretty, definitely more modern. And the lack of bean soup references," Nell replied. "I'm not sure about the slogan, though."

"Not sure about what slogan?" They turned to find Ned standing behind them, shrugging out of his jacket. He smiled and slid into the seat beside Ana, tucking his arm around the railing of her chair and leaning so he could see the screen better.

Nell said, "Ana's doing a trendy, minimalist thing, which I like, but I don't know about that slogan."

"Hmmm, how about 'Let the Winds of Fate Blow You Here?'" Ned asked. "It sounds more active."

"I think if you listen to that a few more times in your head, you'll realize how bad that is," Nell deadpanned. "And you can't just change one word in the slogan—while making a unintentional oral sex solicitation, I might add—and then act like you did something."

Ned shrugged. "OK, but is it the *right* word?"

"I think I've mentioned several times that it's not," Nell told him.

"This felt like such a grown-up conversation until the oral sex solicitation," Ana mused, chewing on her burger.

"Don't be impressed, Nell only knows the word 'solicitation' because I help her with crossword puzzles," John said, approaching from behind Ned's chair and kissing Nell's cheek.

Nell scoffed as John sat in the last available chair at the table. "You're not with me for my crossword skills."

"Should you be drinking that?" Ana asked, nodding at his beer and then made a vague gesture at his deputy uniform.

"Who's going to tell me any different?" John asked.

"Your dad?" Ana suggested.

John jerked his thumb over his shoulder, where his ancient

father, also in uniform, was finishing off a bottle of Bud. Ana laughed. "That makes sense."

"Speaking of dad, would you care to explain why he told me he would be skipping out on half of his shifts because he's going to be working the forges three days a week for 'as long as he damn well pleases?'"

Nell nodded. "I meant to ask—as of this morning, we have an order for more than five hundred weather vanes pending from the gift shop website. I wasn't even aware that we had gift shop website."

Ana grinned, pulling out her phone and showing Nell her Instagram account and a post that featured a photo of her fish-shaped weather vane, shown to perfection in the light of the setting sun. "I just happened to post this exclusive preview of the renovations I'm doing to my new 'island hideaway' and how I found this amazing vintage weather vane to top my meditation turret. How it was only available from artisan craftsman here on Espoir Island and I'd only managed to get one after being on the waitlist for months. But if you wanted to get on the waitlist, you could click on the link I provided."

"What kind of horse shit is that?" Nell demanded. "It's going to take us months to make all of them. Won't that slow down orders? We need something that will sustain us over time."

"Oh, trust me, the kind of people you want for customers *love* waiting lists. It makes them feel like they're getting something exclusive and difficult to attain. And once the trend runs through my New York contacts, it will make some sort of list in a magazine or a vlog and the West Coast will follow suit. And the tourism dollars will get pulled along with it."

"That's your strategy, making trendy social climbers jealous?" Ned asked, his expression dubious.

"I made snail mucus facials and indoor juniper groves *the* thing last year. Don't doubt my powers," Ana retorted.

"That's gross," Nell told her.

"I'm just glad you're on our side," Ned marveled.

"What about 'The Struggle is Real?'" John suggested. "Nell said that's part of your 'theme.'"

Ana was oddly touched that Nell talked about this at home. She was part of the conversation here on the island and not in a tragic, gossipy way. She liked it. She liked the way Ned and John just joined them, casually, because they were comfortable with each other. All that discomfort and resentment with Ned, it was just...gone. They were, well, she couldn't completely define their relationship, but things were definitely better.

She liked their relationship. She liked her relationship with Nell—and she never thought she would call anything involving Nell a 'relationship.' And yes, eating a casual cheeseburger would have made her break out into anxiety hives six months before, but she preferred this. Sitting in a familiar, cozy place, eating unpretentious food, with people who cared about her. And she realized that John was staring at her, waiting for a response. "It's funny, but a little *too* trendy."

Ned pulled a face. "I think that makes it sound like coming here is a struggle."

He turned to Ana. "What were some of your backups?"

"It's quite the list," Ana warned him, opening the file.

Ned shrugged, sipping his beer. "We've got time."

SPRING ROARED ONTO THE ISLAND LIKE A PISSED OFF LION, bringing high winds and surging storms. May squalls were notoriously rough on Espoir, as the island seemed to lie on some sort of invisible line where warm and cold fronts collided over the water. It was one of the reasons Ned insisted on replacing the windows early in the renovation, even when it meant exposing the house to frigid temperatures. They couldn't risk the spring rains soaking the walls or floors during replacement.

One such rainy afternoon, Ana walked into the parlor, watching as Ned inspected the finish he'd applied to the floors the day before. Ana did much of the pre-finish sanding herself, going over the wood in circles until her arms ached with the vibrations of the power sander. Rain was pouring over the house in sheets, flooding the road. It appeared that the lake was trying to reach up to smack the house off the hill.

She'd become so used to him being in the house with her, it felt empty without him. The rooms smelled like him after he left for the day. His tools were spread all over. He'd started letting himself in without knocking, so that sometimes she came down the stairs in the morning to find him already working. While he was still somewhat distant, seeing him every day brought back that feeling of connection, the comfort of having Ned in her life. She wasn't sure she deserved that, but it was nice to have.

"It's starting to look like a real home again," she said.

Ned stood, cracking his back, as he grinned at the shiny maple floor. "Yeah, it's really coming together."

"I've got a pot of chicken noodle soup ready, if you're hungry. The road's flooding anyway, so you might be stuck here for a while."

"Did you make the soup?" he asked, his brows raised.

"Yes. I am capable of putting food items in a pot and leaving them alone," she said, shaking her head at him.

"Well, I thought you'd forgotten how to do things like that for yourself, what with all the servants," he said, crossing the room to put away his tools.

Her voice was as dry as dust when she told him, "Well, life skills like tying my own shoes are slowly coming back to me."

Ned's head whipped toward her. "You had someone to tie them for you?"

"No!" she scoffed. "I had someone to pick them out for me. A stylist who would coordinate outfits for us."

"You couldn't do that on your own? Go shopping?"

"Oh, I did, but I never found stuff that suited me as well as she did."

"What about buying groceries?" he asked.

"The chef did that. I had a housekeeper to keep the apartment clean and running, a driver, a florist who delivered flowers every week, a laundress." She paused and started giggling. "I had an assistant who opened my mail for me. I had a personal mail sorter. How stupid is that? How removed from your life do you have to be, not to open your own mail?"

"Are you having some sort of hysterical episode?" he asked.

"No, I just realized how ridiculous it all is," she said, wiping at her eyes. "I mean, I'm not going to lie and say I got lost in the glamour and the money. I found myself. I found who I wanted to be. Someone who was strong and independent and used the money she had to help people. I worked for charities. I volunteered. I said the word and things happened. I will say that I probably got so caught up in that, that I didn't recognize what was happening around me."

He nodded, his lips pressed together. "I can see how that would happen."

"And when you asked me, if ever I thought about you? I thought about you a lot. When things were difficult with Bash, and in the last couple of years, that was more often than not, I would wonder what you were doing, what my life would be like if I stayed."

"How did you think it would have turned out?" he asked. "Because I pictured the house looking like this—maybe a little better than this—us living here, our kids, being happy."

She scoffed. "Oh, I never got that far. I dried my tears with hundred-dollar bills and forgot about it."

"Smartass," he said, grinning at her as she cackled. "I forgot what a smartass you are. And you were never sorry about it."

"Not once," she said, shaking her head.

Suddenly, he surged forward and captured her mouth with

his. His hands were just as big and warm and *rough* as they'd been years before, when they closed around her jaw. He pulled away, bending his forehead against hers while he panted over her skin.

"Please don't stop," she whispered. "Please don't talk yourself out of this."

"I'm not," he swore. "I'm just trying to figure out if I can get away with carrying you up the stairs."

"I think we're both of an age where it's better not to risk it," she said, laughing as she backed away, while stripping out of her shirt. He chased after her, damn near tripping as he tried to kick off his boots on the way up the stairs. He caught her just before they reached the big master bed, tugging her jeans down her thighs and knocking her gently back across the mattress.

She tried not to think how different she looked from the last time they were together, what he might see that he didn't like. It had been a very long time since anyone had touched her and she *would* enjoy this. No thinking about former husbands and their hands when perfectly good hands were already on her body willing to reach between her thighs and do that thing with his thumb. He'd always been so good at that thing with his thumb. Hell, from what she heard around the hallways, Ned was one of the few boys at their school who knew *where* to put his thumb.

She wouldn't worry about the bed not being made or what underwear she was wearing. She wouldn't worry about which positions would hide her flaws. There was only touch and taste and the smell of his skin as he hovered over her, palming her breasts and kissing the place at the hollow of her throat that always drove her crazy. His hands shook ever so slightly as he touched her, like he was afraid she would disappear again. He nibbled his way down her bared rib cage—and sliding his arms under her hips, pulling her to meet his mouth. He slipped his fingers inside her, plunging and curling them just so, while warm tension built in her belly.

She refused to be embarrassed, at how quickly that lovely heat spiraled into a full-blown, toe-curling, eye-crossing climax. It had been months since Sebastian had touched her and Sebastian certainly hadn't known how to do the thing with his thumb. Or his other fingers. Or his tongue.

He crawled his way up her body, his eyes darkened and full of determined mischief. The lights sputtered out in the hallway, plunging them into darkness, as he sank into her with a reverent sigh.

LATER, LONG AFTER THE LIGHTS FLICKERED BACK ON, SHE sprawled across Ned's sweat-sheened chest, her hair plastered across her face.

"So, we're still pretty good at that," he panted.

"Well, yeah." She pushed up on her elbows, peering down at him. "*That* was not the problem. You were never the problem. It was all of the things that came along with you."

He pushed her hair out of her face. "Is this an apology or a multi-layered insult, because it's very difficult to tell the difference."

"It's not that I don't want you. I wanted you then and I want you now. And you've always been better than me. Kinder. Less selfish. More thoughtful."

He raised his head to glare at her, but there was no real heat in it. "Those are all the same thing."

"I mean, it was *here*. This place, the island, the responsibilities, the permanence."

"Why wasn't *here*, enough?" he asked.

"Because I wanted to see the outside world. And at first, it was enough. There's so much out there."

"Did any of it make you happy?"

"Yes," she told him, making him snort. "Tropical islands. The

Eiffel Tower. Five-star restaurants. The Grand Canyon. Day spas, *regular* spas. It all made me very happy."

He gave her a knowing look.

"OK, it made me temporarily very happy. And then I would go back to my life and I would realize what was missing in my marriage and in my home. And I would frantically try to fix it, and it never worked. So I would try to focus on those things that made me temporarily happy. They were distractions. You were never a distraction."

"And do you still feel that *here* isn't enough?"

She jerked her shoulders. "I don't know. It could be. It helps that I'm not running around, chasing distractions. I just need more time to work everything out in my head."

Ned chuckled, tucking her against his side. "You're still terrible at apologizing."

"I accept that."

7

*A*fter months of work, Fishscale House was finally market ready. Or at least, it only looked way less haunted. The doorbell was changed something far more bell-like, for starters. Ned had painted the interior walls a softer white, the kind of finish that looked good in firelight and bold summer sun. The floors shone bright in the light pouring through the windows. The staircase gleamed, polished and good as new. She'd used lemon-scented wax on all of the wood surfaces and it smelled clean and new, like home.

Ned was in the parlor, installing some sort of new grate in the fireplace. It was the very last piece to be installed. She'd started walking into the parlor to show him her redesigned poster for the new genealogical center, but she stopped to watch him work, with a little smile on her face...which had a lot to do with how he was bent over in the fireplace, his denim-clad butt pointed towards her.

She sat on the bottom step, contemplating the interior of Fishscale House... and Ned's rear. She could spend the rest of her life staring at that butt. She balanced her chin on her hand, smiling to herself. A long-term relationship with him would probably require a little more of her—conversations, probably; emotional availability, sex, commitment, spending way less time on social media or worrying about public opinion, locally or globally. But she thought maybe she could handle that. Ned was a lot of things she'd been missing for years—open, kind, loyal. He understood that Ana had emotional needs that couldn't be met by airline upgrades and dinners at chefs' tables. He talked to her, almost to the point of exhaustion, when he was bothered. She'd never have to worry about him betraying her or ignoring her existence. She could even consider maybe thinking of one day discussing the subject of marriage.

But she wouldn't mention that to him because it felt way too soon…Also, she would never call him 'open, kind and loyal' to his face, because she doubted he would appreciate being described like a golden retriever.

She glanced around the foyer, so polished and pristine compared to what she saw walking into Fishscale House months before. It was such a beautiful house, but it could be more. People might actually pay to stay in a house like this. Back when she was still trying to fix things with Bash—she really had to stop defining the timeline of her life that way—she'd booked weekends in B&Bs that didn't have the charm that Ned had given to Fishcscale House.

The Seacliffe Inn was the only other hotel on the island. Part of the reason tourism was limited on the island was that when the inn was full to capacity, that was the limit of Espoir's accommodations. If she could convince other people with historical, non-creepy homes to offer something similar, that would be even better. Competition created a stronger market.

Ana had proven she could deal with self-promotion. And hosting guests couldn't be worse than hosting some of Bash's colleagues…or his family. She would hire someone on for the cleaning. And probably the cooking.

That was for the greater good.

She would have to ask Jackie about the licensing and insurance issues involved in opening your house up to the public. Also, she would have to get some furniture.

Her cell phone buzzed in her back pocket. Jackie's name and number flashed on the screen. Speak of the devil. "Hey, I've been meaning to call you."

"I have news!" Jackie crowed. "Your ex messed up!"

Ned turned at the bright, loud voice, which was easily heard even across the room.

"I know, we've been through this. He made a huge mistake, leaving me. It's lovely that you want to validate me, Jackie, but—"

"No, I mean, he messed up on an epic, *international* scale. His new lady friend convinced him that they absolutely had to visit some salt cave yoga retreat thing in the Virgin Islands, forgetting of course, that it's called the *U.S.* Virgin Islands and that they're more than willing to extradite wanted felons back to the mainland."

Ana stifled a snort. "Well, geography was never Bash's strong suit."

"His legal team will be meeting him at a very low-profile airport in New Jersey—"

She winced. "Oh, he'll hate that."

"And then he will appear before an extremely irate judge. And because said legal team doesn't want the distraction of dealing with a high-profile divorce with an extremely uncooperative spouse who will be unlikely to do anything besides cause trouble in the press, Houston is offering you a handsome cash settlement."

"How handsome?"

"Well, it depends on where you're planning to make your life. If you're planning to live in New York, you will be comfortable through your old age. If you want to stay a little closer, say Espoir Island, you could live like a queen for several lifetimes."

Looking at Ned, she smiled and said, "Either option sounds really good, but I think I'm going to go with royalty. I do live in a Queen Anne."

"That was terrible," Jackie told her as Ned's brows drew together.

"I'm aware."

"I'll email you the details of the settlement."

"Thanks!" Ana grinned at Ned as he stood.

"Did you just say what I think you said?"

"I don't want to go," she said. "I still don't *love* it here. But I really like this house. And I do love you. I've always loved you."

He took her hands in his, squeezing them gently. "As much as I love hearing that, I don't want to hold you here. I don't want you to resent me."

She kissed him quickly. "Trust me, I know what resentment feels like, I know where it comes from. It comes not listening, from not caring, from thinking that what you want is more important than what the other person wants, from ignoring them, from making them feel small. The things I had before, I don't need them anymore. I don't need those people. And I damn sure don't need to be on TV."

"You're sure?"

"I'm sure of you," she told him. "What I'm not so sure of is the idea of turning this place into a bed and breakfast. What do you think?"

"Well, you might consider that Nell is planning to ask you to take over Mrs. Larsson's position at the museum-slash-genealogical center," he said. "She was sure you'd stay months ago, after the historical society meeting."

She laughed as he kissed her. She'd expected to resent it, the idea that Nell had figured her out before she did. But instead, she found that she was pleased to have options. She was wanted here. Her skills were needed. She had a place. It had been a long time since she'd had a place.

"We'll take things slow," he said. "I will not move into the house or give you any type of jewelry until you're sure you want to stay."

"Knock, knock!" she heard a voice on the porch.

"Come in!" she called back.

Dougie Jergenson opened the door, his arms full of Jergenson and Sons Realty signs for her front lawn. "Hey, Ana! I have the listing papers all ready to sign and…"

Dougie took one look at her face and Ned's arms wrapped around her waist and said, "Oh, shoot."

"I'm so sorry, Dougie," she said. "I don't think I'm going to need your services after all?"

Dougie dropped the signs and threw his arms out. Ned let go long enough to let Dougie envelope her in a hug. "That's such great news! I can't wait to tell my Bonnie!"

"Can we wait a bit before we tell Bonnie?" she asked, making Ned laugh.

Her phone buzzed again, making Dougie jump. "I'll let you take your call. Ned, can you help me carry all this back to my car?"

Ned pressed a kiss to her temple. "Sure."

Ana glanced at the screen, gasping when she saw Chloe's contact photo filling the space. It was all she could do not to burst into tears at the sight of her baby girl's face, but her hand hesitated over the glass. What should she do? The last time Ana checked Chloe's Instagram, she was back in New York, working for a stylist and living in a two-bedroom with three other girls. She hadn't answered Ana's calls in months. What if this was a butt dial? It would be even more painful to find out Chloe never meant to call her, didn't want to talk to her.

But what if Chloe needed her?

Ana made a frustrated noise and swiped her thumb across the glass. "Chloe? Honey? Is that you? Are you OK?"

Her voice cracked just the slightest bit on the word, "OK,"

and for a moment she panicked. What if the distress in her tone made Chloe hang up? The girls hated it when she "guilted" them. What if—

"Mom, Mom, it's me." Her daughter's voice filled her ear, warm and strong and making Ana's eyes fill with tears. "I'm OK. Mom, I'm so sorry I haven't called. I'm so sorry I haven't answered your calls, but with Dad—"

"It's all right," Ana promised her. "I know this has been hard on you and Arden. I'm not mad. I'm just glad you called."

"Where are you?" Chloe asked.

"I'm in Michigan."

"On Grandma and Grandpa's island? You said you'd never go back there!"

"Well, honey, I didn't have a lot of options."

"Ugh, I'm so sorry, Mom. I can't believe I was slumming around that lame villa in the Caribbean with dad and his bimbo girlfriend while you were forced to go back to some awful hillbilly backwater. I feel like such an idiot."

"OK, OK, first of all, you have to have hills to have hillbillies," Ana responded, grinning when she heard Chloe snicker. "Espoir isn't so bad, really. I'm sorry I kept you girls away from here for so long. And no, what you did wasn't great, but I get that this has been confusing and stressful time for you girls, and that you were afraid of losing your dad's..."

"You can say 'money,' Mom, I won't be offended."

"Love and support?" Ana offered.

"That's nicer than I deserve right now. And there's not going to be much of anything coming our way with *Wren* in the picture." Chloe seethed.

"I don't know if I want to hear this."

"Mom, she's *terrible*." Chloe complained. "Back in the islands, she was already talking about not wanting us around on holidays when they have *their* kids, and making sure Dad adds protections to his will so *their family* is provided for. Dad's so blind to it. He just nods and smiles."

A small petty part of her was filled with righteous relief, to hear her daughter's rage, the contempt for Wren. And she was so tempted to add all of her nasty opinions of Bash and Wren. But instead, she took a deep breath and said, "Well, honey, I think they both know what they're getting into."

"I don't even care about the money anymore," Chloe said. "I've talked to one of the paralegals in Dad's lawyer's office and she said Dad *has* to provide for Arden until she's eighteen and that we both have trust funds from Grandpa we can access when we're twenty-one. Apparently, there's some sort of provision in Grandpa's will about college tuition, too. So Arden's covered."

She huffed out a laugh. "You infiltrated Houston's law firm?"

"Yes, I did. It could be lean for a few years, but eventually, we'll have the sort of money to set up the life we're used to. Besides, maybe we need to learn to live with a little less."

Ana smiled as Ned walked back into the house, his expression curious. "Well, I can't say it's hurt me."

She showed Ned the phone screen and his eyes went wide, giving her a silent thumbs up before kissing her.

"Are you sure?" Chloe asked. "I hate to think of you out there on some tiny island all alone."

Ned mouthed the word "alone?" and clutched at his chest as if he was wounded. Ana laughed. "Oh, you don't need to worry about me. But how about you and Arden come out and visit me over the summer? There's some people I'd like you to meet."

"Wait, you mean you're not coming back to New York? You're staying out there?"

She slid her arm around Ned's waist as he tucked her head under his chin. "Yes, I'm staying."

THE END

THE LAST CHANCE MOTEL

KAREN HAWKINS

"Ideas, like ghosts, must be spoken to a little before they will explain themselves."
—Charles Dickens

1

EVAN

ighting the urge to cuss up a storm, Evan Graham watched as the tow truck pulled his car out of the parking lot of The Last Chance Motel. The late afternoon sun glinted off his beautiful Jaguar, steam still slipping out from under the shiny blue hood.

Evan's cell phone rang and he glanced at it, ASHLEY C flashing on the screen. Ashley Carr was the new Vice President of Graham Industries. Evan had promoted her just last week after his previous Vice President, Brad King, had been stolen away by a corporate headhunter.

That loss had been a shock, an ugly one. Although Ashley was sharp and more than capable of doing the job, Brad had been with the company since Day One and Evan missed him.

His cell rang again, seeming shrill in the empty parking lot. Evan hit *answer*. "Hello. What's up?"

"Uh oh," Ashley said. "You sound mad."

"That's because I am. My Jaguar broke down." Evan watched as the tow truck turned a corner and disappeared from sight. "I'm stuck without wheels until tomorrow, and maybe longer if the mechanic can't get the parts." *Which is just great.*

"Should I send a car?"

"You can't. I'm not in Atlanta. I'm in North Carolina."

"Ooooh. You went to see Jess."

To Evan's growing irritation, he detected a hint of hope in Ashley's voice.

When it came to his wife, it was painfully obvious which side his employees were on, and it wasn't his. Not that he blamed them. Jess had one of those warm, funny personalities that people instinctively loved. She made people smile just by walking through the door. And by "people" he meant everyone, including him.

His chest tightened. God, these last two weeks since Jess had left him had been hell. "Look, Ash, I've got to go. Did you need something?"

"The Goodman/Feingold merger contract came in. I thought you'd want to see it, but it can wait."

"Send it on."

Ash hesitated. "Are you sure? It's Friday afternoon and you're there to see Jess. Surely you aren't going to—"

"Send it," Evan said impatiently. "I want to make sure the new provisions were included."

"Yes, but I can do that so you can focus on Jess." At his silence, Ash gave a sharp sigh. "Sending it now."

"Thanks. I'll let you know if I see any problems." He hung up and then slipped his hand into his suit pocket where a jewelry box and two first class plane tickets rested. He hadn't come to just see his wife, but to sweep her off her feet. If everything went as he hoped, he and Jess would be back home by this time tomorrow, packing for their coming trip. He'd have plenty of time to look through the contract then.

He glanced up at the sign that hung over the old one-story motel. Sprawling 1950s font spelled out *The Last Chance Motel*, half of the neon lights either broken or burned out. The name of the motel made him wince. *I hope this isn't my last chance, not with Jess. I can't accept that.*

Two weeks ago, he'd been at his desk, neck deep in a conference call when a military-looking man had walked into Evan's office. "Evan Graham?" The man had held up a large manila envelope with a signature receipt taped to the top.

Evan, still on the phone about a legal issue involving a new client, had figured the guy was a courier. They saw plenty of them in the office, so Evan didn't think much of it. He just took the envelope and, without looking at it, scribbled his name on the receipt. The guy took the receipt, nodded his thanks, and went on his way.

While still listening to the client, Evan had opened the envelope, expecting to see contracts or perhaps a memo detailing some phase of one of their many projects. Instead, what he'd found was a set of divorce papers.

A few years before, Evan had been in a business meeting in San Francisco when an earthquake hit, the entire building swaying wildly. He'd never forgotten the unsettling feeling of the floor moving under his feet, but seeing those papers had shaken him even more.

He'd headed home immediately, ready to promise to go to whatever counselor Jess wanted, only to discover that she'd already moved out. Seeing the divorce papers had rattled him; but standing in her empty closet in their silent house had chilled his soul.

He couldn't say Jess hadn't warned him. She'd been asking him to go to a marriage counselor for over a year, and he'd meant to— he really had. But what with the new investors, the mergers he was overseeing, and a million other things, the request had gotten shuttled to a back burner, and he'd eventually forgotten about it.

To be honest, he didn't believe they needed a counselor, so much as a little time to reconnect. He loved Jess and always had.

And he was certain she felt the same. Or he had been until he'd gotten those papers.

It hadn't taken him long to figure out where she was. For the last four months, Jess had been working on an old motel she'd bought, planning to turn it into a boutique sort of B&B. The motel was in Dove Pond, a tiny-almost forgotten town that sat at the foot of Black Mountain about a half hour outside of Asheville. Since he and Jess lived in Atlanta, she'd been spending a week now and then at the motel overseeing the renovations.

Jess had an affinity with Dove Pond as it was close to where she'd grown up and most of her family still lived nearby. In fact, she used to speak fondly of having family reunions in this very town, at the house of a favorite aunt and uncle.

Once she'd gotten the renovations moving on the motel, she'd asked Evan to come with her and check out the property, but he'd stupidly laughed it off, saying he was sure she had everything under control. He winced as he remembered the disappointment on her face as he'd shrugged off her request. He hadn't done it just once either, but multiple times. *I'm a fool, that's all there is to it.*

And now she was gone. Despite dozens of phone calls and bouquets of flowers, none of which had made a difference, he'd been left behind, alone with a manila envelope of papers he didn't want, and a house he used to love but now found as cold and welcoming as a tomb.

So here he was, standing in front of Jess's big project, The Last Chance Motel. It didn't look like much, this old motel. In fact, if he had to describe it, the words "decrepit" and "ramshackle" came to mind.

"Woo, boy!" called out a rough, craggy voice. "I about cried, seeing a car like that being towed off."

Evan turned to see a grizzled old man sitting on a bench beside the motel office door, his long white hair uncombed. He wore overalls and a faded red T-shirt, his feet encased in a pair of worn work boots. His clothes and the rake that leaned against the wall at his side identified him as hired help.

Evan realized the old man was waiting for an answer, so he forced a smile. "She's a terrific car."

"A real pity to see a nice car broken down like that." The man leaned back and stretched his legs in front of him. "What sort of car was that, anyway? I don't believe I've seen one like it."

"A 1974 Jaguar E-Type Series III Roadster." Evan didn't mention that Jess had given him the car for their fifth wedding anniversary. She'd always given him the most phenomenal gifts. He wished he could say he'd done the same, but after the first four or five years, he'd gotten so busy that he'd fallen into the regretful habit of having his secretary order "something sparkly" from Cartier.

An all-too-familiar feeling of regret pressed against his chest. No matter the circumstances, even knowing he deserved it, the thought of spending the rest of his life without Jess was painful.

"Easy there," the old man said. "Looked more like steam coming out from under the hood than smoke. Reckon all she needs is a radiator hose. That shouldn't cost much."

Cost wasn't the problem. "I hope it's a swift fix."

The old man nodded in agreement, his bright blue gaze assessing Evan as if taking his measure. "Your car reminded me of one I used to have. I called her Gertrude."

Evan eyed the old man with new interest. "You had a Jaguar?"

"Lord no, but Gertrude was that exact same shade of blue. I loved that car." The old man, still reclined against the wall as if he had nowhere to go and nothing much to do, laced his hands over his paunch. "I don't believe I introduced myself, did I? I'm Doyle Cloyd. Nice to meet you."

"Nice to meet you too," Evan said, trying to swallow his impatience. "You'll excuse me if I seem distracted, but I've got to figure out what I'm going to do now that my car is out of commission."

"Left you high and dry, did she?"

And then some. "The second I drove past the Welcome to Dove Pond sign, something under the hood popped and steam came rolling out. Even worse," Evan added sourly, "it appears there's only one mechanic in this town. I hope he knows what he's doing."

"Trav Parker's as good of a mechanic as his dad Bob was, maybe even better. And old Bob Parker kept Gertrude on the road for years. She was a 1983 Cutlass Supreme and a class act. I think of her every time I see that pond."

Evan's gaze followed the old man's. A crystal blue pond sat at the end of the long parking lot. Tall maples and oaks clustered to one side, while a deep green expanse of velvet grass led to an inviting dock. The old, one-story motel might be run-down—paint peeling, shutters hanging from broken latches, weeds and daisies poking through cracks in the asphalt parking lot—but the land it sat on was stunningly beautiful. "This is a gorgeous piece of property."

"Yes, it is. That pond's spring fed and clear as glass, too. When my poor Gertrude was fifteen feet under that water, you could still see every rivet."

"Your car ended up in this pond?"

"She went in right there by the dock." Doyle chuckled ruefully as he stood and picked up the rake. His work boots crunched on loose gravel as he crossed the parking lot and came to stand beside Evan. "My wife Barbara and I had just had a huge fight. She stormed out of the house and got herself a room here. This place was something back then. Always busy." The old man's gaze moved back to the motel, and a soft, half smile rested on his craggy face. "These walls have seen it all—love and betrayal, happiness and sadness, new and old. A little bit of everything."

"It's hard to believe it was ever successful with a name like The Last Chance Motel."

"From the 1950s until well into the '70s, if you were on your way to the Blue Ridge Parkway from the main road, this motel was your last chance for a room."

Evan supposed that made sense. "I didn't realize the Blue Ridge Parkway was that old."

"They started building her in 1935 over on Cumberland Knob, so I'd guess you could call her 'old.'" Doyle rested his crossed arms on the top of the rake handle. "I've always treasured old things. I guess that's because I am one."

Evan had no idea how to answer that. "That's all very interesting, but do you happen to know Je—"

"Yup, I lost Gertrude right there," Doyle said as if he hadn't heard Evan. "I came to see Barbara after our argument and found her standing at the end of the dock. I thought she was reflecting on our life together, but nope, she was staring down at poor Gertrude and was still mad as a wet hen."

Despite being impatient to find Jess, Evan couldn't keep from asking, "Your car ended up in that pond on *purpose?*"

"Barbara said she accidentally left Gertrude in neutral and didn't realize it. But I don't know." Doyle scratched the white whiskers on his chin, the sound surprisingly loud. "Barbara wasn't the sort of woman you should cross."

"I'd be furious if that happened to one of my cars."

"It was just a car. To be honest, Barbara had a right to be mad. I was young and stupid and said some things I shouldn't have." The old man's eyes twinkled. "We don't always make the best decisions when we're young and stupid, do we?"

The old man couldn't possibly know why Evan was here today, but the question, rhetorical as it was, felt oddly pointed. "Whatever happened, I'm sorry to hear about Gertrude."

Doyle flickered a sad smile toward the pond as if he could

still see someone standing out on the dock. "I miss my wife a heck of a lot more than I ever missed that car."

Evan's chest tightened. The last two weeks had given him a brief look at life without Jess, and it was hollow and colorless. He'd lost his appetite completely and hadn't been able to sleep more than a few hours at a time, their king-sized bed cold and empty. But it was even worse to think about Jess being really gone, forever out of touch. "No."

The old man's pale blue gaze locked on Evan. "Pardon me?"

Evan flushed. He hadn't meant to say that out loud. "I'm sorry about your wife. They become a part of us in a lot of ways." *Sometimes in ways you don't even realize.* The need to see Jess was suddenly that much stronger. "I'm looking for Mrs. Jessica Graham. Do you know where she is?"

"Graham?" Doyle leaned on his rake, his brows knitting. "Don't know any Grahams."

Evan frowned. "She has to be here. She owns this motel."

"Oh. You must mean Miss Jessica Cho."

Evan bit back a string of invectives. *Jess is already using her maiden name. I haven't even signed those stupid papers yet!* His gaze dropped to his hand where his wedding ring glimmered in the late afternoon sun.

He suddenly realized Doyle was watching, so Evan forced himself to shrug as if he hadn't just been emotionally gut punched. "Jessica Cho. That's her."

"She's in the office." Doyle slanted a curious look at Evan. "I guess you knew her when she was married. Whew, that man must have been a piece of work, to let a woman like Miss Jess go."

"Maybe it wasn't up to him."

"Baloney. If he'd wanted to keep her, he'd have found a way to do it, just as I found a way to make things right with Barbara."

Impatient, Evan looked at the office. The windows and doors of the motel had been replaced, although only the office door had been painted. It was Jess's favorite color, a teal blue, the word OFFICE written across the frosted upper glass in welcoming yellow script.

Their house in Atlanta had touches of teal here and there, but until this second, he hadn't realized how much he'd associated that color with Jess.

It hit him that he'd been quiet for far too long, so he turned to say goodbye to Doyle, but only a wide expanse of empty, cracked parking lot met Evan's gaze.

The old codger must have wandered off, which was just fine with Evan. There was only one person he wanted to talk to, and it wasn't Doyle Cloyd.

Evan adjusted his silk tie and walked toward the lobby, pausing when he caught sight of the rake leaning back beside the door, where it had started. How had that old man replaced the rake without Evan seeing him? *That's odd.*

Shaking off an uneasy feeling, Evan reached the lobby door. The second he stepped inside, he forgot about the rake. As broken down and worn out as the exterior of the motel was, the lobby was as luxurious and inviting as any high-end boutique hotel in New York or even Paris. The floor was a dark, gleaming hardwood. A mahogany check-in counter stood across from him, topped with a thick slab of Carrara marble that gleamed under hand-blown red pendant lights. The lounge area to his left featured a sumptuous leather settee flanked by two heavily stuffed red chairs and a thick oriental rug. Every surface suggested bespoke opulence and left Evan feeling as if he'd walked onto a movie set rather than an old, already-dead motel.

"Evan?"

The low, honey-toned voice hit him like a ton of bricks. He closed his eyes and took a steadying breath before slowly turning around.

Jess stood in the doorway behind the counter, her long black hair pulled into a ponytail that hung over one shoulder, her copper-framed reading glasses low on her nose. Holding a spreadsheet and a red pen, she wore jeans and a faded blue UNC-Asheville sweatshirt, her hazel eyes wide with surprise.

God, but I've missed her so much. He'd known that, of course, but seeing her made him realize yet again the depth of aching loneliness she'd left behind.

Her surprise melted into a frown. "What are you doing here?"

His heart thumping an odd gait, he managed a grin. "Surprise, Sunshine!" When they'd first gotten married, he'd called her Sunshine more than Jess.

She apparently didn't care for the reminder, because a flicker of irritation crossed her face before she turned away, moving past the desk. Her hip brushed a file perched there, knocking it to the floor. Papers scattered everywhere and she gave them a quick, impatient look, but made no move to gather them, instead locking her exasperated gaze on him. "Why are you here?"

That was less than welcoming. He wished he could call her tone "warm," but there was enough ice in it to cut. "I came to see you."

"Evan, no." She dropped her spreadsheet and red pen beside the family photos that surrounded her computer. "I don't want to see you. Not yet."

His gaze moved to her left hand. No rings shimmered on her finger where they belonged, which made his chest ache anew. He moved his gaze back to her face. "Come on, Jess. We have to talk. Face-to-face and not on the phone."

"I told you last night that I don't have anything more to say." She started collecting the papers that had been knocked to the floor. As she stacked them back on the desk, he noticed that her hands trembled the slightest bit.

He wished he knew how to take that—was it a good sign? A

bad sign? He wasn't sure. Damn, when had he lost the ability to read her? *Maybe I never could.*

At that depressing thought, the now-familiar wave of uncertainty gripped him, the same one that had held him since the moment he'd seen those stupid divorce papers.

That was the problem with being the one left behind. It put a dent in one's confidence that matched the size of the person who'd walked away. And although Jess was barely five feet tall, she had a personality as big as a mountain.

"I should have known you'd come anyway." Looking suddenly weary, Jess slid the papers back into their folder and returned them to the desk.

"I didn't have a choice. Our phone calls weren't getting us anywhere." *I came because I had to see you. Because there are things I need to say but can't find the words. Because I miss you so badly that my chest aches just being in the same room with you.*

But no. Blurting all of that out would just send her running. He couldn't afford to blow this. He took comfort from the weight of the jewelry box and tickets where they rested in his pocket. *Easy, Graham. Remember, you have a plan.* "I had business in Asheville and figured that, since I was nearby, I might as well take a look at your project."

"I've been working on this place for months and you never once bothered to visit."

"That was my mistake. One of many."

Her gaze locked with his. For a second, he thought he saw a waver, but then she shook her head. "I don't need your opinions anymore."

He crossed his arms and leaned against the counter. "For what it's worth, I think this lobby is something else."

She glanced around, her expression softening. "It turned out even better than I'd hoped."

"This area is amazing. Especially after seeing the outside."

"The company I hired for the exterior will start in two

weeks. They've already put in new doors and windows. Next, they'll put in the trim, paint the exterior, and redo the sidewalks and parking lot." She waved her hand. "And all the rest."

"If it looks as good as this lobby, it'll be something else."

Her eyes warmed, and she gave him a reluctant, if stiff, smile. "Thank you."

He wanted to reach across the counter, pull her over it, and into his arms. He'd give up every car parked in his garage for just one brush of her lips over his. Before he could stop himself, words he hadn't yet meant to say tumbled out. "Jess, I don't want this divorce. I don't want to live apart. I want you back and I'll do anything I ha—"

"Stop!" Flushed, she moved back from the counter.

It was a tiny move, a half step and no more, but it felt to Evan as if she'd just run back across a heavy drawbridge and slammed it closed behind her. His throat tight, he had to swallow before he could speak. "There are things I would do differently, Jess. So many things."

Her gaze narrowed. "Like?" As she spoke, she readjusted the reading glasses, which had slipped even lower on her nose.

God, how he'd missed seeing her do that. Seeing her reading glasses always so precariously perched on her nose used to annoy him. So had the way she'd left her shoes under every table, and how she'd used her headphones to talk to her family in what seemed like an endless one-sided conversation that he was never a part of. *What a fool I was.*

Her mouth thinned impatiently. "Great. You can't name one thing you'd do differently."

He could name a hundred things, and he had the evidence in his pocket. But it would be unromantic to just pull out the gifts he'd brought and throw them down on a cold, marble counter.

He needed to take control of this situation. "Jess, what can it hurt if we sit down and discuss things? At the worst, we're right where we are now, ready to sign our lives away on matching pieces of paper. And at the best, we figure out what went wrong and find ways to keep it from happening again."

She crossed her arms over her chest. "I'm not going back to Atlanta."

"I'm not asking you to. Not now." He spread his hands wide. "I just want to talk. That's all."

Her expression softened the tiniest bit. For a wonderful and hopeful moment, he thought she was going to agree.

But then she shook her head. "It won't help. I tried to talk to you for years and you've never listened, not even a little. I'm done, Evan. Have a nice drive back to Atlanta." With that, she sat down in the chair, spun it toward the desk, and picked up her spreadsheet.

He stared at the back of her head, her ponytail hanging well past her shoulders. When they'd been hot-blooded, wildly-in-love college students, there'd been nothing he'd liked more than sinking his hands into her silken hair and splaying it over both of them.

And now she wouldn't even talk to him.

Was this it, then? Were they finished?

Forever?

He suddenly remembered the sadness in poor Doyle's face when he talked about his wife being gone. Evan couldn't accept this was the end for him and Jess. He just couldn't.

He slipped his hand into his pocket and gripped the jewelry box. "Jess, I'd go back to Atlanta if I could, but my car broke down."

She looked over her shoulder at him, suspicion clear in her hazel gaze. "You're kidding."

"I'm serious. Some guy who looked like Jason Momoa took it to his shop."

"That's Trav Parker from Parker's Garage." She sighed and spun her chair so that she faced him once again. "Which car?"

"The Jag. It conked out just as I crossed into town, so I'm stuck here until tomorrow."

"Here? You mean—no. You can't stay here. There aren't any hotels close by, but there are several nice B&Bs in town. You can stay at one of those."

"Not if they have those old, antique beds that—"

"—creak. I know, I know." Her mouth, which had been so tight, eased with a flash of wry humor. "You've always hated those."

"I'm not a quiet sleeper, as you know. Look, Jess, I don't have a choice here. I'm stuck, and you have rooms. Ten of them, from the look of things."

"Yes, but..." She shook her head impatiently. "Take an Uber to Asheville. There are plenty of hotels there."

"I could. Or I could stay here one lousy night—just one—and then leave first thing in the morning when my car is ready."

She was beginning to fold; he could see it in her eyes. "I mean it, Jess," he added softly. "I promise I'll stay in whatever room you assign me while you'll be—" he gestured "—wherever it is that you live now."

She glanced at one of the doors behind the desk. "I had the manager's apartment redone at the same time as the lobby."

That was something. They'd be on the same property, at least. It wasn't much, but it was better than being in two different states. *One step at a time,* Evan told himself. "What do you say, Jess? Just one night. What could it hurt?"

After a long, painful pause, she let out an exasperated sigh. "Fine. Just one night and then you'll go. But you have to promise you won't try to talk me into going back to Atlanta with you."

Damn, but he hated making a promise he wasn't sure he could keep. But maybe, just maybe, if he could win one night, then he could win another. And then another.

Patience, Graham. She's worth it. "Fine. I promise not to belabor our separation, but *only* if you'll have dinner with me."

She frowned. "We have nothing to talk about."

"No, but we both need to eat. I'll even let you pick the place."

She hesitated, and so, for good measure, he added, "Unless, of course, you're afraid..."

He didn't have to wait long.

Her mouth tightened. "I'm not afraid."

"Really? You look afraid."

That did it. Her chin lifted and her eyes sparkled as she snapped out, "Fine. Dinner. But nothing more." She opened a drawer and tossed him a large metal key. "Room Ten. It's nowhere near as grand as the Carlyle, but it's clean."

The Carlyle was his favorite New York hotel. It had also been the site of their honeymoon. "There's no hotel like the Carlyle." *And no woman like you.* He took the key and held it tightly, the edges sharp against his palm. "Shall we say dinner at seven?"

"Six. I need to get back early, too." She opened another drawer, pulled out a small plastic envelope that held a tooth-brush, toothpaste, mouthwash, and the rest of the necessities. "You're lucky these sample kits came yesterday."

He took the kit and flashed his best smile. "Thanks, Jess. See you at six." Feeling more hopeful than he had in two weeks, he left before she could change her mind.

Evan stepped into the late afternoon sun, the door swinging closed behind him, the jewelry box still satisfyingly heavy in his pocket. He looked around the broken and faded parking lot, noting a clump of rather worn dandelions trying to make their way through a large crack in the asphalt. "I know how you feel, buddy. I know how you feel."

Still, despite Jess's less-than-warm welcome, his heart hummed with hope as he walked down the sidewalk toward his room. He wasn't through yet, not by a long shot.

2

JESS

*D*uring her twenty-nine years on earth, Jessica Cho Graham had learned many things. She'd learned to trust her instincts as they rarely led her astray, that changes (even good ones) could sometimes be incredibly painful to make, and to never underestimate the power of a well-fitting red dress.

She slipped a jeweled clip into her straight, black hair and then stepped back from the mirror so she could see her entire form, turning this way and that. The short red dress clung to every curve, revealing an interesting amount of cleavage. *Take that, Evan Graham.* There was nothing quite as satisfying as seeing regret on the face of an ex. It was like caramel buttercream icing on a very delicious chocolate cake.

She hadn't planned on dressing up tonight, but when she'd returned to her apartment after a quick trip to the bank to file some paperwork for her business loan, she'd found the red dress crumpled on the floor of her closet. She must have accidentally knocked it off its hanger earlier but hadn't noticed it until then.

She'd picked up the dress, intending to rehang it, but as she did, she'd caught sight of herself in the mirror and had winced at the faded sweatshirt and her lack of makeup. The desire to show Evan she wasn't just fine without him but was terrific—better than terrific—took hold, and so now, here she was, dressed to kill.

"Or maim. Maiming would be enough." She tugged the dress down a bit, liking how the V-neck molded over her breasts. If she used the woefully inadequate chart that hung in most doctors' offices, then she was twenty-one pounds overweight. Fortunately, she *liked* those twenty-one pounds, every last one. She was healthy and took spin classes three times a week, so she didn't feel particularly pressed to lose her curves. In fact, just last week she'd gone to see Dr. Bolton about her sleepless nights, and he'd said that, except for some predictable divorce stress, she was as healthy as a horse and to keep doing whatever she was doing.

She glanced at the clock. She still had fifteen minutes before she was to meet Evan. *Fifteen minutes before he's facing this red dress. I almost feel sorry for the man.*

Well, she sort of felt sorry for him. Right now, her primary emotions where Evan was concerned were anger and fear. Anger at him for looking so darn *good* without even trying and fear at the way she'd responded to seeing him standing in the lobby, looking as if he'd just stepped off the pages of GQ.

Even after all they'd been through, the man only had to look at her and *whoomph!* up she went in flames. *I don't think he saw it, though.* She eyed her dress with satisfaction. *Now he'll be the one going up in flames.*

She couldn't fault herself for reacting to Evan in such a way; most women did. Over the years, she'd seen it time after time. He was tall, broad shouldered, and handsome with dark brown hair that always looked just so, even when he raked his hand through it repeatedly (a bad habit that was also instantly adorable) and the bluest eyes she'd ever seen. He could have been a model or an actor, but he'd been fascinated by corporate intrigue early on. Spurred by burning ambition and an instinctive knack for boardroom politics, he'd jumped feet first into the corporate world and had been wildly successful. He was now the President and CEO of his own company and rightly proud of his accomplishments.

Jess had been at his side during the first years of the company's journey. Early on, she'd served as the Marketing Director, running the digital channels and keeping the website and other external communication up to date. Eventually she'd started yearning for her own project, rather than just being a part of her husband's ever-increasing team, so she'd bowed out and had started purchasing properties and flipping them. She'd had great success, although it couldn't measure against Evan's company, which had doubled and then tripled in size.

She couldn't blame her husband's ambitious nature for their problems, because she was ambitious, too. But there was a price for his continued success; one he was willing to pay, but she wasn't. His time away from home grew with each additional win and had eventually chipped away at their marriage. The bigger the company got, the smaller their marriage seemed to be, until one day it dawned on her that she was in it alone.

"If I have to choose between having half of a husband or none, I'll choose none," she muttered under her breath. She met her own gaze in the mirror, wincing at the sadness she saw there. Leaving Evan had been the hardest thing she'd ever done. She'd loved him dearly, and still did, and thought him as sexy as ever, as her reaction to him this afternoon had clearly proven. But...that was the problem; there were just so many "buts."

"You shouldn't be going out to dinner with him," she told her reflection. "You couldn't say no, could you?"

With a grimace, she turned away from the mirror. She'd better get this over with and quickly. She grabbed her phone and purse and left her apartment, her heels clipping sharply on the floor.

She entered the lobby and came to a surprised stop. A spectacular bouquet of muted lavender, periwinkle blue, and soft pink flowers in a large pale green vase sat on the long table by the entryway.

Jess's heart thudded a little faster. *Had Evan—*

"Gawd help us all, but I hope you registered that dress as a weapon, 'cause it is one."

Jess recognized her florist's familiar raspy voice. More disappointed than she should have been, Jess turned and offered up a friendly smile. "Hi, Flora. This must be the sample bouquet you were talking about earlier this week."

"I had a delivery to make on this side of town and figured I might as well stop in and see what you think of this particular arrangement." Flora Fellows was aptly named as she owned *Flora's Fauna and Flower Shop*, which had opened on Main Street in Dove Pond a mere six months ago. As sharp in tone as she was round in shape, the older, iron-gray-haired woman was known for her willingness to give her opinion on just about any topic whether you wanted to hear it or not. "I didn't realize I'd be interrupting your date night, or I'd have called first. Where are you headed dressed up like that?"

"To nail a coffin closed."

The older woman's eyebrows shot up, her deep brown eyes bright with curiosity. "Oh ho! The ex, is it?"

"I'm meeting him at six for a final Verbalization of the Grievances."

"I figured you had an ex. You've got that air."

One of despair? Sadness? Freedom? Jess shot a curious gaze at the florist. "You were once married, weren't you?"

"Once. It lasted about a month too long."

"How long were you married?"

"Two months." Flora gave a deep bark of laughter at Jess's

surprise. "I was a young idiot and desperate to leave home. Sweet heaven, the trouble being both of those at the same time can get you."

"I got married while I was still in college, which was a risky move, but I was oh-so-in-love. I think I was blinded." Jess shook her head. "Evan was a handsome senior and drove a BMW; I was a freshman with a bike. A broken, borrowed bike."

"Hot and had money. That's hard to resist."

"I was completely bewitched. Plus, he was an only child and his parents were quite a bit older, so he adored my big, noisy family."

"A triple threat. You didn't stand a chance."

Not even a little one. The way he'd loved her family had sealed the deal for her, and they'd loved him in return. In fact, her brothers and sisters, who all lived within an hour of Dove Pond, were as upset over the pending divorce as she was, maybe more so.

"Although he deserves it, I pity the man who has to face that dress." Flora's gaze narrowed. "Did the fool cheat on you?"

"No. He just loves his job more than—" Jess's chest tightened, but she pushed the words out. "More than he loves me."

"A total and deserving fool," Flora said firmly. "I hope he sees you in that dress, catches on fire with desire, and dies of deep and wrenching regret."

"That would be nice," Jess said wistfully. She wondered for the hundredth time when she'd lost her place in Evan's life, but there wasn't one crystal clear moment. Instead, over the years, she'd slowly found herself left behind, one event and deed at a time, until the anniversaries and birthdays he started missing were simply a part of their marriage.

"Whatever happened before, he'll pay attention to you tonight." The florist picked up the box she'd used to bring in the flower arrangement. "I'd put my last dollar on it."

"Thanks. I have a few things to say to him, and I didn't want to look weak."

"What you look is hot. I'm going to leave this arrangement while I consider some other options. You have to see these things in place to know if they'll work, you know?"

Jess nodded as if she did know, although she had no idea. She could picture materials together—marble, wood, tiles, fabrics. That had helped her design the lobby and the other rooms. But she was at a loss when it came to live plants, which was why she'd decided to hire a professional.

"Oops. I almost forgot." Flora reached into her pocket, pulled out a small brown bottle, and placed it beside the arrangement. "Keep the water to the level you see now, use a few drops of my secret sauce every day or so, and the flowers will stay fresh a whole week."

"Will do," Jess promised. Everyone knew that Flora's 'secret sauce' was really a mixture of vodka and Sprite, her favorite drink. But whatever it was, it worked.

"Before you put in your final order, I want to try another color mix." Flora stared at the arrangement and pursed her lips. "And maybe something a touch larger. I'll bring it in a few days and see which you prefer."

"I think this is lovely, but you know what's best. Thanks, Flora."

"Sure. See you in a few days." Flora headed for the door. As she went, she called over her shoulder, "Good luck burning that fool to the ground!"

Luck was exactly what Jess needed. She waited for the door to close before she turned to the mirror over the entry table. "You know the rules," she told herself. "Don't look directly into his eyes and you'll be fine." *Right. I know how to do this. No eye contact. Focus on his chin. That'll keep my mind functioning.* She straightened her shoulders and, feeling as if she were going into battle, went outside.

Evan was just coming out of his room, still dressed in the same suit he'd worn earlier and looking better than any man had a right to.

Of course he's wearing the same suit, she told herself impatiently. Since he hadn't known he'd be staying overnight, all he had with him were the clothes on his back.

She winced to think of how wrinkled that suit would be by morning. Silk and wool blends weren't made to be worn multiple days. It was a good thing she'd had those sample toiletry kits, though. The only thing Evan didn't have, besides a change of clothes for tomorrow, was pajamas, which shouldn't be an issue as he usually slept in the nude.

Evan. In the nude.

Hot and spicy memories flickered through her mind, and her heart skipped a beat.

Stop it! She couldn't afford to lose herself in memories that left her with weak knees and the inability to think straight. *Keep your mind on the prize, Cho,* she told herself sternly, trying to calm her galloping pulse.

Still, seeing Evan attired in his suit made her doubly grateful she'd decided to wear her red dress.

She took a steadying breath, locked a casual look on her face, and then said in what she hoped was a cool and uncaring tone of voice, "Ready for dinner?"

He looked up, one hand on the doorknob, the other on the key. His eyebrows shot up before his gaze moved up and then down her, lingering on her neckline and legs.

She'd wanted to see deep, authentic regret. What she got instead was an instant, heated *Damn, baby!* look that made her tingle in all the wrong places. *No responding!* she admonished herself desperately. *That's not how you want this to go.*

Evan dropped the key into his pocket and walked toward her. "Jess, you look…" He shook his head slowly.

There it was, the regret she'd wanted to see. *Jess: Score One.*

His blue gaze returned to her face. "You look beautiful."

And you look good enough to eat. The thought flashed through her mind and she barely had time to keep it from tumbling from her lips. She managed to say instead, "I hope you're hungry. It's meatloaf special night."

"I'm hungry." His gaze moved back over her, leaving a tingle everywhere it touched.

"Let's go then." She turned on her heel and walked toward the two vehicles parked in the back of the lot, an Audi sports car and a pickup truck.

Evan fell into step beside her. "Thank you for agreeing to have dinner with me."

As if she'd ever been able to tell him no. He'd been her weakness, her kryptonite. *Was. Not anymore.* "We're going to the Moonlight Café. It's not fancy, but the food's great." She was wildly overdressed for the casual atmosphere of the small café located on Main Street, but that was okay. She'd already gotten the reaction she'd wanted, so the night was already a win. Now all she had to do was keep Evan a decent distance away, and she'd have no regrets about allowing him an hour or so of her time.

"I take it this café is your new favorite place."

"One of them. You know how I feel about meatloaf."

His dimple flashed as he grinned. "You've used the words 'love' and 'passionate' when talking about meatloaf."

Oh God, the dimple. Don't look at it.

"I'd offer to drive, but my car is—" He winced, refusing to say the word.

"Broken," she said in a relentless tone. He was crazy about his cars. When he didn't think anyone was around, he sometimes spoke to them, which she used to think was cute. *It's probably still cute. I just won't see it.*

Her heart ached at the thought. *Stop that.* "I don't mind driving." As she spoke, they reached the two vehicles.

Evan walked to the passenger door of the Audi.

She opened the door to her truck and waited.

"Oh." He looked from the new Audi to her white 1994 pickup, which was creaky, dented, and a little rusty. "Sorry." He walked around the back of the truck toward the passenger door. "I thought the Audi looked more like you."

She could tell he thought that was a compliment. She opened the truck door and, tugging her dress up her thighs a bit so she could move, swung up into the seat. Once there, she pushed her skirt back in place and settled onto the cushion she used so she could see over the steering wheel.

He opened his door and climbed in, his gaze locking on the thigh she'd just covered. "But then again, I can see the benefits of having a truck."

"They're useful. The Audi belongs to my sister Emily. She's just keeping it here while she's having her driveway repaved."

"Did she leave the keys?"

"Yes, but I like my truck better." Jess buckled up, waited for Evan to do likewise, and then cranked the truck on.

"Your sisters' restaurant must be doing well."

"It's doing great. Emily and Mariah have turned it into one of Asheville's most popular brunch destinations."

"I'm not surprised. They make a mighty team."

"They do. They've been helping out here when they can."

He watched as Jess drove out of the parking lot. "I have to say, driving a truck suits you."

She glanced his way, expecting the Evan kidding-but-not-kidding look, but his expression was serious.

She yanked her gaze back to the road. She kept getting fleeting impressions that there was something different about him. He was more serious, his gaze more searching; that much she knew. But she had no idea what that *meant*, if anything.

They reached Main Street and she pulled the truck into the lot beside the town hall, unwilling to attempt to parallel park her beast of a truck in front of Evan. She turned off the engine, undid her seatbelt, and hopped out, tugging her skirt back into place before dropping her keys into her purse.

She looked up to find Evan beside her.

He frowned. "I was going to open your door for you."

"Thanks, but I got it." She bumped the door closed with her hip and then breezed past him. "This way." She didn't wait to see if he followed but headed across the street and down the sidewalk to the café.

She loved this little place. The red-and-white-checked gingham tablecloths were comforting, and she adored the mason jars that the café used in place of drinking glasses. But best of all, after spending only a few months here in Dove Pond, every time Jess went to the café she found that she recognized some, if not all, of the other customers.

Right now, Arnie Gonzalez and his wife Camila sat in a corner booth with their three girls. Across the café, the new dentist, Abby Lews, was splitting a piece of pie with the town's mayor, Grace Wheeler, and her best friend, local librarian Sarah Dove. When Jess had first arrived, Sarah had brought over a stack of business books and had yet to ask for them back.

Waitress Marian Freely looked up from where she stood behind the counter cutting a cherry pie into eight uneven pieces. "Why, there's Miss Jess!" she said in a welcoming tone. At well over seventy years old, the waitress was tall and angular, her improbably bright red hair an uncanny match to the cherry lipstick that traced her thin lips. "You're all dressed up, too." She looked past Jess to Evan. "Well, well," the waitress said under her breath and yet loud enough to make Jess blush.

Every eye in the place was now on the two of them, moving from her to Evan and then back. Her face still hot, she had to fight the urge to cross her arms over her chest. "A table for two, please."

"You look like a thousand bucks," Marian said proudly. "But you couldn't miss meatloaf night, could you?"

"Not in a million years."

"Don't blame you. A table for two, right? That would be for you and..." The waitress looked at Evan and waited expectantly, but he didn't answer.

Marian's smile faded. She sniffed and then turned back to Jess. "Pick your seat, sweetie. I'll be right there."

Jess started to head for a table but then realized that the depth of a booth would help her maintain a healthier distance from Evan, so she turned away and found a booth instead.

When they got there, Evan waited for her to sit before he slid into the seat across from her, but his dry look let her know he'd realized her strategy.

Well. Here they were. Sitting on opposite sides and silently taking each other's measure. Jess rested her folded hands on the table, locking her gaze on Evan's chin. "So. What did you want to talk about?"

"A lot of things." He selected a menu from the ones stuck in the holder by the wall and then glanced through the plastic-covered pages. "I take it you're getting the meatloaf. What else is good here?"

"Everything."

"That's quite a recommendation."

"You'll see. This place is—"

"Here you go." Marian placed a paper placemat, a mason jar of water, and a wax paper packet of silverware at each of their places.

"Thanks," Jess said. "I'll have—"

"The meatloaf dinner." Marian's mouth split into a wide grin. "With green beans, garlic mashed potatoes, and an iced tea."

"You know me too well."

"There's something to be said for routine." Marian scribbled the order on her notepad. "What about you, Mr...?" The waitress eyed him expectantly.

"Graham," he said.

It was obvious the gossip-hungry waitress was dying to know far more than a mere name, so Jess added, "Evan is an old college friend of mine."

Evan shot Jess a hard frown.

"Graham." Marian pursed her too-red lips, which deepened the wrinkles around her mouth. "I don't believe we have any Grahams in Dove Pond."

Evan said, "There's one. She—"

"He's staying at my motel," Jess said. "His car broke down so he's stuck here until it's fixed, which will be soon."

Marian eyed Evan with new appreciation. "You must drive that Jag sitting in front of the Parker Garage. I saw it on my way into work today."

"That's mine." Evan smiled politely as he spoke but Jess could tell that his mind was elsewhere, probably mentally rehearsing what he was going to say once Marian left.

That was the thing about Evan. He was an expert in getting people to see things his way, and he rarely spoke unless he'd planned every word and already knew the answer to any possible objection. It was that skill, along with a certain dimple and her heart's tendency to soften whenever he was around, that had made their marriage uneven in some places, and downright unfair in others.

Jess had learned a lot about herself when she'd started rehabbing houses, mainly that she was a savvy negotiator and an excellent communicator. Sadly, she'd been neither of those in her married life. When it came to personal matters, she couldn't seem to untangle her thoughts from her emotions long enough to say what she really meant.

When the time came, her ineptitude at expressing herself, coupled with Evan's tendency to approach every aspect of his life as if he were in a high-powered negotiation, meant that she'd lost almost every argument they'd ever had. Not once in their entire marriage had he ever stumbled or hesitated to say what he thought. Meanwhile, over that same time, she'd forgotten how to do just that.

But no more, she told herself firmly.

She realized the waitress was looking at her expectantly.

Evan leaned forward. "She asked if your motel was open yet."

"Oh. Sorry. I was just thinking about—" She caught herself just in time. Face warm, she added quickly, "The motel's not open yet. I made an exception for Mr. Graham as he was stuck, but he's only staying one night."

Marian said kindly, "Well, I hear you're doing wonderful things with that place."

"She is." Evan closed his menu and slid it back into its holder. "I'll have the meatloaf special, too, but with fries and a coffee instead of mashed potatoes and iced tea."

Marian wrote down his order and then slid the pad and pen back into her uniform pocket. "I'll bring your drinks right out." With a last curious glance, she left.

Evan's gaze locked on Jess. "So now I'm just an old college friend."

"That's true."

His eyebrows lowered. "I was more than that and you know it. Come on. Stop this." He leaned across the table and captured her hand where it rested beside her mason jar water glass.

A hot jolt rippled up her hand to her arm and beyond. Fighting a gasp, Jess pulled her hand free.

He frowned. "Darn it, Jess. I love you."

"If love was enough, I'd still be living in Atlanta. But love isn't enough, Evan. You know that." She tucked her hands in her lap and leaned back, away from him. "Why are you here?"

"Because I don't want this divorce. I thought I'd made that clear."

"What part of our divorce don't you want? Is it about the money or—"

"No! Nothing like that." He scowled, looking a little hurt that she'd even suggested such a thing. "Although I don't like the idea of selling one of our homes."

Part of their divorce agreement had involved selling one of their three houses. She wanted nothing from her old life. That Jess was gone.

"It's going to take a while to sell the house." His blue gaze never moved from her face. "It could take months."

She sighed. "Brad was right. He told me I should have just asked for the monetary equivalency, as having to wait for property sales could slow down our divorce."

Evan's expression froze. "You talked to Brad about our divorce?"

"Why wouldn't I?" She shrugged. "He didn't have a lot to say, except that he wasn't surprised." She'd known Brad since the year she and Evan had married. During their early years, it had often just been Evan, Brad, and her working into the early hours of the morning, making the most of the business opportunities Evan was so gifted in drumming up. After she'd left the company, she and Brad had stayed friends. They'd met at company events at least every other month, and always spent the time catching up. They also texted each other on birthdays and holidays, and randomly sent each other funny memes. Brad's offbeat sense of humor reminded her of her oldest brother Jay, who could always make her laugh, even on her darkest days.

Evan's gaze dropped to his water glass, which he was absently turning in a circle. "Did Brad mention work?"

That was an odd question. "No. Why?"

Evan sighed and leaned back. "I guess I might as well tell you. I'm sure Brad'll do it the next time he calls. He resigned, Jess. He's no longer with the company."

"What?"

Evan winced. "I was shocked, too."

"When did he leave?"

"Last Friday. And Jess, he went to McTavish."

"That's your biggest competitor!"

"I know," Evan said glumly. "I should have seen it coming; he was upset about a lot of things. Someone at McTavish must have gotten wind of it, because they called him and offered three times what he was making."

"You didn't match their offer?"

"I would have, but he didn't give me the opportunity."

This time there was no mistaking the hurt she saw in Evan's eyes. "Ouch," she said softly.

He flashed a crooked, rueful smile that was more grimace than anything else. "It's been rough," he admitted. "He was like a brother to me."

"You've known him a long time. What was Brad upset about?"

"He didn't say anything when you spoke to him?"

"We didn't talk very long. He called to ask for that risotto recipe I made at Christmas. I told him about the divorce and he got super quiet." She shrugged. "He likes both of us, so it put him in a bad spot. He asked what I was going to do and if I had enough money, and then he offered to look through the divorce papers for me, if I felt I needed it. That's it."

Evan sighed. "I thought he might have mentioned that he was thinking about leaving the company."

"Not a word. What happened?"

"A few days before he resigned, he—"

"Here you go!" Marian set down an iced tea for Jess and a cup of coffee and a small bowl of creamers for Evan. "I'll be back with your meal. Need anything else right now?"

"No, thank you." Jess barely waited for Marian to head to another table before saying to Evan, "Go on."

Evan opened three creamers and poured them into his coffee. "Brad and I have been on the outs recently about promotions, new contracts, client expectations—a lot of things. Last week, we finally had it out and he said some things he probably shouldn't have, and then I said some things I probably shouldn't have. You know how it goes. But before I could apologize, he left for McTavish." Evan's regret was obvious. "I haven't seen him since."

Oh no. "I'm sure you've tried to call him."

"At least a dozen times. He doesn't want to talk to me." Evan shrugged, although nothing on his face echoed that dismissive gesture.

Jess had to fight the urge to reach across the table and hold his hand. "You miss him."

Evan's stiff expression softened, his eyes darkening. "Of course I miss him. He was—is—my best friend." Evan pulled his coffee forward, cupping it with both hands as if savoring the warmth. "Brad said some ugly but true things. But it wasn't what he said about me or the company that hurt so much; it was what he said about you. He said I never should have let you go. That it was the biggest mistake I'd ever made." Evan's mouth thinned.

"He wouldn't leave the company because of that."

"There was more to it than that. He said I'd lost my focus. That I was getting too caught up chasing acquisitions, and that the board had become my 'Little House of Pawns' and weren't doing their due diligence. Among other things, he thinks I've been spreading our assets too far."

"You do love a good acquisition."

"Of course I do," Evan said impatiently. "That's what's made us so successful. And it's not like I've been making those decisions myself. Every time we do an acquisition, I run it by the board and they—"

"—always say yes because they've decided you're some sort of financial wizard who turns everything you touch into gold."

He scowled. "It's not like that."

"They're yes-men, Evan. Every one of them."

"They are not," he shot back, his face reddening. "Our Board of Directors has been lauded for their independence. You know that."

A few months ago, if Evan had gotten upset or displeased by something she'd said, Jess would have promptly swallowed her own opinion and turned to a more soothing, less controversial topic of conversation. But that was the old Jess.

The new Jess, the one wearing the power dress and who owned her own business, put down her iced tea, letting the mason jar thump on the table with such satisfying firmness that tea sloshed over the lip. "Brad was right about it all, wasn't he? That's why you got so mad at him."

Evan's expression darkened, but as he opened his mouth to speak, Marian appeared at their table, a tray balanced on one hand. "Two meatloaf specials!" Her bright gaze told Jess that the waitress knew she'd interrupted an argument and was dying to know more.

The waitress set a plate in front of Jess. "Garlic mashed potatoes. And for the gentleman, French fries." She put Evan's plate on the table, near but not in front of him. "I see the iced tea is holding up. More coffee?"

"I'm good for now," Evan said impatiently.

Marian's eyebrows rose, but she stayed where she was. She put her hand on the bottle of Dot's Hot Sauce that peeked out of her apron pocket. "Maybe some hot sauce or—"

"We're fine," Evan replied tersely, sliding his plate in front of him.

Jess forced a smile. "I'll have some hot sauce. Thanks, Marian."

"*You're* welcome." Marian put the bottle on the table as she said pointedly to Jess, "I'll come back to see if *you* need anything else."

"Thank you."

The waitress looked at Evan, said "Humph!", turned on her heel, and left.

Evan reached past the hot sauce for the ketchup bottle that was already on the table. He slid the bottle to Jess.

She took the ketchup, opened it, and tilted it over her meat-loaf. As she waited for it to pour out, she caught him watching her. "I know, I know. Me and my ketchup."

"You've poured ketchup over every beef dish we've ever had, even in Paris."

"And you hated it."

"I used to." His blue gaze met hers. "After you left, every time I opened the fridge, your ketchup was right there in the door where it belonged, waiting for you."

Darn it, she'd looked into his eyes. *This is how I lose.* She ripped her gaze from his and locked her attention on her plate, her heart beating so fast her throat felt tight.

"Jess, the ketchup is still in the fridge. It'll be there when you come home."

Home. Her heart lurched and she was inundated with memory after memory of her life in Atlanta, of the early years and the good times she and Evan had had. Without trying, she could remember dozens. *But all of them are a long time ago. I can't remember a single one in the last two years.*

Not one. "Throw that ketchup away. It's going to expire."

His gaze darkened. "I'm leaving it." He picked up his fork and listlessly took a bite of his meatloaf. Almost like magic an expression of surprised bliss settled on his face. "Oh wow."

Relieved the conversation had moved to a painless topic like meatloaf, she gave a knowing nod. "Ambrosia, isn't it?"

He dug in, and she had to admit that it was satisfying to see her opinion validated.

They were quiet for a few minutes as they enjoyed their meal, although the tension between them never lessened. Every once in a while, she could feel his gaze on her, but she kept her attention on her plate.

He finally broke the silence. "Why did you choose to stay in the motel, instead of finding a place closer to your family?"

"They're not that far away."

"Staying out of the hot zone, are you?" His smile flickered as he spoke, that damnable dimple as beguiling as ever.

"Barely, but yes." She dropped her gaze back to her plate and wished she'd never agreed to have dinner with him. It was every bit as painful and awkward as she'd feared it would be.

Silence soon fell again. After several, too-long quiet minutes, Evan put down his fork, the metal clanging against the heavy china. "This is ridiculous. Jess, I didn't just come here to talk. I brought you something." He reached into his pocket.

"Evan, don't—"

His phone rang and he grimaced as he reached into his other pocket instead. His gaze locked on his phone as he silenced the ring, murmuring an absent, "Sorry."

And there it was. That instant pull he felt whenever someone from the office reached out to him, an almost insatiable desire to swoop in and control every last aspect of his company.

"You should get that." The words were thick in her throat as she turned her attention to her plate.

"I won't be long, I promise. I sent a contract back to the office with some comments, and I bet Ash just read them and has a question."

Jess waved her fork. "Go ahead." She took a bite of her meatloaf even though she'd lost her appetite the second he'd reached for his phone. Here she sat, waiting on him, just as she'd waited all of those other times.

Darn it, she'd sworn to herself that she wouldn't be in this position again, and yet here she was—

She suddenly realized Evan wasn't talking. She peeped up at him.

He was watching her, the phone blinking from where it rested on the table beside his plate.

"I thought you were going to get that."

"I was going to, but then I saw your face." He looked at his phone, a deep crease between his brows. "I work too much."

She raised her eyebrows. "Do you, now?"

He flushed. "I know, I know. We've talked about this before. But I have responsibilities, people who count on me. And you know I'm competitive. I've always been that way."

"It's not bad, being competitive. It was the imbalance of our lives that I hated. When it came down to the company or us, it was always the company."

"Not always. Damn, Jess. You make it sound as if things were horrible. I'll admit the last few years weren't as good as they could have been, but they weren't terrible."

But they were terrible. Terribly sad. Terribly lonely. Terribly the same. "Things were good early on, sure. But then two things happened. First, you got too caught up in your work, and second, I stopped telling you what I thought."

He looked surprised. "You've always been honest with me."

"I was always nice to you. Always polite to you. But I wasn't always honest."

"About what?"

"About how angry it made me when you put work before us. Angry, Evan. *Really* angry." Her voice quivered with her feelings. "I still get furious every time that stupid phone rings."

He looked stunned. "Jess…I had no idea it bothered you that much. You should have let me know."

"I might not have been clear about how angry it made me, but I repeatedly asked you to leave your work at the office, and the answer was always the same." She lowered her voice and did her best impression of him. *"I can't. I have responsibilities. I'll only be a moment."*

His eyebrows lowered. "I should have noticed how upset you were."

"And I should have been more honest. By the time I figured out what was happening to us, the marriage was already gone."

"Gone? No! What we have isn't gone. It's damaged, sure. I messed up, but I can fix this. I'll change things, Jess. I promise I will."

Right. And she was a unicorn.

Her disbelief must have shown, because his expression grew dark before he suddenly straightened. "Look." He reached into his pocket and pulled out a box marked Cartier and a heavy cream-colored envelope that bore the logo of their favorite travel agent. "I brought these. I wanted to show you how serious I am about us, about our marriage. We'll go away, just the two of us. And I promise, there will be no phone, no laptop. Nothing like that."

She looked at the box and the envelope but didn't move. Really? He thought he could just throw some bling her way and suddenly everything would be okay? And it wasn't as if she hadn't heard this particular promise before, either.

Evan muttered something under his breath, reached over, and opened the box, and then placed it in front of her. A gorgeous sapphire and diamond bracelet twinkled up at her, heavy and luxurious, like something a real princess might wear.

"And look." He opened the envelope and pulled out two first class tickets, placing them beside the bracelet so she could read the destination. "Paris, Jess. You've always loved Paris." He watched her, his expression so earnest that her heart ached.

This was so hard. She knew he loved her, and she loved him, too. But love wasn't enough. She'd had that, and it had left her hollow and empty.

She tightened her grip on her fork, and her gaze moved

from the gifts to his phone, which even now sat on the table beside his plate. The gifts were lovely, but she hadn't left him because there weren't enough gifts or planned vacations. She suddenly realized he was doing with their marriage what he did at work—when there was a problem, he negotiated in the direction he wanted things to go, pushed and pulled until he had what he wanted, and if that didn't work, then he threw money at it.

She put down her fork, closed the lid on the bracelet, placed the box on the tickets, and slid them back to his side of the table. "I can't accept these."

Surprise flickered across his face, followed by hurt. "You don't understand. Things will be different from now on. I'll—" His phone buzzed and his gaze instantly dropped to it. He read whatever message appeared, frowned, and muttered something under his breath. To give him credit, he didn't pick up the phone, but she could see he was sorely tempted.

Jess looked across the room and waved at Marian, trying to get the waitress's attention, but she was too busy chatting to another customer to notice.

"What are you doing?"

"I'm going to ask for the check." Jess pushed her plate away. "We're finished here, Evan. I'm done being second to your work."

"Jess, I didn't even answer it!"

"But you wanted to."

"It was the lawyer working on the Sanchez case, and I thought I should let him know—but you're right. I shouldn't have even looked at it." Evan put his phone into his pocket, and then placed his hands flat on the table. "Done. Over with. I won't touch it again."

She shrugged, her entire body weighted as if with lead. "We should go. I've got things to do back home."

His frown was instant. "Our home is in Atlanta."

"Not mine. Not anymore."

"Damn it, Jess." He sighed. "You never liked Atlanta, did you?"

"I liked it, but we had three houses, Evan. Three."

"I have offices in Atlanta, San Francisco, and Miami, so we needed places there."

"Needed? We never stayed anywhere more than a week or two at a time. We were like nomads."

He frowned and picked up a fry, only to put it back on his plate. "I didn't know you felt this way."

It bothered him, she could see it. "That's because I never told you. See? A lot of this was my fault, too. I wasn't honest about things. Not even a little. And that doomed us just as much as your working habits." She felt miserable admitting it.

He stared down at his plate. After a long while, he looked up, his gaze dark. "I don't understand why you just want to quit. We were great in the beginning, Jess. That's something."

"In the beginning, yes. But name one time in the last two—no, three years that we spent together, just the two of us. Something that wasn't interrupted by your work."

"Okay. We spent a week in Jamaica—" He stopped and winced. "I was in the middle of the Davis merger then, wasn't I? I was on the computer part of the time."

"*All* of the time."

"It was complicated, but yes, that's a bad example." He rubbed his jaw, thinking. "What about that weekend in Montreal where we—oh. The Bradford/Parks contract. That was a mess though. We almost ended up in court over the—" He threw up a hand when she rolled her eyes. "Okay, okay. But what about—" He paused, obviously culling through a long list of memories.

After a moment, his shoulders fell, his sigh deep.

She picked up her fork and stabbed a green bean with more

force than was warranted. "We didn't have a single vacation where you weren't pulled away by work."

Evan was quiet a long moment. Finally, he said, "All I know is I love you. I can't accept this is it. I just can't."

"It wasn't working, Evan. We tried and we failed. It'll be easier for us both if we just leave things as they are and move on." She should have been used to those words by now, because she'd thought them a thousand times, and yet they burned as if they were acid. Tears clouded her eyes and she looked down at her plate to keep him from knowing how hard she had to fight to keep her emotions under control.

"We could try a marriage counselor or—"

"Evan, stop it. I'm done. I'm exhausted and worn out and I just can't."

He winced and then leaned back in his seat, raking a hand through his hair. "That's harsh."

"It's the truth." She hated how her words hurt him. Hated it with a passion because his pain was hers. It took all of her newfound strength to fight the urge to blurt out something soothing just to ease the hurt she saw in his eyes. When had she become more worried about his feelings than hers? Whenever it was, it was over. While she cared about him, she had to be honest about who she was and what she wanted.

Suddenly tired, she stirred her mashed potatoes. "I don't want to talk about this anymore."

She expected him to argue, but after sending her a deep, brooding look, he said, "Fine. But can we at least stay for the rest of the meal? You were right about the meatloaf."

She supposed it was the least she could do. "Sure."

He collected the jewelry box, returned the tickets to their envelope, and put them back into his pocket.

"There." He picked up his fork. "What should we talk about?"

"Something positive."

"Why don't you tell me about the motel? What's your overall plan?"

She was more than willing to talk about the motel and had a lot to say. For the next thirty minutes they talked, and Evan's tense expression relaxed as he listened. She liked that the questions he asked were both sharp and thoughtful, although he couldn't seem to help himself from suggesting ways to "better" her plans.

Eventually, they segued from the motel to Brad's defection and what that had meant to Evan. Jess was glad he didn't refer to their relationship again. Tomorrow, his car would be fixed, and he'd leave, and she'd go back to making her own dreams come true. But tonight, they were doing something they hadn't done in a long, long time—sharing their lives without anyone else being a part of it.

While he spoke, she watched him, and decided that now and then, there was something un-Evan-like in his expression. Something almost vulnerable.

Marian stopped by to clear their table and to try and talk them into dessert. They refused, so the waitress left the check, offering to wrap up the rest of Jess's meatloaf so she could take it home.

The waitress had just taken Jess's plate when Evan's phone buzzed.

Jess waited for him to dig his phone from his pocket, but he didn't move. "Aren't you going to answer that?"

"Not this time." He sent her an almost tired smile and then picked up the check. "Allow me. It'll salve my bruised ego." He pulled out his credit card and placed it on the tray. "I owe you for the room, anyway."

Jess wished she'd given him one of the redone rooms. She'd wanted to discourage him from staying, so she'd given him one of the original rooms, one with ugly, burnt orange carpet and chipped, white lacquered furniture older than her pickup truck.

At least the room was clean, although that was the only good thing about it.

Still, she felt a little guilty as she said, "Thank you for dinner."

His gaze darkened. "Any time."

She ignored the seriousness of his gaze and a few moments later, they were on their way out of the restaurant. Evan must have tipped generously, because Marian smiled brightly at him as they left.

They went to Jess's truck and she drove them back to the motel. Jess filled the awkward silence with comments about the town, pointing out the new businesses that were springing up here and there. She was glad when they finally got home.

Home. The old motel with its endless possibilities, colored as it was by her fond memories of its better days, felt more like home than anywhere she'd lived in the last five years.

"Here we are," Jess announced as she parked the truck. She collected her purse and leftovers, and then hopped out. She walked to the back of the truck and into the relative safety of the wide-open parking lot, where Evan joined her.

The evening breeze whispered through the trees overhead and tugged at the bottom of his suit jacket and rippled across the bottom of her dress.

Evan's gaze locked on her. "I guess this is it."

She nodded, feeling achingly alone.

"Trav is supposed to call in the morning with an update on the car, so I'll let you know what he says."

"Sounds good. Thanks again for dinner."

"Sure." He put his hands into his pockets, looking oddly lost, standing there under the humming light that lit the parking lot. "I don't suppose you'd be up for a drink? It's still early."

She had to swallow twice to keep herself from agreeing. "Not tonight."

He nodded as if he'd expected her answer. "I'll watch some TV. Maybe there's a game on."

"There's no cable yet, but there's Wi-Fi. The password is—"

"BrunoMarsIsMyLovah."

She had to smile. "That's it."

His gaze lingered on her mouth. "At least some things are still the same."

Too much so. Jess ached with the pain of walking away, of leaving him alone, of being alone herself. For a wild moment, she imagined tossing all caution to the wind, throwing her arms around his neck, and kissing him the way she used to, passionately and without the pain of a long, long list of rejections.

But that wouldn't be fair to either of them, so instead, she tucked her purse under one arm and clasped her leftovers with both hands, which kept her from making such a grave error.

His gaze slid over her, lingering on her mouth. "I'll see you in the morning?"

"Sure. I usually set out coffee and a light breakfast in the lobby around eight for the various workmen coming through. There'll be more options once the place is open."

"I'm sure they appreciate it, as will I." A smile, polite and tired, flickered over his face. "Good night, Jess. Thanks for the talk, and the honesty."

"You, too." Her eyes burned from the weight of the words she'd spoken, and those she'd heard, too. "See you tomorrow." Without giving herself time to say anything else, she turned on her heel and went back to her apartment, far too aware that he watched her every step.

3

EVAN

*T*he cell phone rang into the silence and jerked Evan from a deep sleep. He rolled to his side and blindly reached for his phone, accidentally knocking it off the nightstand. Cursing, he leaned over the edge of the bed and retrieved his phone from the floor.

Ashley C flashed across the screen.

He rolled to his back and hit the answer button. "Hello."

"Good morning!" Ash's voice spilled into the silent room. "I sent the changes you marked to Legal and, except for a few tweaks, they were all okayed. I believe his exact words were 'Good catch.'"

"Good." Evan rubbed his face and then glanced at the windows. He'd drawn the shades before he went to bed, and they were surprisingly effective. It was a pity the bed wasn't as well designed as the blinds. The ancient thing sagged in the middle so badly that he felt as if he'd been sleeping in a ditch. "What time is it?"

"Eight." There was a surprised pause and then she said, "You aren't up yet?"

"I'm getting there." He stifled a yawn and supposed he

couldn't fault Ashley for her surprise. Since Jess had left, he'd started going to the office at six and sometimes earlier, including weekends. Anything was better than sitting in his echoingly empty house.

"Will you be in later today?" Ashley asked.

"I don't know yet. I'm still in Dove Pond at Jess's motel."

"Oh Evan! That's—have you and Jess—"

"No. Not yet." *And probably never.* His chest ached as he thought of Jess's face last night during their talk, how furious and then sad she'd looked. He'd spent most of the night in his uncomfortable bed, staring at the ceiling, and thinking about that very thing.

"Are you making any progress?"

"If I keep answering this phone, no. Apparently she hates that."

Ashley made an impatient noise. "Then stop answering it."

"You're the one who called me," he retorted. "And on a Saturday, too."

"You work Saturdays, so we have to work Saturdays."

Evan frowned. "I've never asked you guys to do that."

"Yes, you did. I got an email from you just last night asking for the details on the new lawsuit. You said you needed them for the Monday morning conference call."

Evan didn't think it was possible, but now he felt even worse. "Sorry, Ash. I didn't mean to force you into the office on a weekend. Starting today, I'll be more careful."

"Thank you. To be honest, everything you needed for the conference call was already in your folder."

He rubbed the sleep from his eyes. "I'm an idiot. I should trust you guys to get things done."

"You should. I wouldn't have sent you that last contract except you asked to see it."

"Yeah, and if I hadn't looked at it—"

"—then I would have looked at it instead, noticed the issues with it, made the necessary changes, and sent it on to Legal exactly as you did. But no, you wanted to see it for yourself and so I sent it to you."

Evan could almost see her frown. He sat up and swung his bare feet to the floor. "Brad hated it when I did that."

"And now he's gone," Ashley said in a flat tone.

God, why was every person he knew suddenly intent on pointing out his flaws? It was getting annoying. "You think I should let you handle the rest of this deal."

"I do. And while I'm working on it, you can work on fixing things with Jess."

"Leave Jess out of this, Ash," Evan growled.

"I know, I know. I shouldn't say anything about your personal life, but you've been miserable since she left. Everyone here in the office can see that."

"That's my business."

"Not when you bark at people the way you've been doing for the last two weeks."

"I haven't been that bad."

"Not that bad? Evan, you have no idea how bad you've been. Please, put the phone away and go spend some time with Jess. You know you want to."

"I'm going to." *If she'll let me.* "Still, I'm not leaving that contract out to dry. Promise you'll call if anything else comes up."

"If that's what you want."

"It is. Talk to you later." He dropped the phone back on the nightstand and then stretched, wincing as his back protested. This old mattress was hell on a body. Still sitting on the bed, he scuffed his foot over the ugly orange carpet. It was older than he wanted to think about, as was the painfully thin blue-and-orange-striped bedspread. The furniture was covered in a weird white lacquer that was chipped in places, revealing cheap press-board beneath. The bathroom was even worse as it was decorated a dull turquoise blue with bright orange stripes, the colors unfortunately echoed in the sink and counter.

The whole place reeked of the 1970s and not in a good way. It was a million miles away from the perfection of the lobby, but not for long, if what Jess had told him over dinner was true.

Last night, after he'd reluctantly agreed to talk about less painful topics, Jess had given him the lowdown on the motel. She had an in-depth, well-thought-out plan for the property, which didn't surprise him as she'd always been an ace planner. What *had* surprised him was the way her face had lit up as she talked about this funky old place.

She loved this rickety motel and was excited to bring it back to life. Watching her face glow, Evan realized that it had been years since he'd seen her so excited. In fact, last night as he'd stared at the ceiling for hours on end, it had dawned on him that *he* hadn't been that excited about anything in a long, long time, either.

He sighed and eyed the nearly flat pillows piled four deep beside him. Maybe if he slept another hour, he would be able to think clearer and—

Bang!

Bang!

Evan scowled at the closed door.

Bang Bang Bang!

"What in the heck," he growled, reaching for his pants and yanking them on as he hopped toward the door. *Who in the hell hammers on things at this time of the morning?* Muttering a curse, Evan stepped outside.

The morning sunlight made him shade his eyes as he clenched his jaw against the chilly air.

Standing on a ladder on the sidewalk, hammer in hand, was Doyle. The handyman was dressed in a fresh set of overalls that sported a ripped knee, and a white T-shirt splattered with red paint. An ancient-looking leather toolbelt hung around his rotund waist.

Doyle pointed his hammer at Evan. "You forgot your shirt."

"You're lucky I stopped to put on my pants. What in the hell are you doing, banging away at this time of the morning?"

"I didn't know anyone was in that room." Doyle climbed down the ladder. "So Miss Jess put you in Room Ten, did she?"

Evan rubbed his cold arms, frowning at the amused grin on the old man's face. "What's wrong with this room?"

"Nothing, I guess." Doyle chuckled as if he'd just made a joke. "I don't know if you've noticed, but it's the farthest room from the main office."

A fact Evan had noticed but hadn't admitted to himself. "So?"

"Also, it hasn't been updated. Rooms One and Two have been updated, but Miss Jess didn't give you the key for either of those, did she?" Doyle laughed and slapped his knee as if he'd just made a huge joke.

Evan suddenly remembered that last night Jess had mentioned how she'd completed two rooms and was working on two more. But it hadn't occurred to him that she would stick him in the worst room available. *Making a point, were you?*

Doyle snickered, shaking his shaggy head. "But other than that, it's a fine room. A wonderful room. Best one on this end of the parking lot."

Evan glanced over his shoulder at the depressing condition of Room Ten. "Apparently Jess didn't want me to get too comfortable."

"You think?" Doyle chuckled.

Evan's mood, already ruined by Ashley's call, grew worse. "I've been had."

"'Had' is a strong word. I'd just say you were 'put in your place.'" Doyle's eyes twinkled. "That's a tad more accurate."

Evan cut the old man a hard look. "You don't need to sound so damn chipper about it."

"I hear some 'tude in your tone, boy." The handyman put his elbow on a ladder rung and leaned on it, still grinning from ear to ear. "I'm getting that cranky-before-coffee vibe from you."

"I didn't sleep well last night. That bed—" Evan arched his lower back where a dull pinch had grown into a deep ache. "I feel like I've been kicked down ten flights of steps by a herd of angry cows."

Doyle winced in commiseration. "That bed's not much younger than me."

"It's probably older. If you don't mind, I'm going to try and catch up on some sleep. Could you hammer somewhere far, far away for a few hours? Like maybe in South Carolina or Georgia? Hell, I'd be happy if you wanted to try the Florida Keys for a week or two. I hear they're nice this time of the year."

"I've got to change out this light, but lucky for you I'm done with the hammer. At least for now."

That was something, Evan supposed grumpily. He wondered why Doyle would need a hammer to change a light bulb anyway, and then decided he didn't care enough to ask. "Thanks," he muttered and turned back to his room.

"How was your date with Miss Jess?"

Evan stopped and slowly turned back around. "How did you know about that?"

"I saw the two of you getting into Miss Jess's truck as I was leaving yesterday. I've never seen her so glammed up. That dress—" Doyle gave a silent whistle.

"It wasn't a date." Evan couldn't keep a sour note out of his voice. Jess had looked good last night. Better than good.

"You soured up just now as if you'd swallowed a bad lemon," Doyle said. "Or maybe it was a bad date."

"It wasn't a date," Evan repeated. At the old man's curious gaze, Evan found himself admitting, "But I wish it had been."

"Can't blame you for that." From the bucket that rested at his feet, Doyle picked up a small box and removed a light bulb.

"Judging from the reactions I've seen from various bachelors in this town, you aren't alone wishing that."

Evan had just crossed his arms over his bare chest against the morning chill, but now he cut the old man a hard look. "What bachelors?"

Doyle placed the bulb on the top of his ladder and dropped the empty box into the bucket. "There are quite a few single men in this town. More than there used to be, what with all the new businesses opening up because of Mayor Wheeler's initiatives. She's a sharp one, our mayor."

"Except for you, I haven't seen any other men roaming around here."

"Not yet, but they'll come. And trust me on this; they've already noticed Miss Jess. But you had to have expected that. I mean, you've seen her."

Evan scowled. "Before you say another word, you should know that Jess is my wife."

Not one iota of surprise appeared on the old man's face. "You mean ex-wife, or soon-to-be ex-wife, don't you?"

What in the hell? It seemed like every person Evan spoke to this morning was determined to drag him down. "You already knew I was Jess's husband."

"I might've suspected it," Doyle admitted.

Evan eyed Doyle sourly. "Yesterday you called me 'a piece of work' and 'stupid.'"

"I might have said the first one, but I only implied the second." Doyle chuckled, unrepentant. "Lord, the things I say sometimes. No filter at all. I used to drive poor Barbara nuts."

"I can see why." The morning breeze blew a piece of paper across the cracked parking lot. Evan rubbed his arms again. "It doesn't feel like April."

"You've got thin blood. It's cooler up here than it is down in Atlanta."

"It gets cold in Atlanta, too."

Doyle cocked his eyebrow. "I take it from your grumbly and acrid disposition that things didn't go well last night."

Evan didn't reply. After they'd left the rocky conversation topic of their relationship, he'd gotten to talk to Jess, *really* talk to her, and in a way they hadn't done in years. Although that too-brief, but wonderful part of the evening didn't erase the part where she'd made it clear—*very* clear—that she still wanted this divorce.

Which was the real reason he'd spent last night tossing and turning in the ditch-like bed. He had to find a way forward. He *had* to. When he thought about it, he'd learned a lot about Jess over dinner, things he used to know but had somehow let drift out of his daily consciousness. He'd learned that Jess's hazel eyes, which were beyond beautiful, glowed when she was excited about something. He'd learned that her business acumen was as sharp now as it was when, freshly married, they'd worked together at his new company. He'd learned that her laugh still made him feel as if he'd just struck gold.

But more than anything else, he'd learned that despite all of the barriers she'd thrown up, all of the hard truths she'd thrown at him, he still wasn't ready to walk away from this marriage, not by a long shot.

He suddenly realized Doyle was watching, and the understanding on the old man's face softened Evan's temper. "I'll be honest; I'm worried. I came here to get Jess back. I had a plan— gifts, a romantic getaway, everything."

"She wasn't interested, eh?"

"Not even a flicker. I've messed things up badly and now I'm at a loss on how to proceed."

"Wives are complicated beings, aren't they?" Doyle climbed the ladder, pulled his screwdriver from his tool belt, and reached over his head for the light cover. "There were times I thought Barbara and I spoke different languages."

"I get what Jess is saying. I've been too tied up with work, which is my fault, and something we've fought about before."

Doyle glanced down at Evan. "She warned you, did she?"

"Yeah, but I didn't listen. I'm the head of my own company so I'm busy, maybe too much so, but—" Evan winced. "She's right. I let things go that I shouldn't have. And now I don't know how to convince her to give us another shot."

Doyle replaced the bulb and put the cover back in place. "Can-Do people like Miss Jess aren't about pretty gifts and vacations and such. Can-Do people like other Can-Do people."

"So?"

"So you have to be a Can-Do person and not an annoying, whiny Can't-Do person."

"What makes you think I'm a Can't-Do person?" Evan asked stiffly.

"Can't-Do people are about words and not deeds. They're the sort of people who, when you tell them it's cold because they're in the mountains at around 3600 feet above sea level, will reply that it gets cold in Atlanta too, thankyouverymuch, and will then stand where they are, shivering in the cold, instead of putting on a shirt."

Evan's face grew warm. He had done that, hadn't he? "Sorry."

"It's nothing to me. But to Miss Jess? She's a mite pickier than me, as she should be." Doyle eyed Evan closely. "My advice is this: Don't *give* Miss Jess something. Any fool with a credit card can do that. *Do* something *for* her. Let her see you for what you will be, a man of action instead of empty promises."

Evan considered this. "That's decent advice." He looked at the old man standing on the ladder. "But it's not just up to me. Jess has to want us to work, too."

"Then convince her of that. You're a salesman or something like it, aren't you? You have the air."

Evan often had to convince a room full of skeptical board

members to take big chances, and it was a rare day he didn't get his way. "I guess I am a salesman of sorts."

Doyle shrugged. "So sell yourself. And do it like it's the day before Mother's Day and you're one of a thousand boxes of chocolate sitting on the shelf." Doyle tightened the final screw. "But first, before all that, you gotta fix whatever it was Miss Jess decided was unfixable."

"It? There was more than one thing." Truth be told, there were so many that Evan was at a loss where to begin.

"I daresay she's willing to put up with some of your faults. Women will do that if you do the dishes and such. But it sounds as if there was a sticking point she wasn't willing to let slide by. Fix that, and you're home free."

"You make it sound easy."

"It's never easy, not when women are involved." Doyle replaced the screwdriver in his tool belt and then climbed back down the ladder. "It's pretty obvious you've dug yourself a hole. Miss Jess gets pretty het up when she hears your name."

"Great. Just great."

"Which is why you shouldn't be wasting time standing here." Doyle folded the ladder, leaned it against the wall, and placed the bucket of light bulbs and empty boxes beside it. "I'd run for that breakfast buffet if I were you. Flora Fellows just brought in another flower arrangement and when it comes to bacon, Flora's never been known to be shy. I once saw her gobble down a pound of it at the Baptist Church Barbeque without blinking."

Evan looked toward the office and realized that just past it, he could see the back of a dented white van with the words "Flora's Fauna" written on the side. Through the lobby window, he could make out Jess's dark hair as she spoke to a short, round woman holding a huge vase of flowers. *Who in the hell sent Jess flowers?*

He took a step toward the office, and then realized that he

was only wearing pants, and nothing more. Muttering to himself, he turned. "I'd better get dressed before—"

Doyle was gone. Evan looked around the parking lot, but the handyman was nowhere to be seen, although he'd left his ladder and bucket behind. *He should clean up his stuff.*

No matter. Evan had bigger fish to fry. He returned to his room and threw on his clothes. Within minutes, he was hurrying down the sidewalk, his hair hastily combed, his mouth now minty fresh. As he reached the lobby door, the delivery van was just pulling out of the parking lot.

Evan tucked his shirt into his suit pants, wishing he had something else to wear. His first order of the day, after sleuthing out who'd sent Jess flowers, would be to get some clothes— something more comfortable than his suit, which was getting too wrinkled to wear.

He pushed open the door and found Jess standing beside a table in the lobby's entryway, studying the flower arrangement on display. She was dressed in jeans, tennis shoes, and a red T-shirt with the words *Dove Pond Spring Fling* written in script over a picture of a pie. She nodded coolly, her reading glasses perched on her head. "Good morning."

Her voice was as impersonal as the words, so he decided to go the other direction. "Good morning, Sunshine."

Her polite smile sank into a chilly frown. "Don't."

Damn it. He took a steadying breath and turned to the flowers. "Nice. Who sent them?"

"Someone." Her hazel gaze pinned him in place. "That's all you need to know."

It wasn't all he needed to know. He needed to know who'd sent them, what she thought about the guy, and how many punches Evan might have to deliver to convince the idiot to never again send a bouquet to another man's wife.

"Breakfast is on the table by the fireplace." Jess dropped her glasses into place on her nose and headed for her desk behind the check-in counter.

"Jess, wait. I—" His phone rang, but he ignored it. "Can we talk? Last night, we left things—"

She stopped and turned toward him. "Answer your phone."

"I'm not going to answer any calls while we're talking—"

"*Evan!*"

"What?"

She pointed to his pocket where his phone was ringing. "That's probably Travis."

"Who?"

"The mechanic. The one who has your car. He's supposed to call this morning, remember?"

"Right, right," Evan muttered, feeling like a fool. He grabbed his phone. "Hello."

"Mr. Graham? Trav Parker from the garage."

"Yes?" Realizing that Jess was close enough to hear the mechanic talking, Evan moved away, walking a dozen or so steps into the lobby. "What's the news?"

"I got the part in this morning as I'd hoped and the Jag is good to go."

Damn it. Evan looked at Jess and shook his head. "That's too bad."

"Too bad?" The mechanic sounded annoyed. "It's done. Runs like a top. My shop manager is here, so we could bring it to you around noon, if you don't have a way to—"

"How long will it take to get the part?"

"The one I already got and is in your car?" The man muttered something under his breath that sounded like "bad connection."

Across the room, Evan met Jess's gaze, and he noticed how her reading glasses framed her eyes. God, those eyes. He felt as if he were sinking into the silky warmth of a hot bath.

Doyle was right. If Evan wanted to win Jess back, he'd have

to work at it. Which meant he needed far more than one day, or even two. He faked a frown and said to the mechanic, "Not until Friday? You can't get it done sooner than that?"

"Are you drunk?" Trav's voice couldn't have been more bewildered. "I said today, not Friday."

"I understand. I guess I'll just have to wait until Friday, then."

Jess was looking concerned, so Evan sent her a helpless shrug before saying to Trav, "Since it'll be at your shop for so long, I'll pay for storage, of course."

There was a long silence, and then the mechanic said, "You're looking for an excuse to stay in town. Is that it?"

Relieved, Evan said, "Yes."

"I suspect there's a woman involved, but I really don't want to know."

"Thank you."

"Okay, then. Now we're on the same page. I won't charge you storage as it's only a week, but after that, we're going to have to talk."

"Deal. And seriously, thanks. I owe you."

"Yes, you do." Trav hung up.

Evan dropped his phone into his pocket as he turned back to Jess. "Too bad."

"You're stuck," she said, her jaw tight.

"I guess I'd better get used to that dip in the mattress in my room."

"What? No. You can't stay here."

"Why not? From what I've heard, I'm in your least rentable room."

She bit her lip. "Sorry about that. It was rather childish of me, but I didn't want to encourage you."

He rubbed his lower back. "Message received."

She tucked a stray strand of hair behind one ear, her brows drawn. "I don't like this, Evan. Not even a little."

"Sure, but can we talk about it after breakfast? I'm starving and you know I can't think until I've had coffee."

She didn't look happy, but she shrugged. "You might as well. I've things to do, anyway."

Relieved she hadn't said "you can't stay here" more than once, he went to the buffet table and found a collection of fresh muffins and bagels in a box marked *The Magnolia Café*, a bowl of ice displaying an assortment of yogurts, and a small chafing dish holding fluffy scrambled eggs and bacon. An urn of hot coffee sat nearby with pitchers of half-and-half and milk. He picked up a plate. "This is all for me?"

She was already at the computer, her fingers flying over the keyboard. She didn't look up as she replied, "It's been good practice for my opening. Plus, the workmen love it."

Evan had only seen one workman so far. From what he could tell by the still-generous portion of bacon left, it didn't appear that Doyle had yet stormed the breakfast buffet. That was a good thing because Evan suspected that, given the chance, the plump handyman would eat more than his fair share. Evan poured himself a cup of coffee and then piled eggs and bacon on his plate. The tempting smell made his mouth water.

He carried his food and coffee to the check-in counter and set them on the marble surface. "You said last night that you wanted to open in September."

She turned to look at him. "In time for leaf season, yes. But you're not staying that long, car or no car."

"I wasn't suggesting I should. I was just thinking that September isn't that far away, and yet you've only finished two rooms. You have a lot to do before then." He picked up his fork and attacked his eggs.

Jess frowned and then pointed past him to the seating area. "There's a table and chair right there in the corner."

"I'm good here." He took another bite of the delicious eggs, aware that Jess was still frowning at him from the other side of the counter.

The moment stretched and became heavier.

He sighed and put down his fork, eyeing his cup of coffee with regret before turning his attention back to Jess. "You're upset."

"You can't stay here until Friday. I can't—" She closed her lips over the words and shook her head. "I'll drive you to a car rental place. There's one about twenty minutes from here in Marion. You can go back to Atlanta for the week and return when the car's ready."

"I want to stay here, in Dove Pond."

"Then I'll take you to a local B&B. There are several really nice ones in town. And don't tell me you can't sleep in a creaky bed. The one in your room last night couldn't have been any better."

"It was pretty brutal." He stretched his back, wincing a bit as he did so. "Made me think of that lumpy bed we slept on our first year."

When they'd first gotten married, they'd been broke but deliriously happy. While her family had welcomed him from the beginning, others had warned them about the dangers of getting married "too soon." His parents had made impassioned pleas for him to rethink what they'd believed was a hasty decision. Meanwhile, their friends, all of whom were either focusing on graduation or were neck deep in the party life, declared them both crazy to marry so quickly.

But he and Jess had ignored them all. They'd been madly in love and determined to make things work, and they had. For a while, at least.

His throat tightened. Doyle had pointed out that Evan was a salesman. So now was the time to prove it. He idly twirled his coffee mug on the counter and said, "Hmm."

He waited.

Jess sent him an annoyed look but didn't say a word.

He cleared his throat and said it again, but louder this time, "Hmmmmmm."

She rolled her eyes. "Stop that. I'm not going to ask what you're thinking."

He grinned. "I guess I should just tell you, then. Let's strike a bargain. I'll pay you top dollar for the room. I won't even ask to stay in one of the updated ones."

She slid her glasses back to the top of her head. "Evan, go home."

"Without a car? Plus, I hate being at the house since you left. I feel like a loose pebble in a huge, empty box."

"You'd feel the same here." Her gaze was hooded, cautious. "I'd rarely see you. I have a To Do List as long as my leg."

"That's fine," he lied. "I have to work every day, too. Although, if I *do* find myself with some extra time, I could help you out. Do a few chores around the place, maybe—"

"No. This is *my* project, Evan. Not yours."

He frowned. "Of course it is. Who said otherwise?"

Her gaze narrowed. "You know how you are when you get enthusiastic about things. You take over, even if you don't mean to."

He opened his mouth, ready to argue, but the anger he saw in her eyes made him stop. *She makes me sound pushy. I'm determined, sure. And capable. And like all good leaders, I like to be in control, but only because I know more than everyone el—*He winced as he heard himself.

I'm pushy. Ouch.

Now that he thought about it, Brad had said something similar, claiming Evan had "a tendency to bulldoze."

Evan scowled. "Fine. Maybe I do tend to take over. I don't mean to, though."

Her eyebrows rose and she leaned back in her office chair. "I never thought I'd hear you admit that."

"It wasn't easy." He had to take a drink of his coffee to get the bitterness out of his mouth. "I understand why you're hesitant to let me stay, but here I am, and Trav isn't bringing my car until Friday. If your biggest concern is that I'll take over, why don't we do this? Let's come up with a safe word."

"A what?"

"A safe word. I promise I'll do my best to stay out of your way, but if at any time you feel that I'm infringing in some way, just say the safe word and I'll back off, no questions asked."

She eyed him with suspicion. "Is this a new trick of yours?"

"*What?*" He shook his head. "I would never try to trick you."

"You attempted to bribe me last night," she pointed out. "So why wouldn't you also try to trick me?"

"I wasn't trying to bribe you," he replied stiffly. "I was trying to prove my sincerity. But I can see now that bringing you gifts was a stupid move on my part."

"It wasn't smart," she agreed. "In fact, it was a remarkably asinine move."

"Point taken. You don't need to belabor it. Between you and Brad, my ego is taking a beating this week. If this coffee wasn't so good, I might be reduced to tears."

"I'm glad you have the coffee, then." As she spoke, her lips quirked, and he could tell she was hiding a smile.

He'd take amusement over sadness and anger any day of the week, even when it was at his own expense. "Come on, Jess. Let me stay." When she hesitated, he added, "What will it matter? You made it clear that we're over. Why would my being here make any difference?"

"Because you'd be standing right here, bothering me."

"I would not."

"You'd stay out of the lobby?"

"For the most part, yes." When she hesitated, he pointed to his coffee. "I have to be here some of the time."

She regarded him for a long moment. Finally, she sighed. "I

suppose you're right; it won't make any difference. But a safe word is a good idea."

Yes! Yes! YES! He forced his voice to a calm level. "All right, then. Pick an unusual word, one you wouldn't use in a normal, casual conversation."

She bit her lip and stared into the distance as if reading from a list. "Rhino."

"Rhino. Got it."

"Good." She slid her glasses from the top of her head back to her nose. "Now, if you'll excuse me. I have work to do."

He picked up his plate and coffee cup. "I'll leave you to it, then. But if you need help, I'd be glad to—"

"Rhino."

"Hey, I was just saying—"

"*Rhino!*" she yelled, but she shot him an amused glance as she did so, one he hadn't seen in forever.

Laughing, Evan backed away from the counter. "Okay! Okay! I'll just head over here to this lonely corner and finish my breakfast which, by the way, is excellent."

She rolled her eyes as if she didn't believe one word of his compliment, but before she turned back to the computer, he noticed that her cheeks had pinkened.

Well. That was something, wasn't it? Last night had been an abject failure, but all in all, it had been a good morning. He'd gotten permission to stay on-site for another week, they'd found a safe word to keep him from accidentally making an ass of himself, and he'd made her both laugh *and* blush. Doyle would be pleased, Evan decided. *Not bad for one morning.*

Smiling to himself, he retreated to a table near a large window, ready to enjoy the rest of his breakfast while thinking of ways to spend time with the woman he loved more than life itself.

4

JESS

$\mathcal{L}$ater that afternoon, her truck window rolled down to let in the spring breeze, Jess rested her elbow on the door and pretended she wasn't obsessively watching the people leaving Target. A half hour ago, Evan had worn his wrinkled suit into the big store, his wallet at the ready.

The sunlight warmed her face while a noisy bee hovered outside the front windshield, searching for a way inside and too silly to realize both side windows were wide open.

Sleepy from the sun, she leaned against the headrest, the scent of fresh cut grass and sun-warmed asphalt wafting into her truck as she wished for the hundredth time that Evan would hurry. She'd brought him here so he could buy clothes and toiletries and whatever else he needed to make it until Friday. She hadn't meant to offer to drive him, but he'd looked so un-Evan-like standing there in her lobby with his wrinkled white shirt and creased suit pants, his face darkened by a five o'clock shadow, that she'd folded. And so, here she was.

She was being way too nice to him. Had she any sense, she'd have just left him to make do with the clothes he'd shown up in. After all, he was the one who'd wanted to stay in her motel. But somehow, when he'd asked, before she could think, she'd heard herself agree to drive him here.

"I'll be fast," he'd said.

She glanced at her phone to check the time. To be fair, he'd only been gone about thirty minutes. Still...

She dropped her phone back into the cup holder. *I'm so weak. But at least I have the safe word. All I have to do is use it on myself.* She snorted at the thought. So far, she'd only had to use it once but she suspected she would be saying it to him at least a dozen times before the week was over. *I should embroider "rhino" on a pillow and just throw it at him when I need to.* Thunk! *Right in the head.*

The vision was satisfying and she found herself smiling.

A robin flew to a tree beside the parking lot and she watched it hop along a branch, scolding a nearby squirrel. If she was honest—which she didn't really want to be where Evan was concerned—she'd admit that only he could make a crumpled suit and a lack of a razor look hot. *Hot. Stop that. Don't think of him that way. Don't think about him at all.*

She'd be better off thinking about other men. Men who were the opposite of Evan. Men like the guy who was even now walking through the parking lot two rows away. His jeans rode low on his hips, his flannel shirt hung open, revealing a colorful T-shirt, his broad shoulders and narrow waist a perfect balance. A baby blue Tarheels ballcap cast a shadow over a face with a pleasingly square jaw. *Mm-mm. Now that's the way to wear jeans and flannel—*

The man suddenly stopped and glanced around, obviously looking for his car and unable to find it. She started to grin but then she got a glimpse of his profile. The man was Evan.

Oh God, no, no, no! She covered her eyes and slunk lower into her seat. *What's wrong with me? I know the cost of that poison.* And yet...and yet, she couldn't seem to walk away from it. She was like an addict, yearning for the very thing that could hurt her. *He's worse than chocolate. I can't get enough.*

"I hate parking lots." His voice came from the open passenger window. He opened the door and set his bags into the floorboard. "Do you know how many trucks are parked in this lot? Dozens. And they all look alike." He slid into the seat.

"All done?"

"All done. Except for getting lost, it was relatively painless."

Speak for yourself. She started the truck, ready to head home where she'd chill her overactive imagination with a deep dive into the ice-cold reality of refinishing the furniture she'd bought for Room Number Four. She didn't have time to lollygag in the Target parking lot with a man she should be avoiding like the plague. She backed the truck out of the parking space.

"Where are we going now?" Evan asked.

"Back to the motel."

His smile slipped. "I thought that since we're in Asheville, we might as well grab some lunch and—"

"No." She hit the brakes as a Honda Civic backed out in front of her. "We can do a drive-through on the way home if you want, but I need to get to work. I have a lot to do." *And you don't.*

She didn't say it, but he must have known she thought it because he slanted her an amused look that made his eyes crinkle in the darnedest way. "I have work to do too," he said. "Or rather I *had* work to do, but I did it this morning while I was waiting on you to finish entering those invoices."

"Good for you."

"Which means I'm free now."

She didn't offer a comment, turning the truck out of the parking lot and heading down the street.

"Since I'm free," he continued, "maybe I can help you with whatever you're doing."

"No." She turned on her flasher, changed lanes, and headed for the interstate.

"Jess, I'm here, so you might as well let me help."

"No," she repeated.

"Why not?"

Because I can't handle being close to you for that long, not without feeling confused and lonely. "Thanks, but I've got it covered."

"Come on. Everyone needs help."

She shot him an annoyed look. "Didn't you promise to leave me in peace if I let you stay until Friday?"

His jaw tightened. "Right. Rhino. No lunch and no help. Got it." Looking put out, he tugged his hat lower, rested his arm on the window, and stared straight ahead, leaving her in peace.

Normally, she'd have made the same suggestion—that they grab something to eat, as Asheville was known for its excellent cafés and brunch locations. But she needed some breathing room, especially with Evan dressed as he was now. In his jeans and flannel, he reminded her far too much of the Evan she used to know, the one who'd swept her off her feet and into his bed.

The silence stretched as she pulled up on the interstate and drove out of town. Soon, the buildings of Asheville fell away and then disappeared altogether. Moments later, they were surrounded by blue and green mountains, the sunshine spilling over the dashboard.

Evan shot her a glance. "Since helping you is out of the question, then what should I do to kill time until Friday? I can't sit in that motel room the entire time. I'm not a hundred percent sure, but I'm starting to believe that orange carpet is alive and possibly hungry."

"Don't you have mergers to oversee and contracts to argue about and stuff like that?"

"A few, yes. But this morning I realized that meetings were eating up a lot of my time, so I called Ashley and asked her to handle them for the next few days."

That was surprising. Jess shot him a curious look. "All of them?"

"Every last one."

"Really? You're going to let Ashley attend every meeting, decide what needs to be done, and then make it happen."

"Not exactly. She's taking notes, but then she's to call me and we're going to develop an action plan."

And there it was. "You're still going to be making all of the decisions."

"Yes, but I'll have a *lot* of extra time in between those decisions, which could be to your benefit."

She didn't answer.

Undaunted, he flashed his smile, his damnable dimple enhanced by his shadowed face. "Just come up with a list of things you want done, and I'll get to work."

"No, thank you. There are other ways you can keep busy that have nothing to do with my motel."

"Like what?"

"You could read a book. There's a library in town. You have time. They have books." She shrugged. "Sounds like a perfect match."

"I need something more active to do. You said you were working on Rooms Three and Four."

"Exactly. *I* am working on those rooms. *You* are not."

"Jess, I've got to do *something* to kill the time, and I'd rather be helping you than sitting in your lobby just staring at the back of your head while you're working on the computer."

She cast him a dark look. "You promised you wouldn't hang out in the lobby."

"Well, in the parking lot, then. There's a bench right there by the door, which is convenient. You know I can't stay in that motel room. It's depressing."

She couldn't argue with that. She still felt a little guilty for putting him in the worst room.

They drove on in silence as she turned the truck off the interstate and onto Highway 9. To be honest, if anyone else had offered to help, she'd have taken them up on it. She had tons of work to do, far more than she could handle. There were carpets that needed pulling, walls that needed painting, and (worst of all) furniture that needed refinishing. She planned on hiring professionals to do the bigger jobs, but she could save both time and money by jumping in where she could. *So much to do and so little time.*

His soulful sigh broke the silence. "What if I promise not to talk while I work?"

She couldn't keep from grinning her disbelief. "Are you serious?"

"As serious as a heart attack, although I'm not sure why it would matter."

"If you couldn't talk, then you couldn't convince me to do something stupid like taking two hours of my precious time and driving you to Target so you can buy clothes and a razor." She turned off Main Street and headed for the motel. "By the way, how did you get them to let you change clothes right there in the store? I'd think that was against some sort of policy."

His grin returned. "The manager happened to walk by just as I was checking out. I explained that my car had broken down and I was stuck and I really, really wanted to change out of my suit. She was very understanding."

Looking the way he did, Jess would bet every woman in that store had been "understanding." It was a wonder they hadn't offered to help him tug on his new jeans, too. Heck, for all she knew, maybe some of them had.

She turned the truck into the motel and parked near the lobby, then she climbed out and waited while he collected his bags.

He joined her on the sidewalk, resting the bags at his feet. "Thanks for the ride. I don't know what I would have done without it."

She shrugged. "It was nothing." Which was a lie. Just sitting in the truck with him had stirred emotions she'd thought and hoped and prayed were long gone.

"Jess, can I ask you something?"

She wanted to say no, that they'd already talked way too much. But she didn't want him to realize how something as simple as talking to him affected her, so she stiffened her resolve and said in what she could only hope was a cool, unconcerned tone, "What's that?"

"When I offered to help, I meant I was willing to do the things you hate. You understood that part, right?"

"Really? You'd strip old wallpaper off of walls?"

"Sure."

"And rip up dirty orange carpet?"

He grimaced, but said, "Why not?"

That was promising. "What I really, *really* hate is refinishing furniture. There's a lot of sanding involved."

"Sanding?" His smile was almost dismissive. "That's not hard."

Oh, if only he knew how hard sanding could be. This was getting to be a difficult decision. The only real problem with accepting his offer was that it threatened to soften the anger she'd been holding onto.

She needed that anger. She needed to remember how lonely she'd been, how lost. She needed to remember all of that so she wouldn't fall back into the same hole again.

Still, she was painfully aware that her To Do List was growing by the minute. Just a half hour ago, while sitting in the Target parking lot, she'd thought of five more things that needed to be done.

He rubbed his chin, his fingers scraping over his shadowed jaw. "Let me remind you that I'm pretty good with a hammer."

"Used to be," she corrected.

"Hammering skills are permanent, like teeth." He grinned as he spoke.

She had to fight an answering laugh. To be honest, he'd been good at everything he'd ever put his hand to, including her.

Rhino! she told herself. *Rhino! Rhino! Rhino!* She took a steadying breath.

See? She could handle this situation, and him, too. All she had to do was keep her feet firmly on the ground. *You can do this,* she told herself. *Just be honest and set firm boundaries.* "All right, Graham. Let's see what you can do."

He looked as if she'd just given him a gift, something wonderful like a bottle of the most delicious, expensive wine in the world. "You mean that?"

"I do, but there are rules. *Lots* of rules."

"Fine. Just tell me what you want done, and I'll do it."

"*If* I let you help—and that's a big *if*—then you have to do what I tell you to do, the way I tell you to do it. No taking over. No changing things. No 'here, this is better' or 'I did it this way because I know better than you.'"

As she spoke, his smile had grown dimmer. "Do I sound like that?"

"Telling people what to do is how you make your living. I don't want to be talked into or out of anything, so just keep your bright ideas and thoughts to yourself. And no talking about our relationship. Not a peep. If you mention us just one time—" She swiped her finger across her throat.

"Noted." He adjusted his ballcap, his awkward laugh oddly endearing. "Just point me in the direction of this furniture that needs work and I'll get it done."

"It's not that easy. I'll send you some videos that'll explain what needs to be done. Don't touch anything until you've watched them. I have a vision for each room, and the furniture is key."

"I'll watch every video. I'll even take notes."

"You'll probably mess up your new clothes," she warned.

"I'm willing to make that sacrifice." As he spoke, he grinned, his eyes crinkling at the corners in that way that made her melt like butter.

Rhino, rhino, rhino! She moved away, trying to ignore the way her heart had just thumped at least four extra beats. "Watch the videos and then meet me at the shed in an hour and I'll get you started. You'll be working alone after that, because I'll be busy elsewhere." Probably hunkering down under her desk in the fetal position wondering what had possessed her to include him in any way.

"I'd be glad for some company—" he began, but at her look, he added in a rushed way, "—but I understand you're busy."

Boundaries, limits, restrictions, those were her friends, not his. So why did he look so pleased while she felt as if she'd just fallen into some sort of trap? She shook off her uncertainties. "See you in a bit."

He saluted and then collected his bags. "On the dot, Sunshine. Don't forget to send those videos."

She managed an acknowledging nod and, suddenly yearning for the quiet of her own apartment, she murmured "goodbye" and left. Head up, she made a beeline for her office, trying her best not to run.

She kept getting glimpses of a different Evan, one who was willing to put the hard work into their relationship that it required. One who wasn't as obsessed with his business as he used to be.

Was he *really* different?

And if he was, did it matter?

Her head said no, but her heart—ah, that fickle thing, said *maybe, just maybe.* And that was what scared her the most.

5

EVAN

*E*van stepped out of the shower and grabbed a towel. Say what he would about this old motel, the water pressure was pure perfection. Of course, that could be because he was the only guest, but for now, he'd celebrate every positive he could find, despite their scarcity.

The last several days had been challenging. His efforts to win his way back into Jess's good graces had left him with scraped knuckles, a matching set of splinters in one thumb, and a bruised knee from where he'd banged it on an open drawer of the old mahogany bureau he'd been sanding.

And sanding.

And then sanding yet more. He was pretty sure he no longer had fingerprints on his right hand. Even worse was the deep ache in his lower back. And his knees—*good Lord, listen to me moan!*

Evan had always thought of himself as fit. He exercised often and avoided most carbs, but wrestling a dresser day after day that weighed as much as the Audi even now sunning in the parking lot was proving how inadequate his fitness routine was. He'd never, in his entire life, had back issues. But between the ditch-like bed he'd been sleeping in, spending hours stooping over ancient furniture, and trying to slide that same furniture around so he could reach a "better sanding angle," his back had turned into one large ache.

He stopped getting dressed long enough to do some stretches, groaning as he did so. *If I keep this up, by the time I'm forty, I'll be using a cane.*

Damn. He hoped he wasn't still living in this ancient motel room trying to win Jess back when he was forty, but hey, if he had to do it, he'd do it, bad mattress and all.

He tossed his damp towel over a wobbly hook on the back of the bathroom door and was just pulling on his jeans when his phone rang. Still dressing, he let it go to voicemail, remembering Jess's expression when he'd reached for his phone his first night here. That flicker of disappointment had cut to the quick.

A jingle told him a voicemail was now waiting and he was irked by his instant impulse to grab the phone and throw himself back into work.

But no. His time with Jess was running out, and he had to do something different, *be* someone different, if he wanted her back. The question was, could he do it? Was it possible that for today at least, he could let work take care of itself? He'd hired a rockstar team. Maybe it was time he used them.

A week ago, he couldn't have imagined himself thinking such a thing, but in the last few days, Evan had realized that old man Doyle had been right—it wasn't enough to promise Jess changes. Evan had to show her those changes, and that meant trusting his company to the people he'd trained to run it.

His phone beeped, an email landing in his inbox. He flexed his fingers against the urge to check it. Ash was great at her job, he reminded himself. She'd handle whatever had arisen. He was sure of it.

Before their fallout, Brad had referred to Evan's management style as "effective overkill." Evan had been proud of the "effective" part and had ignored the "overkill" portion. He now knew that had been a mistake. Being away from the office was giving him startling new clarity, and he was beginning to realize that although he'd chosen and trained excellent people to run his company, he'd never given them the chance to do it.

The things you learn when you stop long enough to get some perspective. Brad was right, as usual.

It would be nice to call Brad right now and get his opinion on Jess and the direction Evan was taking to win her back. But apparently Brad was busy learning the ropes at his new job, too tied up to take a call from an old friend. *I'll call him again tonight and hopefully this time he'll answer. Jess was right; I miss that guy.*

But then Jess was rarely, if ever, wrong. *Except about us.*

Evan grabbed one of his new T-shirts from the drawer, a bright blue one with a Lion King logo and the words *Hakuna Matata* written in even brighter pink beneath it. He pulled on the shirt and donned his socks and sneakers.

Unable to resist, he checked the message from Ashley and was reassured that he'd been right. She'd answered her own question and was already effectively dealing with the situation.

Evan zipped off a reply email telling her he agreed with her decision. At the end of the email, he wrote something he never thought he'd write: *I'm taking off the rest of the week. I trust you'll make any decisions necessary. Feel free to call if there's an emergency, but otherwise, I'll talk to you Monday.*

He started to hit send but his thumb hovered over his phone screen. He trusted his people, but this was a big step. A huge step. *I'll send it later.*

Maybe.

Frowning, Evan closed his mail app, dropped his phone into his jeans pocket, and then went outside. He took in a deep breath of cool morning air, welcoming the smell of dew and freshly cut grass as he watched the morning mist roll across the pond. There was something to be said about mountain life.

He turned to walk toward the office, noticing that the lightbulb he'd watched Doyle replace was still burned out. *Come on, Doyle. You had one job.*

To be honest, Evan wouldn't mind seeing the old guy. For the last few days, Evan had been confined to the shed as he worked on the antiques Jess had gotten from an auction. They were complicated pieces, covered with nooks and crannies and ornamental hand-carved wooden scroll thingies, which were all a pain in the ass to sand. Fortunately, he'd had Jess's expert help.

Not that he'd needed it. Before he'd picked up the first piece of sandpaper, he'd watched a number of videos on the Hows and How Nots of refinishing antiques. By the time he'd begun, he'd felt surprisingly knowledgeable about the whole process.

Or he had until he'd begun the actual work. No video accurately represented how slow, grueling, and time-consuming sanding could be. Still, he'd been determined to do it and do it well.

To his surprise, sometime during the second day, he'd realized that he was enjoying himself. It wasn't just the satisfaction of working with his hands, although that was part of it. It was also because Jess kept stopping by to check on his progress. Although she'd pointedly told him that he would be working alone, she'd been there most of the time.

He wished he could say she kept returning to the shed because she couldn't keep away from him, but it was painfully obvious that she thought he needed supervision. That realization had been a blow to his ego, although he'd seen the irony of the situation, too.

Jess was every bit as focused on her motel as he'd been focused on Graham Industries. For the first time, he realized how belittling that must have felt, to be standing right there, working shoulder to shoulder, and yet your partner's attention remained fixed on the project alone. He'd never thought he could be lonely while in the company of others, but that's what he'd felt, and it had made him even more aware of what he'd put Jess through.

Evan rubbed his chest where a dull weight pressed over his heart. Every day, the weight grew, and he knew his time was running out. Friday would be here before he knew it.

Frowning, he neared the lobby, his stomach growling as the scent of fresh grass was replaced with the delicious smell of coffee. Yesterday, as he'd walked to the lobby, he'd noticed that the door nearest the office had been left open, probably by Doyle, who had a bad habit of leaving tools and ladders here and there. When Evan had reached in to close the door, he'd realized the closet not only held cleaning supplies and freshly folded towels and linens, but that it was far larger than it appeared. To one side of the door was a washer and dryer, while a workbench sat along the back wall, a pegboard hung over the top that held a number of tools.

Seeing the stacks of clean linens, Evan had taken the opportunity to go back to his room and change out his towels and sheets. To make things easier for Jess, he'd washed the old ones, returning later to fold and replace the ones he'd taken from the shelves.

He knew Jess had noticed because she'd thanked him later that day. He'd told her it was nothing, but he'd have washed and folded a thousand towels and sheet sets just to see that smile again.

Evan glanced at the closet now as he walked past it, the door securely closed. He was going to have to wash his new clothes soon as sanding was a messy business. He reached the lobby and was just getting ready to open the door when he heard a familiar deep voice behind him.

"Getting ready to belly up to the breakfast bar, are you?"

Evan turned to find Doyle standing on the sidewalk just

outside the supply closet. One of the new floor lamps from the lobby sat in front of him, listing heavily to one side.

"Good morning." Evan went back down the sidewalk to join Doyle. The handyman was wearing his usual overalls augmented by a bright red T-shirt featuring a rippling American flag, his toolbelt filled with so many tools that Evan wondered how it stayed in place. "I haven't seen you around lately."

"I've been here." Doyle squinted at the lamp, rocking it back and forth on its wobbly base.

"It looks broken," Evan offered.

Doyle's teeth flashed as he grinned. "Either that or it's as drunk as Cooter Brown." The handyman shot Evan a measuring look from under his bushy eyebrows. "How're you doing? I've seen you working around the place. Sorta wondered if you were after my job."

"Hardly. I've been helping Jess refinish some furniture."

"Sanding your way back into her heart, are you?"

"I wish," Evan said.

The old man's sharp gaze narrowed. "You don't sound too sure of yourself."

"I haven't been sure of anything for the last few weeks except that I miss her and want to be a part of her life again, but she hasn't been very encouraging. Quite the opposite, in fact." He raked a hand through his hair and sighed. "I'm trying, Doyle, but I don't think it's working."

Doyle snorted. "Trying. That's a weak word, isn't it?"

"What else should I do?"

The old man moved the tall lamp until it stood in front of Evan. "Try and pick that up."

What the heck? Evan looked at the lamp. "What do you mean 'try' and pick that up? I just—" He grabbed the lamp and lifted it.

"Exactly. Don't 'try' and make things right. Make 'em right, whatever you've got to do. It's time for actions, boy."

"We're back to the Can-Do and the Can't-Do, aren't we?" Evan said, trying not to show his frustration.

"You'd think hearing it once would be enough, but it doesn't look as if it took." Doyle shook his shaggy head. "So here you are."

Here he was, indeed. Evan wondered what it would take to show Jess he meant what he said about fixing the mistakes he'd made. *Really* meant it. Meant it with all of his heart and all of his soul. "I'm not sure what it will take."

"You'll figure it out. But let me say one thing, and you need to trust me on this. When you're old like me, you won't regret the things you *did* do near as much as you'll regret the things you *didn't* do."

Evan was struck by the sadness he saw in Doyle's bright blue eyes.

Evan's gaze dropped to the leaning lamp. It looked so out of place there, a modern if broken piece sitting on the grayed and cracked sidewalk of the old motel. It exactly represented how he felt. He sighed, rubbing his lower back where the persistent ache matched the one in his heart. "She's not making this easy. I've founded a huge company and expanded it dozens of times, but trying to reach her is way more difficult than anything I've done so far."

Doyle snorted. "Running a company is a lot simpler than talking to your wife, as there are rules and laws and such. Plus, when you're dealing with a woman and it's just you and her, you're outnumbered before you even begin."

Evan had to smile at that. "Jess is a force of nature. When I first started my company, she was right there." He remembered the long days and longer nights when they'd worked side by side for hours upon hours. "She had a thing for spreadsheets even then. She set one up for almost everything. Our accountant loved her." And so had he. Deeply and desperately. *And I still do.*

"Those early days were something else, weren't they?" Doyle lifted the lamp and turned it upside down, examining the wobbly base with an expert gaze. "Things seem simple at the beginning. Easy, even. Although the truth is, you're just too young, too excited, and too in love to know better. You just *think* the whole world is yours to conquer."

"We did conquer it. And we had it all. But somehow, like an idiot, I got distracted and stopped paying attention to our marriage. I don't know how I let that happen."

"Life'll do that all on its own. When Barbara and I were first married, we were thicker than thieves. We liked all the same things—picnics, swimming, fishing. But then, after we had kids and we both started working, we drifted apart. Once the kids moved out, we had to fight our way back to normal."

"We don't have children, not yet."

"You have a company," Doyle pointed out. "It's a distraction, just the same. That sort of thing can punch holes in the walls of your marriage. But if you get to it quick and plaster those places up, then those cracks won't reach the foundation."

"Everything is a construction metaphor to you, isn't it?"

"If it works…" Doyle shrugged.

"I suppose." Evan thought about what the handyman had said. "What if those cracks have already reached our foundation?"

"Then it'll take more than mere plaster to fix them. It'll take a bigger effort, something memorable."

"Like what? I already tried to give her jewelry and a trip to Paris, but she wouldn't have it."

"You'll have to figure that out. It was easy for me because Barbara was a romantic. She loved flowers, especially live ones." The old man's face softened. "Over the years I bet I bought her a gazillion pots of flowers. We had the prettiest front yard in town. If I'd really messed up, though, I'd do something bigger. Like maybe write her a song."

"Really?" At the old man's proud nod, Evan asked, "What do you play? Guitar? Piano?"

"The accordion. I played that thing every year at our summer family get-together."

"You must have been good."

"Oh, hell no. I was horrible." Doyle chuckled and scratched his bearded cheek. "I never learned how to play that stupid thing. Barb and I bought it at a garage sale one day on a whim, just for fun. I planned on learning how to use it but never had the time. Anyway, every summer Barb's family from Asheville, the whole lot of them, would come to Dove Pond and spend a week here. They'd stay in tents, cabins, some even stayed in this here motel back when it was open."

"A family reunion."

"Yup. They did it so the kids could all get together—cousins don't often get to see each other, you know. Anyway, that accordion had been languishing in our closet for years when, out of the blue, I heard Barbara telling everyone that I knew how to play it."

"But you didn't."

"Not even a little." Doyle chuckled. "She was a scamp, that one. Never missed a trick. She got everyone to beg me to play a song. Swore up and down that I was the best accordion player she'd ever heard. That much was probably true because I don't think she'd ever heard one in person, just on the television."

"She had a good sense of humor."

"The best. She was usually one step ahead of me, but not this time. She expected me to admit I didn't know how to play that silly thing, but I decided to make her pay." He laced his hands over his stomach and laughed, his eyes shining. "I told the whole family that she was right and I was a maestro accordion player. After dinner, I launched into the biggest bunch of grinding notes you ever heard. Just to make it authentic, I even sang a bit, screeched like an owl giving birth to a coffee table."

Evan laughed. "Ouch!"

Doyle chuckled. "You should have seen their faces. They looked as if they were all in pain, but because Barbara and I were their hosts, they acted as if they enjoyed it. It was all Barbara could do not to burst out laughing, but she managed and led the applause. Even asked for an encore."

"No one called you out on it?"

"Not a single person. Barbara's family are good people, the whole lot of them, but too polite by far. Later that night, after we were alone, Barbara and I laughed until we cried about everyone's reaction. From then on, every time her family got together, she'd suggest I bring out the accordion. It got to be too much for her relatives, though, and they started finding reasons why I shouldn't. One time, after the family weekend was over, we found that accordion hidden behind a couch in the den." The old man laughed. "Lord, the times we had, Barbara and I."

Evan looked past Doyle to the glistening water. "And then there was the day she drove poor Gertrude into the pond."

Doyle followed Evan's gaze, his smile widening. "That was during a spackling-the-walls phase. After all was said and done, it was worth it."

Evan wondered how much his and Jess's marriage was worth. *A hell of a lot.* "Thanks, Doyle. You've given me a lot to think about."

The old man's shaggy gray eyebrows rose. "If you decide you need an accordion in order to win Miss Jess back with a love song, I might have one to sell you."

Evan grinned. "I bet you do. Thanks for the advice, Doyle. Getting Jess back was feeling like an impossible task until we had this little talk. She's been throwing up walls faster than I can tear them down."

"You'll figure it out." Doyle carried the lamp into the closet, moving a pair of pliers off the old workbench before resting his project on the scarred, wooden surface. "If I were a betting man, I'd bet on you."

"You have a lot more faith in me than I do."

"Pssht. Even a blind hog can find an acorn now and then."

"Thanks," Evan said dryly.

"You're welcome. And now, if you'll excuse me, I have work to do. Meanwhile, you'd best grab you some breakfast while you can. That coffee won't stay hot forever." With a wink, the old man picked up a screwdriver and started to work.

Evan looked at the lobby. Through the window, he could see the top of Jess's head where she sat at her computer, queen of her spreadsheets. *And of me, too.*

Doyle was one hundred percent right. The crack in Evan's and Jess's relationship was deep, and it would take more than mere spackle to fix it. Now was not the time for mere words. Now was the time for action, something far bigger than sanding a few pieces of furniture.

He turned to tell Doyle goodbye, but the handyman was nowhere to be seen, the lamp abandoned on the workbench. Evan frowned and stepped into the closet, but it was empty.

How had Doyle gotten out of the closet without using the door? Evan was still standing there, trying to figure it out, when his grumbling stomach reminded him that breakfast was only a few yards away. Shrugging, Evan left the closet, closing the door behind him. *There must be another door somewhere.*

Hungry and anxious to see Jess, he headed for the lobby, Doyle and the closet forgotten.

Evan went inside, his gaze instantly locking on Jess. "Good morning."

She didn't look up from her computer. "Morning."

He noticed the stack of folders at her elbow, the ever-present row of family photos watching over her as she worked.

"Looks like it's going to be a nice day," he said.

"Uhm hm." Her fingers flew over the keyboard.

Undaunted, Evan poured himself a cup of coffee and helped himself to some breakfast. Today, there were three fresh bagels in a basket, as well as fluffy scrambled eggs, sausage, and some deliciously browned breakfast potatoes. He helped himself and sat at the table, the lone guest in a luxurious lobby.

As he ate, he watched Jess. He could just see her from the shoulders up, but even that was inspiring. Her thick black hair was pulled into a ponytail that covered the nape of her neck. He remembered how she used to love it when he kissed her there, how she would shiver and moan. An answering flash of heat raced through him, so strong that he had to bite his lip to calm his body. She was the sexiest woman he'd ever met. Then and now and forever.

Doyle's right. I have to do something big.

Evan put down his fork, pushed away his plate, picked up his coffee cup, and carried it to the counter. He tried to think of a scintillating topic to start a conversation, but nothing came. How did one begin a conversation that one wanted to end with *"we belong together"*?

Maybe he shouldn't say anything at all. Maybe he should just—

"What are you doing?"

He realized she was looking over her shoulder at him. He pointed to his cup. "I'm drinking my coffee."

Her gaze narrowed. "Right." She turned her chair to face him, crossing her arms over her chest. "You're staring."

Okay, fine. He was staring. A lot. "You're worth staring at."

"Great. What do you want?"

You. A future. Some promise that this will all work out and we'll be together forever, the way we were meant to be. "For now, I'd settle for dinner."

Her frown was instant. "That's not part of our bargain. Besides, we had dinner the first night you were here."

"But that meatloaf. I've been dreaming about it ever since and I'd like some more." Which was a lie. Not that the meatloaf wasn't terrific. It had been. But meatloaf wasn't his goal. "To be honest, I'm tired of having pizza by myself every single night. How about we go back to the café this evening? I know it's not meatloaf night, but I expect there will be something equally tasty on that menu."

She was tempted. He saw it in her eyes, in the way her gaze flickered past him to her truck, as if she were asking herself what could possibly go wrong. Whatever "wrong" was, she apparently figured it out, because her eyes held a hint of regret as she said, "I can't, but you're welcome to borrow the truck if you want."

He tried again. "It's more than dinner. I would like to get to know Dove Pond better. Why don't you show me around and explain why you love it here so much." He shrugged. "Maybe then I'd understand what makes this place better than Atlanta."

She eyed him suspiciously. "You don't like small towns."

"Which is why I'm curious about what makes this one so special. That was your word, by the way—'special.'"

She eyed him for a long moment, and then shook her head. "You've only got two more days here and then you're leaving. I'm sorry, Evan, but I don't have time to be your tour guide." She turned her chair back toward the computer and was soon working again.

Evan found himself staring at the back of her head, at the silken shine of her hair, and the delicate line of her neck. Somewhere in the back of his mind, he heard Doyle saying, *Don't try. Do.*

Fine. He'd do, then. "So...I should be done with that dresser and the two nightstands today. They're ready to stain."

She didn't even look up. "And?"

"And I noticed that there was another dresser in the shed. A large one. An ornate one. One with tons of tiny wooden embellishments."

She froze in her seat, her fingers still over the keyboard as she stared straight ahead. "So?"

At least she was listening to him. That was a start. "So maybe I could be convinced to refinish it, too."

She slowly turned her chair back in his direction, her gaze suspicious. "It's a complex piece."

"I noticed that. There are more carved angels on that dresser than the Vatican."

"It's for *Ti Adoro*, the Italian-themed room."

Ti Adoro. The words meant "I adore you" in Italian. He found himself remembering a trip from long ago. The day after he'd signed the papers for his first merger, he and Jess had taken a celebratory trip to Italy. It was their fourth anniversary and Italy had been a dream destination for both of them. At the time, Evan had been working so many fifteen-hour days trying to close the deal that he'd slept through most of their first day. But after that, he'd thrown himself into their vacation.

The next two days had been perfect. They'd stayed at a villa on the outskirts of Florence and had spent two glorious days wandering hand in hand through cobblestone streets savoring perfectly made gelato and shopping in luxury shops. That part of the trip might have been perfect, but the very next day, he'd gotten a call from work about a late complication that threatened to derail the entire merger. He'd tried to handle it by phone, fielding dozens of calls and sending email after email, but eventually he was forced to admit that he needed to address the issue in person. So he'd flown home early, leaving Jess behind.

He'd hoped to return a day or two later but although he'd resolved the biggest issue, he didn't trust the situation enough to leave again. To make up for his absence, he'd offered to fly Jess's sisters to join her, but neither of them had been able to make it. As a result, Jess had ended up staying in Italy by herself for the rest of their vacation. *How did I ever think that was okay?*

"Evan?"

He blinked, yanking his mind back to the present. "Sorry. I was just thinking about our Italy trip."

Her eyes darkened. "The best two days of my life, followed by the worst five days."

He winced. "I meant to come right back, but the deal—"

"Right, right. It was in danger. You had to save it. I'll think about your offer to do the other dresser. Thanks." She turned back to her computer.

He was left staring at the back of her head again, feeling as low as a dead ant. *The cracks in this foundation are deep, damn it. And I made every one of them.* "Jess, let me do this. I've gotten pretty good at sanding. You've seen that."

She sighed and tilted her head back. He suspected she was staring at the ceiling and mouthing *"Just go away!"* or something equally disheartening.

"So," he continued doggedly, "I'll do that other dresser. It's the least I can do to thank you for putting up with me this week."

She pushed herself away from the computer and stood, looking none too pleased. "I appreciate the offer, but there's no need for this. You did great work on the other pieces of furniture—"

"And enjoyed every minute." At her obvious disbelief, he said, "It was nice to fix something with my own two hands. Something more immediate and touchable than a company report."

His answer seemed to surprise her. "You enjoyed it?"

"My back is a bit sore, and I have splinters where I shouldn't. Plus I'm pretty sure the FBI will never be able to get decent fingerprints from me, should the need arise, but it was fun."

Her lips quirked. "Really?"

"Really." He crossed his arms and leaned against the counter. "*Ti Adoro* was the name of the villa we rented in Italy. I may have messed up that trip, but I'm not going to mess up this dresser." *Or us, ever again.*

"Evan, I—"

"You'll see. It'll be perfect. Just like the bureau and the night stands I did yesterday. You have to admit my work has far surpassed your expectations."

The line of her mouth softened yet more. "You did a good job on those."

"Good?" he scoffed. "They were flawless. Picture-perfect. Immaculate—"

She burst into laughter, her eyes sparkling with humor. "Easy there. It wasn't brain surgery."

His soul flew at the sound of her laughter, and he wondered if he could fill the cracks in their relationship with laughter and new memories. *Maybe. Just maybe.*

At least now he understood what Doyle had meant about doing and not just trying. Jess didn't need to hear any more platitudes or promises. What she needed was proof that Evan was serious about making their marriage his main focus, something he should have done long ago.

He leaned against the counter, his smile answering hers. "Let me finish the dresser that's left. You might as well. I'm right here, and I'm bored to death."

"Don't you have phone calls to make, important meetings to call into, contracts to review—stuff like that?"

"I did, but not now." With one elbow still on the counter, he pulled out his phone, found his draft email to Ashley, and hit *send.* "There. I'm off."

Jess's eyebrows rose. "Off what? Your rocker?"

"Off work. I'm officially on vacation. And not just for one day, either. I took the rest of the week off."

"You did not."

"I did. I told Ashley to handle any problems that might come up because I wouldn't be available until Monday. Here, look." He held up his phone so Jess could see the screen.

She read the email and her eyes widened. "That's the most un-Evan Graham thing you've ever done. Ash must be wondering if you've hit your head or have been inhabited by aliens."

"New day, new play. So..." He closed his email and put his phone face down on the counter. "After I apply the stain—"

"And wax."

"—and wax to the furniture I sanded and cleaned yesterday, shall I start on that dresser? I still have fingerprints on my left hand, and my right hand is getting jealous."

Her lips quirked. "Symmetry *is* important."

"It's my life." He returned her smile, drinking in the shimmer of humor in her eyes as if it were his favorite bourbon. *Thank you, Doyle.*

"So?" Evan rubbed his hands together. "Shall we get to it? That dresser won't sand itself."

"We? I thought you were going to do the work."

"I can still use your expert advice. I'm good, but let's be honest, you know more about this than I do. Dozens of YouTube videos can't replace in-person expertise."

"You've watched dozens of YouTube videos? I only sent you four."

"Need I remind you that there's no cable in my room? I get bored late at night, so—" He shrugged.

She glanced from him back to her desk where her folders waited. "I'd help, but there are a ton of things on my To Do List today, and the computer work is just part of it."

"What's on your list?"

She reached behind her and picked up a notepad. "Rake the flowerbeds, paint the kayak stand, fix the loose boards on the dock—" She wrinkled her nose. "Too many things."

"I can help with those too. Or I can if you'll give me permission to leave the shed now and then."

"You don't need my permission to leave the shed. You're not chained there."

"Not physically, no," he agreed, flashing her a grin. "But emotionally, I fear I've become attached to your antique dressers. I'm probably just suffering from Stockholm syndrome, but still."

Her lips twitched as she held back a smile, and her gaze moved over him.

He could feel her taking his measure, and he tried to keep his expression calm. He was glad she didn't know how just the touch of her gaze could send his pulse galloping like a wild horse.

Finally, she shrugged. "I guess it can't hurt. I really could use the help."

"It's a big job, what you're doing here, but it's going to be worth it." He straightened. "I'm off to the shed. I'll get the stain and wax ready."

"We'll need some rags. They're in the white cabinet in the back of the shed."

"Got it." He collected his coffee cup and was backing toward the door. "See you in a few." And with that, he pushed the door open and headed out into the sunlit parking lot.

It was all he could do not to give a tell-tale fist pump as he hurried to the shed.

6

JESS

*J*ess leaned on the broom she'd been using to sweep the sidewalk and shaded her eyes against the late afternoon sun. It was one of those unusually warm April days that felt more like June, which she loved.

Time was flying by. It was already Thursday, which meant that Evan would be leaving in the morning. *It's been a whole week,* she realized with both surprise and bittersweet regret. *A whole week.* It felt as if he'd been there all along, but it also felt as if he'd just arrived.

He makes me so confused. He was just outside the shed, waxing the old dresser she'd bought for the Italian-themed room, bringing the newly stained wood to a soft, warm sheen.

She had to admit that he'd done an exceptional job on the furniture, and now she could check those boxes off her To Do List. But it was more than the furniture. Over the last few days, Evan had been super helpful with other projects too, giving the kayak stand a fresh coat of yellow paint, repairing a few loose boards on the dock, and other things, as well, some that weren't even on her list. She'd woken up just this morning to find him pulling weeds from the parking lot.

He claimed he was just helping out to keep from being bored, but they both knew that wasn't true. Every once in a while, when she least expected it, she'd look up and catch him watching her with a dark, brooding, almost possessive gaze that made her tingle from head to toe.

How she used to love that man. And still did, of course. *But it's different now,* she reminded herself.

Isn't it?

She watched as he applied the last of the wax to the dresser and wondered at the changes she'd seen in him this past week. For one, he was no longer obsessively checking his phone. Last night, he'd even accidentally left it in the shed when they'd ordered takeout from the Moonlight for dinner. He hadn't realized it was gone until hours later when they were saying goodnight.

She'd never thought she'd see that. For once, he'd been true to his word about leaving the office behind. As far as she could tell, he hadn't called Ashley one time since he'd sent her that email.

Working with Evan this week had made Jess remember so many things she'd forgotten. Like how funny he could be, when he wasn't obsessing over work. They'd spent an hour last night laughing at—of all things—the wretched on-campus apartment they'd lived in when they'd first gotten married. The bed had been so small that Evan's feet had hung over the bottom, and when he'd turned over at night, which happened often as he was a restless sleeper, he'd sometimes kick the set of drawers that sat at the end of the bed. The room was as small as the bed so they couldn't move the dresser out of the way, and so his poor toes had stayed bruised for the better part of a year.

It had been such a long time since they'd shared laughter and memories that it felt both familiar and fresh at one and the same time.

Evan put down his wax rag and squinted at the dresser, the

sunlight shimmering on the surface. She could tell from his expression that he was proud of his work. He tilted his head to one side and then bent to buff out a spot he'd apparently just noticed. When he straightened back up, he swiped at his brow with the back of his hand, leaving a long smudge of dark wax in its wake.

She grinned but had to admit that even with his beginning-of-a-beard and his dark hair falling over his brow, he looked good.

Really good.

Too good.

He glanced up, his expression brightening when he caught her looking his way.

She forced a smile. "You did a great job on that dresser," she called.

"*We* did a great job." His gaze traveled over her, making her feel as if she were wearing her killer red dress instead of her usual jeans and T-shirt.

His deep voice filled the parking lot. "Pure perfection, Jess."

He wasn't talking about the dresser, but she refused to acknowledge it. Glad he was too far away to know his compliment had made her flush, she called out, "You have a smudge…" She pointed to her forehead.

He swiped at his forehead with his arm, frowning at the dirt he saw. He dropped the rag into the bucket. "I'll be right back." And with that, he pulled his shirt off and headed for the pond.

Oh dear. Oh dear. Oh dear. She was assailed with memory after memory of curling around those rock-hard abs, of being pulled against him, beneath him and—

Stop it. Rhino, rhino, rhino! I can't—oh God, he's taking off his—

He tossed his jeans on the dock and, dressed only in his briefs, executed a perfect dive off the end of the dock.

Wow. Just wow.

She wet her suddenly dry lips as she watched him swimming back and forth in front of the dock, his muscled arms shimmering as they carved through water. It was hot out here in the sun, more so now that she was watching him, but she bet that pond was icy, at best.

"Lord love me, but I've died and gone to heaven."

Startled, Jess turned to find Flora standing behind her on the sidewalk, holding a large flower arrangement.

Flora's gaze was locked on Evan. "I don't know about you, but that just made my day. Maybe my week, too. Hell, it might have made this year the best year I've ever had."

Jess didn't know what to say. "I didn't hear you pull in. I—I was just thinking about work and stuff."

"And stuff, huh?" Flora nodded at Evan swimming by the dock. "I'd like some stuff like that of my own."

They both watched him swim.

Flora sighed. "My oh my, but he's easy on the eyes, isn't he?"

Yes. Yes, he was.

"If I didn't have three more deliveries today, I'd say we pull up some chairs, crack open some cold ones, and watch a bit. But sadly, I'm too busy for more than a quick peek."

Jess tore her gaze from Evan and turned so that her back was to the water. "Is that the new flower arrangement?"

Flora beamed and held it up for Jess to see. "The holder is wider and lower than the last, which let me put more flowers on display. I think it'll fill that table in the entry better than the round one."

Jess touched one of the deep blue flowers. "Flora, you've outdone yourself. I love it."

"Me too." Flora carried the flower arrangement past Jess and walked toward the lobby. "Let's see how it looks in place."

Jess had to fight the urge to glance at the pond as they went inside.

Flora moved the old arrangement and centered the new one on the table. "Just as I thought. This is much better."

Jess shook her head in wonder. "Every time you bring an arrangement, I think it's perfect, but then you bring a bigger, better one."

"You have to see them in place to know what will work." Flora tilted her head this way and that. "Looks like we finally found the right one. It doesn't get any better than this."

Jess wondered if "seeing them in place" only worked with flowers. Maybe Evan seemed different because he was here, in Dove Pond, cut off from the corporate rat race he was so addicted to. *I'm different here than I am in Atlanta, where I felt so lost and alone. And I want to stay in Dove Pond, to be the person I've become here, but Evan won't.* She appreciated that he'd taken a break from his work, something he should have done long ago. But that was temporary. Which meant that they, and this little truce they'd been enjoying, were temporary, too.

"Honey, you're not going to cry, are you?"

"No," Jess choked out. She pulled a tissue from the box near the counter and dabbed at the tears that had filled her eyes. "I'm sorry. I don't know what's gotten into me."

Flora snorted. "You know exactly what's gotten into you. And don't tell me it doesn't have anything to do with Adonis out there, swimming laps by your dock, because then I'd have to call you a bald-faced liar."

Jess sighed. "I'm confused, that's all."

"Confused by a handsome hunk. Where have I seen that story before?" Flora tapped her chin. "Oh wait. *Everywhere*, that's where I've seen that story before."

Jess had to laugh, glad for the chance to erase a little of her sadness. "It's an old story, isn't it?"

"Older than us." Flora cocked an eyebrow at Jess. "I take it that's the ex you told me about." At Jess's nod, Flora said, "He must want another chance. Otherwise, he wouldn't be here."

"Yes, but I don't know if I can do it. When it was good, it was really good. Better than good, to be honest. But then he threw himself into his work and our marriage disappeared." Trying to control her tears, Jess absently touched one of the verbenas in the flower arrangement. "I don't want to repeat my mistakes, but I also don't want to miss out if things could—maybe, possibly—get better."

"You're hoping."

"I am, and that scares me. It was hard, leaving Evan. Our lives were so tangled, my sense of worth so tied up in us as a couple, that when the time came to go, I felt as if I had to leave a part of myself behind. I loved him, Flora. I still do."

Flora's gaze softened. "So what's making you so sad? He's here, isn't he?"

"For now. We used to be partners in every sense of the word. I want that back, but I don't want it to cost so much this time. I wonder if he can do that. Heck, I don't even know if he's *willing* to do that."

"Men," Flora said, shaking her head. "Biggest pains in the ass I've ever known, and yet there are times, and certain men, who are worth it. That's what you have to figure out, Miss Jess. Whether this particular one is worth taking another chance on."

"I've been asking myself that same question for a week now and I just don't know."

Flora snorted. "You know. You just haven't told yourself yet."

"You think so?"

"I do. There will come a moment when you'll realize what that decision is. You just have to wait for the switch to flip."

"I hope you're right. He's leaving tomorrow, and he's going to want an answer. What if I don't realize what I want until after he's gone?"

"If he's such a sorry piece of work that he bails after one lousy week, well then, you won't have to spend any more time worrying about him, will you?"

"I guess not." *If only it was that easy*, Jess thought. "Thanks for listening, Flora."

"My pleasure. I—oops, gotta go. I've got another arrangement to deliver before five. But you call me if you need to talk more, okay?"

"I will. Thank you."

"Don't think about it. I'm off. Flowers wait for no one." Flora headed for the door.

Jess followed, walking Flora to her van. "Once I open, I'll need one arrangement a week, plus a smaller arrangement for the breakfast buffet."

"You got it." Flora opened her door and looked past Jess to the pond. The older woman pouted. "Looks like Eros has left the water. Call me if he decides to sunbathe naked, will you?"

Jess laughed. "Will do."

"Great. I'll bring a pitcher of my secret sauce and we'll make a day of it." She winked at Jess and climbed into the van.

Jess watched Flora leave and then turned and looked at the pond. The late afternoon sun cast long, golden fingers through the trees and across the sparkling water. Evan's jeans and T-shirt were gone, so she supposed he was in his room, probably taking a shower and getting ready for dinner.

She glanced at the lowering sun. By this time tomorrow, Evan and his repaired Jaguar would be back in Atlanta, and she'd be here alone.

Suddenly, the air felt chillier, the world a little duller, her heart a lot heavier.

What could she do? She couldn't leave The Last Chance Motel. She'd invested her time and heart in this place. She looked around, seeing the motel as it would be—charming, fun, and memorable. A place she would be deeply proud of. If she closed her eyes now, she could hear the excited exclamations from the guests as they saw their rooms for the first time, and the delighted murmur of dozens of conversations as families shared joyous moments. She could see the smiles of happy couples walking hand in hand to the dock where they'd enjoy late afternoon snacks as they dipped their feet in the cool, fresh water.

And all of that would happen because of her vision and her hard work. She couldn't leave here. She'd be miserable if she did. Evan was just going to have to accept that it was her turn to follow her dreams.

And if he couldn't? Flora was right about that; at least then Jess wouldn't be sitting around, weighed down by her own doubts.

She turned to walk back to the lobby but stopped when she noticed the door to Room Two stood partially open. She frowned. She'd been in there only a few hours ago and could have sworn that she'd locked the door as she'd left.

"I must be going crazy," she muttered under her breath and headed for the room.

Before locking the door again, she took a few steps inside to make sure everything was okay. She called this room The French Connection and so far it was her favorite. It needed a more romantic name, one that matched the deluxe brocade pillows and duvet; the luxuriously carved headboard; and the heavy, cream-colored linen curtains, but for now The French Connection it was.

Nothing seemed amiss as she ran her hand over the ornate cherry bureau and bedside tables. She'd gotten them from a dealer, although the ones Evan had just refinished were now every bit as nice.

He'd done an amazing job, and she was grateful. Better yet, he hadn't once tried to Evan his way into taking over. That was different, too.

Maybe, just maybe, there was hope.

Still musing, she'd just started to leave when she heard an odd *drip-drip-drip.*

She stopped and looked at the bathroom door. That sounded like a leak. But surely not. The entire plumbing system was new.

She went into the bathroom, the dripping sound louder. She turned on the light and glanced at the freestanding soaking tub, but no water dripped from the brushed chrome faucet. She rested her hand on the cool Carrara marble countertop and bent to see if perhaps the dripping came from the sink faucet, but again, everything was dry. She opened the cabinet beneath to see if anything was amiss there, but everything looked the way it should.

That left the heavy glass-encased shower. She opened the door and there was the source of the annoying noise. "For the love of—" She stepped inside and reached for the handle, twisting it firmly.

The dripping continued.

She frowned and tried the handle again. Surely if she twisted it hard enough, the water would st—

Clank! The handle came off in her hand.

She stared at it, surprised, when—*whoosh!*—water gushed into her face. Icy cold water pummeled her, stinging like needles. Unable to see or breathe, she stumbled backward, falling blindly—

Strong hands lifted her out of the gushing water and set her on the bathroom floor. She dropped the handle, and it clanked to the floor as she wiped her face with both hands, still gasping for air as she tried to clear her vision.

"Are you okay?" Evan asked over the sound of flowing water.

"I'm fine. Just angry at my plumber." She shoved her wet hair from her face and blinked hazily at him. Evan stood in front of her, his T-shirt splotched with water from where he'd lifted her out of the shower.

At least he was dressed, she told herself, ignoring a flicker of disappointment. "I need a pair of pliers to turn this off." She looked down at her soaked tennis shoes and jeans.

He handed her a towel. "I know where the pliers are. I saw them earlier."

He was gone before she could reply. Muttering to herself, she dried off as much as she could. When the towel grew wet, she dropped it on the floor and then grabbed an extra one from the rack. Nothing was going to completely dry her soaked T-shirt, which was plastered to her like plastic wrap, but at least water was no longer dripping off her elbows.

She pulled her ponytail holder free and had just towel-dried her hair when Evan reappeared in the doorway, holding the pliers. She tossed her towel onto the counter and held out her hand.

"I'll do it." He started for the shower but then stopped and sent her a sheepish look. "I mean, I will if you want me to."

She plucked the pliers from his hand. "I'm already soaked. It might as well be me."

He stepped out of her way. "It's your motel."

"I'm going to kill the plumber who screwed this up." She grasped the pliers firmly, straightened her shoulders, and went back into the shower. This time, she stayed to one side of the icy spray, so she could see what she was doing. It took her several tries to turn the valve stem, but eventually she managed to twist it to the off position.

Just as quickly as it started, the gushing water stopped.

Victory! Jess came back out of the shower and looked down at her newly sopping-wet clothes.

"That was something. Where did you learn about the parts of a shower—oh. Let me guess. YouTube." He shook his head. "You and your videos."

"I have a book on home repair too." She took off her tennis

shoes and drained them in the sink. "Every night, I read a few pages."

"Really?"

"It helps me sleep." She put her shoes on the mat and then grabbed a dry towel from the stack under the sink and tried to sop up some of the water dripping from her newly drenched clothes.

"You're soaked," Evan said.

"It's nothing that a hot bath and a slice of pizza won't fix."

"Pizza and a hot bath. Now you're just teasing me."

She grinned. "I hope the water doesn't ruin your Princess Elsa T-shirt." Every day this week, he'd shown up with yet another Disney T-shirt he'd bought from his Target trip. She rather liked them.

He looked down at his shirt, which was overlaid with her wet imprint, and claimed a towel for himself. "Fortunately for us both, it was cold water and not hot, so the color shouldn't fade." He made a show of delicately patting his T-shirt as if afraid to ruin it.

She had to laugh. "You sound as if you plan on keeping those shirts."

"I've become a fan. I mean, how can you not love Elsa?" He tossed his towel onto the counter and broke into such a screechy falsetto rendition of *Let It Go* that she burst out laughing.

His gaze met hers, and suddenly, their shared humor disappeared. Left in its place was a raw, powerful emotion that made her heart thud wildly.

She couldn't look away from him.

But what was even more amazing was that she didn't want to.

She wanted to be here, with him, in this moment.

An instant, slow warmth formed in the pit of her stomach, fighting the chill made by her wet clothes.

His gaze darkened, his chest moving rapidly. "Jess?" His voice was deep and ragged.

She didn't answer. Instead, she dropped her towel and stepped into his arms, pulling his mouth to hers.

Evan kissed her deeply, his searching hands molding her soft curves to his hard planes.

She opened her mouth under his and, desperate for more of him, tugged at his shirt, pulling it up, sliding her hands up his back—

"*Argh!*" He stepped back, laughing. "Good lord, your hands are *cold!*"

"Are they?" Jess grinned and grabbed the front of his shirt, trying to slip her hand up his stomach as he backed out of the bathroom and into the motel room.

Laughing, he stopped beside the bed, grabbed her wrists and wrapped her hands behind her back, pulling her wet body flush against his. "We need to get you warm."

"That would be nice," she admitted. There was a bed right beside them that was piled high with blankets.

She knew it.

He knew it.

All that had to happen was for someone to mention it.

Jess leaned against him. "Maybe we could—"

His phone rang.

His gaze, so locked with hers, never moved.

She expected him to react as he'd done for the last few days whenever his phone rang—ignore it completely.

But instead he slowly, reluctantly released her. "Sorry, Jess. I need to take this one." He went to collect a towel from the bathroom counter and dried his hands. Returning to the bedroom, he tossed the towel over his shoulder, and pulled out his phone.

And there they were, back to where they'd started.

Disappointment flowed through her, bitter and sad, hitting her harder than the icy, gushing water.

She'd really thought things had changed. She'd *believed* things were different, that he was more committed to their relationship, and less obsessed with his work. The pain of her disappointment told her how much she'd wanted that to be true, for him to be the Evan she'd married and not just the President of Graham Industries.

Her expression must have been telling because he lowered the phone, the ringing loud in the small room. "Jess, don't. It's not like that."

"Answer your phone." She went to the bathroom, collected her wet shoes, and then returned. "I'm going back to my apartment. Your car will be ready in the morning and you can leave then. I'm—"

She was enveloped in his towel and then swept up into his arms, her shoes falling to the floor. "Evan! What are you doing?"

"Explaining something." He carried her to the bed, sat down, and settled her in his lap, his phone finally stopping its insistent ringing. Evan's dark blue eyes were deeply serious. "Jess, that's Brad."

"Brad?" Then it wasn't work. Relief flooded through her. She relaxed, a tiny bit of her hurt melting away. "You've patched things up with him."

"You said I should, so I did. I must have called him twenty times, and last night, he finally answered. We talked for a long time." Evan grimaced. "It was awkward because he told me a lot of stuff I knew but didn't want to hear."

That was something, she supposed. It was warm here on his lap, wrapped in a towel. Perhaps she'd stay another minute. "I'm glad you're talking to him again."

"So am I." Evan's expression couldn't have been more solemn. "Jess, Brad wasn't calling to just say hello. He was calling because I offered him a job. And I'm pretty sure he's going to say yes."

"Doesn't Ashley have Brad's old job?"

"She does. But I didn't ask Brad to be VP. I offered him the job of president."

Jess opened her mouth and then closed it. She had to blink three times before she could speak again. "You offered Brad the job of President of Graham Industries?"

"And CEO. The whole package."

"But...that's your job."

His smile was soft, endearing. "*Was* my job."

"You're leaving the company?"

"I'll still be around if there's an issue, but I doubt there will be many. I'm leaving the company in capable hands. Brad and Ashley know what they're doing, and so do the others."

Jess blinked at Evan. She couldn't imagine him without the company. But then she realized she'd seen what he was like without it these last few days, and he'd laughed more, talked more, and had *been* more.

Oh wow. He *had* changed. He'd changed a lot. "That's huge."

"It is. But it's worth it." His eyes darkened. "*You're* worth it."

Her face heated and her heart, which had felt so very heavy, was suddenly lighter than air. "That's...I don't know what to say." She pushed aside the towel and, wanting to touch him, used one finger to absently trace one of Elsa's eyes. "What will you do now?"

"We need to talk about that." He gently tugged the towel so that it came together under her chin. "The reason I got so caught up in running the company was because, once things were running smoothly, the only challenge left was making it grow."

"Which you did."

"Maybe too much." He grimaced. "One of the painful truths Brad laid on me last night, and one of the reasons he left, was that I was taking too many risks."

"Were you?"

"It's possible."

"Possible?"

Evan winced and then gave a wry laugh. "Fine. It was true. It wouldn't have made me so mad if it hadn't been. This obsession I have is hurting the company, the people I work with—everyone, but especially you." His gaze met hers, his blue eyes shiny with emotion. "Jess, I'm so sorry. I shouldn't have let that happen."

She put her hands on each side of his face. "I don't want to hear the word 'sorry' again. You're fixing things. That's all that matters."

He captured one of her hands and turned his face to place a warm kiss in her palm. "Right now, I only know one thing. Whatever I do from here on out, I'm going to do it here, close to you."

She wanted to say *I'd love that,* but her emotions had closed her throat too tightly for mere words.

His gaze darkened. "I'm not asking you to make a decision this second. I know I still need to prove myself. But I want a better marriage for us, Jess. A better life." He pulled her against his chest and rested his cheek against her wet hair. "That's what I want. For both of us."

He meant what he said. He really and truly meant it.

In that moment, sitting in his lap, his heartbeat steady against her cheek, something moved in her heart, clicking into place as if it had always belonged there.

She wanted this marriage to work. He was making changes, big ones. It was time she did the same. "Let's do this."

He looked down at her. "This?"

There was so much hope in that word that she found herself smiling. "Our relationship. Let's try it again. I can't promise it'll work, but I want to give it a go and maybe we'll—"

He gave a huge war whoop and stood, taking her with him as he swung her wildly around the room.

Laughing, she slipped her arms around him and buried her

face against his neck. She had missed this, missed him, for so, so long. But now she felt as if she were home.

He sighed happily and set her back on her feet, leaving his arms around her. "We're going to make this work. I promise. But Jess, you have to tell me what you want. No more just being nice."

"I'll do my best." She thought about it for a moment and then said, "I don't want to go too fast."

"We'll go slow. We'll move like snails if that's what you want. We should build our foundation solidly and keep the walls spackled."

"What?"

He shook his head impatiently. "A metaphor, nothing more. What else do you want?"

"We shouldn't move back in together until we know things are going to be okay."

He groaned, his hands moving up and down her back. "Fine, fine. I was afraid you'd say that. But I understand."

She placed her hand flat on his chest, enjoying the simple contact. "Also, I want to date. Really date. I want movies and dinners out and—I don't know, maybe even board games."

He laughed. "Done. Done. And done." He bent and kissed her, long and lingering. When he finished, they clung to each other, smiling like loons.

But after a moment, his smile faded, and he cupped her face, his gaze searching. "Whatever you want, Jess, I'll do. I just have one request."

Her heart tightened. "What's that?"

"Please, *please* let me move to this room. That warped bed in Room Ten is killing my back."

She had to laugh. "You got it." And with that, she lifted up on her toes, slipped her arms around his neck, and kissed him once more.

She loved him. She'd always loved him.

And now they could move forward in their lives together, as a couple should.

Happiness, which had seemed so far away a week ago, was here, in this room, within the arms of the man she'd fallen in love with those many years ago.

EPILOGUE
DOYLE

*T*wo months and two days later, their bare toes lightly touching the cool water, Doyle and Barbara sat together on a long, low branch of a huge oak tree that hung over the bank of Dove Pond. To a passer-by, who couldn't see either them or their toes, it would appear as if tiny fish were tapping the water's surface from below, causing small rings to ripple over the glassy surface.

Just down from that huge oak, Evan spread out a picnic blanket near the dock, the scent of fried chicken rising through the air. Jess stood nearby with their basket of food, giving him orders. In the early evening quiet, their laughter rang across the water, lingering in the warm summer air.

"Look at them," Doyle said smugly from his perch, his arm around Barbara. "Another perfectly executed mission."

She sent him a sharp side glance. "You almost drowned my poor niece in her own shower!"

"I wanted to remind her that disasters aren't so tough when you've got a little help."

Barbara snorted. "You just have a thing for water."

"Maybe." He hugged her. "And maybe I was making the point

that even death is bearable if you share it with the right woman."

"Oh shush." But Barbara's cheeks were now flushed a beautiful pink. "You're still in trouble. We're no longer among the living, and we're not supposed to talk to those who are."

"I like talking to people. It's the best way to convince them they're being foolish. Besides, Evan enjoyed my pep talks."

She rolled her eyes. "Yes, well, next time stick to the rules. Having that car break down as he reached town was a smart move. Even the shower mishap turned out well. But when you show yourself, you cause problems. That poor boy thought he was going crazy once he saw that picture of you on Jess's desk, and she told him you were her uncle, and had been dead for years."

"He recovered, didn't he? Look at him over there. He's happy as a clam."

"But now The Powers That Be are threatening to pull you off Romance and put you on Redemption." She cut him a warning look. "You won't like Redemption, Doyle. It's dry, dull work."

"But I like Romance. I'm good at it, too. Just look at them."

"Then you'd best be toeing the line with your next assignment."

"Yes, ma'am," he said meekly.

She shook her head, mumbling "old fool" under her breath the way only Barbara could.

A pair of ducks quacked loudly as they flew low across the pond and landed near the dock just as Evan sat down on the blanket, pulling Jess with him. Their laughter was silenced with a kiss. The two were so lost in their embrace that their basket of food sat forgotten.

Doyle watched for a moment and then, restless, said in a grumpy voice, "That ice cream is going to melt and then their basket will be a mess."

"It'll be worth it," Barbara said, smiling softly. "Jess is a good kid."

"So is that boy. I wish you'd seen his face while they were towing his car away." Doyle sighed heavily. "I know the pain of losing a good car."

Barbara's smile disappeared and she sent him a sour glance. "That was a complete and utter lie. *You* forgot to set that parking brake, not me."

"I set the brake," he protested. "It was broken or something."

"Or something," she said with obvious disbelief.

Doyle chuckled and pulled Barbara closer.

She leaned against him, her gaze moving back to the couple on the blanket. "I think they're going to be okay, the two of them."

Doyle agreed. "He's starting a new company."

"Oh no!"

"It'll be all right. He's going to do market consulting for small businesses, the kind that are growing in Dove Pond."

"Mom and Pop shops," Barbara said. "I love those. They'll benefit from his vision and experience."

"He's promised to keep it simple, nothing too big. He doesn't need the money and wants to keep his time open so he can keep having picnics like this one. Jess is excited about it."

"If she's happy, then he'll be happy."

"Happy wife, happy life." Doyle rested his cheek against Barbara's soft hair and smiled. Sometimes the biggest truths in life were also the simplest.

DISCOVER MORE BY SUZANNE ENOCH

No Ordinary Hero
Hero in the Highlands
My One True Highlander
A Devil in Scotland

Wild Wicked Highlanders
It's Getting Scot in Here
Scot Under the Covers

Traditional Regencies
The Black Duke's Prize
Angel's Devil

Regency Historicals
Lady Rogue
Stolen Kisses

The Bancroft Brothers
By Love Undone
Taming Rafe

With This Ring
Reforming a Rake
Meet Me at Midnight
A Matter of Scandal

Lessons in Love

The Rake

London's Perfect Scoundrel

England's Perfect Hero

Anthologies

One True Love (from The Further Observations of Lady Whistledown)

A Touch of Scandal (from Lady Whistledown Strikes Back)

The Griffin Family

Sin and Sensibility

An Invitation to Sin

Something Sinful

Sins of a Duke

Contemporary Romantic Suspense

Flirting with Danger

Don't Look Down

Billionaires Prefer Blondes

Twice the Temptation (half historical, half contemporary)

A Touch of Minx

Barefoot in the Dark

The Notorious Gentlemen

After the Kiss

Before the Scandal

Always a Scoundrel

The Adventurers' Club

The Care and Taming of a Rogue

A Lady's Guide to Improper Behavior

Rules of an Engagement

The Scandalous Brides

A Beginner's Guide to Rakes

Taming an Impossible Rogue

Rules to Catch a Devilish Duke

The Handbook to Handling His Lordship

Standalone Short Stories

Good Earl Hunting

The Scandalous Highlanders

One Hot Scot (a short story)

The Devil Wears Kilts

Rogue with a Brogue

Mad, Bad and Dangerous in Plaid

Some Like it Scot

DISCOVER MORE BY MOLLY HARPER

The Southern Eclectic Series

(contemporary women's fiction)

Save a Truck, Ride a Redneck (prequel novella)

Sweet Tea and Sympathy

Peachy Flippin' Keen (novella)

Ain't She a Peach?

Gimme Some Sugar

The Mystic Bayou Series

(paranormal romance)

How to Date Your Dragon

Love and Other Wild Things

Even Tree Nymphs Get the Blues

Selkies Are a Girl's Best Friend

Always Be My Banshee

The "Sorcery and Society" Series

(young adult fantasy)

Changeling

Fledgling

The "Nice Girls" Series

(paranormal romance)

Nice Girls Don't Have Fangs

Nice Girls Don't Date Dead Men

Nice Girls Don't Live Forever

Nice Girls Don't Bite Their Neighbors

Half-Moon Hollow Series

(paranormal romance)

The Care and Feeding of Stray Vampires

Driving Mr. Dead

Undead Sublet (A story in The Undead in My Bed anthology)

A Witch's Handbook of Kisses and Curses

I'm Dreaming of an Undead Christmas

The Dangers of Dating a Rebound Vampire

The Single Undead Moms Club

Fangs for the Memories

Where the Wild Things Bite

Big Vamp on Campus

Accidental Sire

Peace, Blood and Understanding

Nice Werewolves Don't Bite Vampires

The "Naked Werewolf" Series

(paranormal romance)

How to Flirt with a Naked Werewolf

The Art of Seducing a Naked Werewolf

How to Run with a Naked Werewolf

The "Bluegrass" Series

(contemporary romance)

My Bluegrass Baby

Rhythm and Bluegrass

Snow Falling on Bluegrass

Standalone Titles

And One Last Thing

Better Homes and Hauntings

DISCOVER MORE BY KAREN HAWKINS

The Dove Pond NC Series

The Book Charmer

A Cup of Silver Linings

Love in the Afternoon

Made to Marry Series

Caught by the Scot

The Oxenburg Princes Series

The Prince Who Loved Me

The Prince and I

The Princess Wore Plaid (novella)

Mad for the Plaid

Twelve Kisses to Midnight

The Duchess Diaries Series

How to Capture a Countess

How to Pursue a Princess

How to Entice an Enchantress

Princess in Disguise (novella)

The Wicked Widows Short Stories

The Lady in the Tower

The Lucky One

The Hurst Amulet Series

One Night in Scotland

Scandal in Scotland

A Most Dangerous Profession

The Taming of a Scottish Princess

The Maclean Curse Series

How to Abduct a Highland Lord

To Scotland, With Love

To Catch a Highlander

Sleepless in Scotland

The Laird Who Loved Me

The Prequel to the Maclean Curse

Much Ado about Marriage

The St. John Talisman Ring Series

An Affair to Remember

Confessions of a Scoundrel

How to Treat a Lady

And the Bride Wore Plaid

Lady in Red

Just Ask Reeves Series

Her Master and Commander

Her Officer and Gentlemen

The Abduction and Seduction Series

The Abduction of Julia

A Belated Bride

The Seduction of Sara

Novellas in Anthologies

The Further Observations of Lady Whistledown

Lady Whistledown Strikes Back

ABOUT THE AUTHORS

A lifelong lover of books, **Suzanne Enoch** has been writing them since she learned to read. She is the author of two well-received traditional Regencies, 24 and counting England-set Historical Romances, four contemporary Romantic Suspense novels, and a growing number of Scottish Highlands Historical Romances including the October 2016 release of HERO IN THE HIGHLANDS (Book One in the No Ordinary Hero trilogy).

A native and current resident of Southern California, Suzanne lives with a green parakeet named Kermit, some very chirpy finches, and a small army of Star Wars figures (including a life-size Yoda). Her books regularly appear on the *New York Times* and *USA Today* bestseller lists, and when she's not busily working on her next book or staging fights with action figures, she likes to read, play video games, and go to the movies with her large and supportive village. Please visit her website, http://www.suzanneenoch.com/ for more information, to sign up for her newsletter, and for fun freebies.

Molly Harper worked for six years as a reporter and humor columnist for The Paducah Sun. Her reporting duties included covering courts, school board meetings, quilt shows, and once, the arrest of a Florida man who faked his suicide by shark attack and spent the next few months tossing pies at a local pizzeria. She is the author of the Jane Jameson series, the Half-Moon Hollow series, the Mystic Bayou series, the Southern Eclectic series, and the Society and Sorcery series, as well as several standalone titles of romance and women's fiction. Please visit her website, https://www.mollyharper.com/ for more information, to sign up for her newsletter, and for fun freebies.

Karen Hawkins is a *New York Times* and *USA Today* bestselling author of over 26 fun and lively Regency historical romances and two humorous contemporary romances. Like Sabrina Jeffries, Julia Quinn, Victoria Alexander, and Suzanne Enoch, Karen's books are renown for their sparkling humor, dashing rakes, independent heroines, and often include freshly retold fairy tales (Cinderella, Sleeping Beauty, Snow White, etc), daring rescues, runaway brides, marriages of convenience, Regency balls, and more! With vivid descriptions, strong characters, and captivating plots, Karen takes her readers from London's Regency ballrooms to the purpled moors of Scotland and beyond.

When not stalking hot Australian actors, pretending to do 'research' while looking up pictures of men in kilts from the Scottish highlands, or teasing her husband (aka Hot Cop) about his propensity to idolize chocolate cake over the other food groups, Karen is busy writing her next book while resting her toes on one of her three large rescue dogs. Please visit her website, https://www.karenhawkins.com/ for more information, to sign up for her newsletter, and for fun freebies.

9 781641 972024